Praise for

Stolen Away

"Ripe with evocative imagery that easily builds worlds touched by magic." —*BCCB*

"Full of fun and memorable characters and positive relationships, this book is an excellent choice for teens who like their fantasy with just a touch of romance." —*VOYA*

"Eloise is a likeable character and readers will find themselves engrossed in her adventure right from the start. Recommended." —*Library Media Connection*

"Breezy and entertaining, with a diverting blend of chills, humor and spunk." —*Kirkus Reviews*

Praise for

HAUNTING VIOLET

"The requisite Victorian romance . . . complete with furtive meetings in the garden and love letters bound with elaborate ribbons." —*VOYA*

"Harvey . . . delivers a fun adventure in the form of a Victorian mystery novel that captures the feel (and the flaws) of the age." —*Publishers Weekly*

Praise for

"Vampires with bite and girls who bite back. A witty, exhilarating, and fresh take on an old tale."
—Kelley Armstrong, *New York Times* bestselling author

"Witty, sly, and never disappointing. . . . Fun, funny, and a relief from Twilight wannabes." —*Booklist* on *Hearts at Stake*

"An action-packed story full of intrigue, suspense, and romance with a great cast of characters."
—*SLJ* on *Blood Feud*

"Will keep readers entertained from start to finish. . . . Fast-paced and engaging." —*VOYA* on *Out for Blood*

"Alyxandra Harvey is the consummate storyteller. . . . It's a rare treat to be involved in a book that is new and can hold my rapt attention in this genre after 40 years of reading about vampires!" —A Bookish Libraria on *Bleeding Hearts*

Stolen
Away

Stolen
Away

ALYXANDRA HARVEY

WALKER BOOKS
AN IMPRINT OF BLOOMSBURY
NEW YORK   LONDON   NEW DELHI   SYDNEY

First published in the United States of America in January 2012
by Walker Books for Young Readers, an imprint of Bloomsbury Publishing, Inc.
Paperback edition published in January 2013
www.bloomsbury.com

For information about permission to reproduce selections from this book, write to
Permissions, Walker BFYR, 175 Fifth Avenue, New York, New York 10010

The Library of Congress has cataloged the hardcover edition as follows:
Harvey, Alyxandra.
Stolen away / by Alyxandra Harvey.
p.   cm.
Summary: Abducted and trapped in an alternate world in which a despotic
ruler threatens both faery and human realms, seventeen-year-old Eloise
must battle to save her aunt, herself, and a society in danger.
ISBN 978-0-8027-2189-1 (hardcover)
[1. Fantasy.] I. Title.
PZ7.H267448St 2012   [Fic]—dc23   2011025043

ISBN 978-0-8027-2188-4 (paperback)

Book design by Regina Roff
Typeset by Westchester Book Composition
Printed in the U.S.A. by Thomson-Shore, Dexter, Michigan
2 4 6 8 10 9 7 5 3 1

All papers used by Bloomsbury Publishing, Inc., are natural, recyclable products
made from wood grown in well-managed forests. The manufacturing processes
conform to the environmental regulations of the country of origin.

*For (just some of) the many writers
who have inspired me without even knowing it:
Terri Windling, Charles de Lint,
Holly Black, and Mary Oliver*

prologue
Eloise

Thursday evening

"I hate this town," Jo complained. "There isn't a single hot guy anywhere."

"Hey," Devin protested mildly, out of habit. We weren't really listening; we'd heard Jo give this same speech about a hundred times, and frankly, my mint chocolate chip ice cream was more interesting. It was too hot to worry about guys. Only Jo could muster the energy to multitask a tantrum while sweating through her T-shirt and eyeing the carful of perfectly droolworthy guys currently ignoring her. Mind you, I'd seen her flirt with a photograph of Ian Somerhalder in a magazine once. A little drought wouldn't stop her.

"I'm hot," Devin added, wiping his forehead. "Literally."

We were at the ice cream parlor where everyone hung out because there was nothing else to do in the bustling metropolis of Rowan, population 8,011. In winter we drove up and down Main Street, and in nicer weather we stood around the parking lot. It was October, and even though the sun had just set, the pavement was still warm and slightly soft under our shoes. I'd already eaten more ice cream during this drought than in the last ten years put together.

"You don't count," Jo told him. "You know what I mean," she added, patting his shoulder comfortingly. "You'd be hot if I didn't know you. And if I hadn't seen you stuff eight Ping-Pong balls in your mouth when you were ten and then spit all over me when you choked."

He just leaned back against the picnic table, his dark skin gleaming. "Halloween dance last year," was all he said.

Jo narrowed her eyes at him. "Shut up."

The stunning and epic failure of her costume was still talked about. I turned red just thinking about it. I'd have died on the spot if the whole gym had turned to stare at me like that.

Something I was considering doing right now, actually.

"Dishy." Jo smoothed back her waist-length hair as a guy I didn't recognize crossed the parking lot toward us. People staring at her never fazed Jo; she got more upset when they ignored her. I much, *much* preferred being ignored.

"I'd snog that." Jo loved anything British, especially slang, which she used incessantly but incorrectly about half the time. Mostly, she used the swear words.

"Do you even know what that means?" Devin asked.

"It means kissing."

"Then *say* kissing."

The guy was still coming toward us as they bickered. He ignored the girls preening in his wake, and the guys snickering. His eyes were the color of moss, an eerie pale green that I could see even from several feet away. His gaze was touching me all over, like rain. He looked awed. That would have been disconcerting enough, never mind that he was wearing brown leather pants and some kind of gold-embroidered tunic. There was even a sword hanging from his belt. He looked like he belonged under torchlight, not streetlight.

And, did I mention? He totally kneeled on the dirty pavement, right at my feet.

"My lady Eloise," he said in a voice just made for long summer nights and acoustic guitars. "Finally, you are undressed to our eyes."

"Whoa." I took a big step backward. "What?"

Jo was trying so hard not to laugh at the look on my face that I thought ice cream was going to come out of her nose, which would serve her right. Everyone around us turned to watch. Some of the girls even edged closer, especially Bianca. She loved nothing more than watching me squirm, all because two years ago Graham defended me when she laughed at me for getting a volleyball to the face in phys ed. She loved Graham. She hated me. Since she'd been the one to throw the volleyball, I wasn't too fond of her either.

"Come," he said to me with polite formality at odds with

the scars on his hands. He didn't even glance at Jo. "We must away, before the others find you."

I knew I was blushing that special shade of red that makes me look like a boiled beet. Nothing like being a pale, freckled girl who embarrasses easily. "Get *up*."

He got to his feet, graceful as water. His hair was dark blond, catching the light. His eyes blazed.

I took another step back. "Um, okay."

Devin scowled at him. "What's with the outfit?"

"Is it some sort of theater thing?" Jo asked. "Extra credit for drama? Who are you supposed to be, King Arthur?"

He didn't glance away from me, not even for a moment. I squirmed. Everyone was still looking at us. The whispers crested, like ocean waves. "You must come with me," he said urgently. "Please. If I have found you, the others will as well."

I nearly snorted. "Yeah, I don't think so." Why do people always assume that if you're quiet, you're also naive? Or downright stupid?

"You are in danger."

Devin shifted so he was standing closer to us. "Dude, not cool."

"I'll go with you, handsome," Bianca purred. She was wearing a tight tank top and some kind of glitter gel on her cleavage. Jo actually bared her teeth. She was a little territorial, not just about me, but about cute guys too. Each and every one of them belonged to her. In fact, for all that she teased

Devin, she was notorious for cornering girls in the locker room if she thought they weren't being nice enough to him.

"Let's get out of here." I grabbed Jo's arm. "Devin, come on."

The guy finally looked away from me, noticing all the curious faces looking him over. "Another time, then."

He bowed. He actually bowed. I could feel Jo fluttering beside me—she loved that sort of quasi-medieval thing. She was probably forcing herself not to curtsy back.

"Soon," he added.

I honestly didn't know if I should take that as a promise or a threat.

We circled the picnic table to get to Devin's car. Jo let me have the front seat, a definite indication that I must have looked as uncomfortable as I felt. She never let me have the front; she considered it her personal territory, to be defended at all costs, like Ian Somerhalder and chocolate macaroons. The guy watched us as we drove away, looking determined.

"Cute," she said as Devin squealed out of the lot. "But what a wanker."

chapter 1

Eloise

Friday evening

We went to Rowanwood Park the next night. There were
parties every weekend since the weather refused to turn cold.
There was a bonfire, but it was mostly for light. No one stood
next to it; it was way too humid for that, even at night. The
air was thick, that kind of sweaty moisture that chills even as
it swelters.

The last thing I wanted to be doing was picking my way
around tree roots in the backwoods of the park, but Jo was
bored and a bored Jo was a force to be reckoned with. She
dragged Devin and me out, despite the fact that I hated parties
and Devin would rather be reading about elves. I'd applied an
extra coat of my mom's favorite red lipstick. It matched the red

scarf in my short hair and the red stitching on my capri jeans. It was my own personal shield; looking tough was a trick my mom taught me for when I didn't *feel* tough. It helped. Not being stuck at a party in the middle of nowhere would help more.

"Over there." Devin motioned to a moss-covered log on the edge of the clearing. To get over to the log, we went around a few dancers and two girls trying to figure out how to work the keg. Devin and I exchanged a look.

"Now what?" I asked. "Are we having fun yet?"

Jo shook her head. "You two have the socializing skills of rabid dogs. Relax. Have fun."

"I *was* having fun," Devin muttered. "Until you made me come here."

"Yeah," I grumbled, and popped my chewing gum for emphasis.

"Fairy warrior women with pink hair don't exist." Jo grinned at Devin. "No matter how many hours you spend playing video games."

Devin pulled a bottle of pop out of his knapsack. "Just for that heresy, you go thirsty." He handed me the ginger ale and got another one for himself, smirking at Jo.

"Maybe *he'll* share his drink," she said, waggling her eyebrows in the direction of a guy I didn't recognize. He had long dark hair, and even from the back he looked like a rock star, the kind who make girls stupid. I groaned. Jo was doomed. "Seriously. He's clearly from out of town. No one here is remotely that yummy."

He tossed his plastic cup aside and left the circle of fire-light, between the trees.

"Oh, hell no, I am not letting him get away," Jo said. "Cover me, I'm going in." She adjusted her bra.

Devin winced. "I did *not* need to see that."

Jo nearly plowed over two guys from our math class in her haste to follow the rock star. For a girl who dressed in long skirts, she could move like a linebacker when she wanted.

Devin sighed. "One day I'm going to have to punch someone on her behalf."

I grinned. "It's only fair. She threatens to kick people for you all the time."

"Seriously, the girl needs a leash. I don't know why people think *guys* are dogs, juggling girls and flirting with anything in a skirt. Jo's worse than any of us."

"Did you just call her a dog?"

He finished his ginger ale, looking only slightly scared. "I'll deny it if you tell her."

I just laughed and drank my own ginger ale. Music blared out of cheap speakers attached to someone's iPod. A girl squealed when a guy pressed a cold beer bottle to her lower back, under her shirt. There was noise from the bushes that sounded suspiciously like someone throwing up.

"Maybe the cops will bust up the party and we can go home," I said hopefully.

"You're so cute when you're deluded."

He was right. The cops never broke up these parties;

they were too hard to get to, hidden so far back in the forest. They only bothered if we spilled out into the actual park, which we never did. At least if I had to be stuck here, I was stuck with Devin. He didn't force me into small talk, like most people. He was good with silences. He pulled a novel out of his bag, a book light clipped to its spine. I leaned against him. The fire crackled, and when the wind shifted, I caught a glimpse of the moon, hanging sideways. A dog barked in the distance.

"I'd better go check on Jo," I said after a while. We could never convince her that chasing after strange guys was stupid, even near a crowd like tonight's. She was so convinced that romance was enough to protect her. She'd say she was more convinced it was the foghorn she carried in her bag, ready to blast someone into deafness, but I knew better. She was a marshmallow. People just assumed she was tough. And people assumed I was a marshmallow because I didn't say much, but I'd been raised by a woman who kept drunk bikers in line at the bar where she tended. And Devin was Devin: kind, unruffled, and uninterested in what other people thought about him.

"Want me to come with you?" he asked, getting ready to stand up.

I shook my head. "Nah. She'll get all pissy if we scare the guy away. If she looks happy I'll just leave them be. And I need a minute away from all this fun."

He snorted. "Whoo-hoo," he agreed drily, and went back to his book.

I ducked into the sparse darkness of the forest. The birch trees glowed in the moonlight, like silver spears between the pines and maples. Fallen leaves crumbled under my shoes. The trees were losing their green summer dresses early this year, taking off their layers in the heat. It was pretty back here, with giant papery mushrooms growing out of the undergrowth and fanning from broken tree trunks. I didn't feel crowded, and I could breathe easily again.

Until Bianca and three of her friends stepped out to block my path. I hated to admit it, but my palms went damp and my heartbeat doubled. She always had this effect on me and she knew it.

"God, could you look more white trash?" she said, sneering, hands on her hips. Her friends snickered. "Is that even a real tattoo?"

Vines of ivy leaves trailed down my left arm out from under my sleeve. My mom had given in and taken me to get it done on my seventeenth birthday. Since she was covered in ink, she couldn't exactly forbid me; she just wanted to make it a bonding experience. And make sure I used her artist because he was scrupulously clean and talented. I'd grown up calling him Uncle Art, even though he wasn't my uncle and his name wasn't even Art. He'd given me a Tinkerbell "tattoo" with a marker when I was four, and I'd fallen in love with his art on the spot. And now I worked at his shop part-time when his receptionist needed a break.

"Well, you dress like a slutty hillbilly," Bianca added. "Just like your mother."

"It's *rockabilly*, idiot." My throat was dry and aching, stuffed with other jagged words I couldn't quite form. She thought I was afraid of her, that I wilted under any kind of assault. The truth was, I had a secret and dark temper. The kind that would be like a hurricane, when you expected a breeze. "And shut up about my mom."

I moved to step around them, but one of them shoved me back. They usually bullied me in public, where the weight of so many eyes crippled me. And I put up with a certain amount of bullying because it was easier to ignore it. People assumed I was fragile because I was so quiet.

Quiet and fragile are two very different things.

"Back off," I said clearly. My heart was still beating fast, but I didn't feel cornered like a wild animal ready to chew its own paw off to get free of a trap anymore. The laughter and the music of the party were muffled.

"Or what?" Bianca asked. "What are you going to do, white trash?" She was close enough that I could see where her eyeliner had smudged at the corners.

A hawk plunged out of a tree, flying suddenly between us and so close that his feathers fanned the hot air over my cheeks.

I jumped, throwing my hands up to protect my eyes. Bianca shrieked and stumbled back. The hawk landed in another tree, powerful claws digging into the bark. His eyes glittered over his beak. Did hawks attack people? Weren't they supposed to be asleep in a nest somewhere? I swallowed and edged back. He gave a piercing, whistling cry that shivered around us.

"Please don't eat me," I muttered.

He lifted off the branch and then dove for Bianca. She shrieked again and knocked her friends aside as she took off at a dead run. They scrambled after her, also screaming. The hawk circled over my head once and then lifted farther into the dark sky until he disappeared.

I stepped off the path into the wilting ferns and hazel bushes, letting them hide me from view. I had definitely had enough of people today. When I found Jo, we were going home. I didn't care how hot the rock star guy might be.

I stayed parallel to the path so I wouldn't get lost, heading toward the caves, where people usually went to make out at these parties. I could see the candles burning between the trees. They were in tall glass containers, usually with pictures of saints on them. They were the cheapest ones the convenience stores in town sold. The smell of smoke tickled my nostrils.

Before I could climb over the huge moss-covered boulders tossed around the caves, an old woman crossed my path. She stopped to dig in the dirt, pulling out pale roots and dropping them into a basket full of acorns. She looked like something from a fairy tale. Her hair was white, her eyes were like black raisins, and she was smoking a corncob pipe. She wore layers of ratty old gray shawls. She stopped foraging to stare at me.

You know, for the woods in the middle of the night, it was getting awfully crowded.

I tried to smile. "Um, hi." She looked like someone's grandmother, but she was probably homeless. I didn't know what to do. Did I ignore her? Did I give her change from my pocket? Was that an insult?

She solved my internal dilemma.

By screaming.

A lot.

I lifted my hands, palms out, as if she had a gun. Her hoarse scream bounced off the trees, off the rocks and the nearby stream. It made my teeth hurt.

"I'm not going to hurt you!" I had to shout, but I wasn't sure if she could even hear me. For someone who looked about a hundred years old, she sure had a set of lungs on her. I backed away.

"You'll get us all killed!" she hollered. "Want Himself to break our bones and suck out the marrow?"

"Um, no?"

"Then go! Get away!"

That was when she started to throw things at me.

She flung the roots out of her basket and they tumbled to the ground, looking like pale, disembodied fingers. She plucked up the acorns and whipped them at my head. The first one bounced off my left cheekbone, narrowly missing my eye.

"Hey! Ow!" Three more followed. "Shit!" I dove behind one of the rocks while she continued to pelt me with acorns. She had wicked good aim. "Stop it!" I fumbled for my cell phone, dialing Jo's number.

"Hello?" She sounded cranky.

I was crankier. "Where are you?"

"In the caves. Is someone screaming?"

"Yes!" I poked my head out. An acorn grazed my hair. "Get out here!" I wasn't sure what she could do to help, but since it was her fault I was here in the first place, she could get walloped with bits of the forest at my side. It was only fair.

"Where are you?"

"Right outside."

I hung up and saw a shadow block the candlelight for a brief moment. "El?"

"Over here."

Jo ran toward me, ducking acorns. She hunkered down beside me, her long hair trailing in the dirt. "Um, Eloise?"

"Yeah?"

"What the hell?"

"Worst night ever."

"I'm getting that." She picked up one of the acorns and threw it back. "Why are we throwing acorns at an old woman?"

"She started it!" I inched to another boulder, in the direction of the path. "Where's the rock star?" I asked.

"Couldn't find him," she said, frustrated. "He disappeared." She shook her head. "Just as well, I guess. He'd really think I was a nutter if he saw us right now."

"You *are* a nutter."

"You're the one getting beaten up by Granny over there."
She tilted her head. "Is she yelling about deer?"

"I have no idea. Count of three and we make a run for it?"
I suggested. "One, two . . . three!"

We ran. An acorn pinged off the back of my head and
then we were on the path, on the other side of a copse of
pine trees and out of range. I rubbed my head where I felt a
bruise throbbing. Mean girls, wild hawks, and crazy old
women were officially too much for one night.

"I'm going home," I muttered. "Because this party just
sucks."

• • •

Mom and I lived on the second floor of a small brick building near Rowanwood Park. The walls were crammed floor to
ceiling with her paintings and photos, with masks and books
of every description. Jo's parents' house had silk wallpaper
and matching furniture from a catalog; under the framed
pictures, our walls were magenta. And Jo soon learned that
all the books were in order of subject matter; the CDs sorted
by mood; and if you forgot to use a coaster on the antique
chest we used as a coffee table, you'd get lectured. And then
lectured some more.

Which was still nothing to the lectures I'd gotten when
Mom caught me trying to pick the chest's lock with a bobby
pin. It had been locked for as long as I could remember; it was
the only thing my exhibitionist mother was rabidly private

about. Irresistible, right? But the stupid lock held tight no matter how much I tried to jimmy it.

Our cat, Elvis, meowed impatiently at the window leading out to the roof. Mom was on a date with some guy whose name I didn't know. I hadn't met him yet, which meant he wouldn't last the month.

"Okay, your highness," I muttered when Elvis batted my hand. We had access to the roof, which the landlord let us use as our private balcony. When I opened the window, he streaked out, racing to the spot where the crows usually hung out. They were safely asleep in a tree somewhere, and Elvis sat on his haunches and sulked.

I flicked on the strings of Christmas-tree lights that draped over the railings. There was a plastic patio set in the center and one of those dining tents for shade. Two chairs were tucked inside, and dozens of silver-shot scarves hung from the ceiling poles, like some Berber desert palace. Mom was into all things Middle Eastern right now: belly-dance music, Afghan silver bracelets, and statues of ancient Egyptian gods. The planters around the tent were empty, except for a few dried-up stalks of mint and basil that hadn't survived the drought. Even the lawns on the fancy side of town were brown from the water shortage.

"Eloise."

I squawked like a chicken being plucked bald. I had the most attractive reactions; I couldn't think why I didn't have a hundred boyfriends eager for my company.

Still, when you found someone hiding in the shadows of your roof garden, a little screeching was healthy. Elvis hissed and darted past me to the safety of the apartment. Fat lot of good he was to me.

"How did you get up here?" The fairy lights caught the silver of his sword hilt. A *sword* hilt. "Did you *follow* me?" It was the guy from the ice cream parlor. His eyes were just as green, just as intense. I didn't think I could beat him to the window, but I edged toward it surreptitiously. If I screamed, would someone down on the street hear me? My heart felt like a plucked guitar string. It was actually vibrating in my chest with fear. I did *not* want to be run through with a theater sword on my own patio.

"I won't hurt you," he said softly, looking as awed as he had in the parking lot. He was still wearing a tunic, like an extra out of some medieval movie.

I glared at him. "Then go away. My mom's just in there, you know," I lied.

He raised his eyebrows. "Lady Jasmine is out front, kissing a man in a leather coat."

"You know my mom?" Fear receded a little under a rush of hot indignation. I tried to cast a glance over the side of the rail to the sidewalk. I couldn't see her, but I did see an entire flock of sparrows perched on the edge of the garbage bin.

"I know your family. The blood of the Hart is famous." The mention of blood made me decidedly nervous. "We honor Antonia's lineage."

I gaped at him, well and truly confused. "Okay, you know my aunt too?"

Aunt Antonia, the Hart wild child, had taken off again and we didn't know where, but that was nothing new. Every spring, she left town and wouldn't tell us where she was going. Sometimes we got postcards; sometimes we didn't. Mom said Antonia had been like that since their sixteenth birthday. Mom might look like the boho free spirit, with her tattoos and combat boots, but she was actually the dependable twin. Go figure.

"Have you seen her? Where is she?"

"Hiding until Samhain, as usual."

"What?" He said it so matter of factly, as if he was making sense. "Look, who are you? Because I'm this close to screaming."

"Your pardon, lady. I am Lucas Richelieu." He looked like he was about to kiss my hand so I snatched it behind my back. "We must go," he said again, urgently. "Anyone can see you now. 'Tisn't safe."

"But going off with some stranger in leather pants is?" I crossed my arms. "Go away, Lucas Richelieu." He looked so taken aback I nearly laughed. "You didn't really think I was just going to blindly go off with you, did you?" He'd obviously never met my mother, even if he did know her name. Not falling for pretty boys was one of the first lessons she'd ever taught me. "You're pretty, Lucas, but not so pretty that I'm going to turn into a drooling idiot."

He sighed, aggrieved. "This was much easier in the old days, when girls were educated."

"Hey. I'll have you know I get As. Well, mostly." I wrinkled my nose. "How old are you anyway? Eighteen? Nineteen?"

"One hundred and eighty-seven."

"Of course you are." I shook my head. I certainly wasn't going to be able to complain come Monday that I'd had a boring weekend. He didn't say anything else, only whirled suddenly when a crow landed on an empty planter. He pulled his sword out of its scabbard.

I stumbled back. "Easy, Conan. It's just a bird."

"A crow," he said tightly. "And a cousin of sorts."

He said something else in a language I'd never heard before as another crow joined the first, and then another. And another. I'd never seen any at night before. I assumed crows went off and slept somewhere, dreaming crow dreams. But maybe they were nocturnal like owls? That was going to bug me; I'd have to look it up in one of Mom's encyclopedias. We'd had our Internet shut down again when we couldn't pay the bill.

"Eloise?"

"Yeah?"

"Take this and go inside," he said very carefully, very slowly, knees bent as if he was about to launch himself into battle. He shoved a necklace at me, and I noticed his hand was covered in burn blisters over the old scars. They were red, fresh. I expected the pendant to be hot, but it was cold, normal. "Go!"

I wanted to tell him he was overreacting, even for a head case, but there was desperation in his voice, enough to have me slipping a leg over the windowsill.

Crows lifted out of the park like a raucous storm cloud, settling back down over the empty planters, the tent, the chairs, the twinkly lights—every available surface that might provide some kind of perch. I shivered despite the rational part of my brain telling me it was just a bunch of birds. But if there really was something weird about them, shouldn't I be out there helping him? I was stepping back onto the roof when he turned his head, barely, toward me. "Don't."

I climbed inside, kneeling on the window seat, where Elvis was hissing, his every hair on end.

Outside, Lucas swung his sword once, twice.

Crows cawed indignantly, a few flying toward the quiet of the park. He was repeating some kind of rhyme, but I couldn't make out the words.

A crow landed on the ledge in front of me. I'd always liked the crows.

I didn't like this one.

His eyes were too yellow, wrong somehow. Elvis swiped out a paw, missed. I could have sworn the crow laughed. A few more joined it—enough of them that I slammed the glass shut and slipped Lucas's necklace over my head. It was heavy, made of iron nails twisted into the surprisingly delicate shape of a leaping stag with some sort of leaf in its antlers.

One of the crows pecked at the glass so viciously that it cracked, blooming like a frost flower. I almost missed seeing Lucas blur, as if he were a watercolor painting soaked too long. He wavered, shimmered, and leaped off the roof.

The crows fled.

"Shit, oh, shit." I rushed outside and peered over the railing, holding my breath. I didn't want to see his broken body on the pavement below. I had to call 911.

I peeked.

He was gone.

"That's impossible," I said out loud. I leaned farther out but there was still no trace of Lucas, just a hawk riding an air current.

Disappearing boys in medieval costumes on top of crazy crows and crazier old women. Clearly *I* was crazy too. Because I should be snuggling under my blanket, dreaming about Robert Pattinson, not on the roof inspecting the balcony for crows and weird cute guys swinging medieval weapons over their head. But there was nothing here: no ladder at the side of the building, no window washer's scaffolding, nothing to explain Lucas's vanishing into thin air.

Nothing.

Only moonlight and the neon glow of the bar sign down the street. All perfectly ordinary; so ordinary, in fact, that

I might have imagined the whole thing if it weren't for the iron stag around my neck.

I went back inside and sat on the lumpy couch, staring out the window. Maybe I had the flu. I felt my forehead. I was kind of warm; it could be a fever-induced hallucination. Of course, the stifling heat inside the apartment could explain my clammy skin just as easily. So maybe it was heatstroke.

Which still didn't explain the very solid presence of the iron pendant.

I scrubbed at my face, as if that could wipe my brain clean.

Lucas had mentioned my aunt Antonia. I had her cell phone number, but she only ever answered it during the winter. She traveled out of the country during the summer months. I dialed it just in case, but there was no answer.

I put the kettle on for rose hip tea. My mom always made it when she was stressed out. An impending psychiatric breakdown was stressful. I was adding three spoonfuls of honey when Mom came in. She raised her eyebrows at the tea, tossing her keys in the ceramic bowl by the door. She'd made it during her pottery phase, and it was painted with pirate skulls. "Bad night, honey?"

I wasn't sure how much to tell her. I didn't want to end up in a doctor's office until I figured it out. Because I didn't feel crazy. Then again, wasn't that a sign of *being* crazy? The iron stag slipped under the collar of my shirt when I moved to put the kettle back on the stove. The cold iron brushed my skin, grounding me. No, there was definitely something going on. It wasn't as simple as a hallucination. Besides, I reminded myself, Jo and Devin and even Bianca had seen Lucas at the ice cream parlor. If nothing else, he was real.

"There's the weirdest thing outside," she said, crossing to the window and climbing out onto the roof. "Come and see."

Oh my God. Lucas's broken body really was on the sidewalk.

I dashed past her and slammed into the railing in my haste to look out. My brain kicked in belatedly. If Lucas was down there lying in his own blood, not only would there be ambulances, but I was pretty sure Mom wouldn't want me to see that kind of thing.

"Look," she said softly, pointing to the telephone wire across the street. Bright red cardinals perched on the line, watching us. Another landed on the corner of the building next door. "Aren't they beautiful?"

We watched them for a long time, their feathers red as raspberries.

"Have you heard from Aunt Antonia lately?" I asked, in what I hoped was a casual, normal tone.

She shook her head. "You know how she is." Her gaze slid away from mine.

"She's not in trouble, is she?"

"Why do you ask that?"

I shrugged. "Just wondering. Her cell phone's off again."

"She's probably out of range. Or she's avoiding collection agencies."

It was a logical explanation.

But it didn't ring true for some reason.

Especially when Mom hurried inside to fill a water bottle for the empty birdbath on the roof. She refused to meet my eyes, rushing so that she sloshed water on the floor. She didn't even stop to wipe it up. She *always* wiped up spills and messes, even the dust visible only to Mom-eyes.

And she was dismissive of Antonia, even though I knew they were close. Whenever Antonia came home for Christmas, they whispered late into the night, as if they were at a slumber party. But neither of them answered direct questions. Why hadn't I noticed that before? I felt strange, as if I were waking up from a convoluted dream I could only half remember.

There was definitely something going on.

Especially when she went straight to her room after a quick good night. She shut the door firmly behind her.

I focused on the few details I had. Lucas. The pendant. Antonia. Antonia was the only mystery I could work on right now. Though I did check the phone book for Lucas Richelieu. Not a single person with that last name in Rowan. I'd have to go to Jo's and use her Internet to google him. In the meantime, I gathered up the family photo albums, even the small one Mom thought I didn't know about. It was the only one with photos of my father.

I went into my room and sat on the bed, flipping through the albums. Mom and Antonia as babies, my grandparents. Granddad looked kind in his faded pin-striped suit. Grandma just looked kind of scary. The prom night pictures of Mom and Antonia were my favorite. The teased and crimped hair alone offered hours of entertainment. Mom at her first art show, sporting a very pink mohawk; Mom selling brownies at the school bake sale last year. We'd had so much fun that day. At the PTA meeting, the principal had suggested that parents dress appropriately, and everyone knew he meant Mom. So she did her hair in rollers and we wore fifties-style dresses and pearls. She looked like Bettie Page or a particularly evil version of Marilyn Monroe. The other moms had sniffed. But Mom was a better baker than they were, so our table sold out before noon.

There weren't a lot of pictures of Antonia after she turned sixteen, and the few I could find were from Christmas. Our purple tree glittered in the background, tilting slightly under the weight of handmade ornaments. They were mostly paintings of Elvis Presley and fifties pinup girls that Mom did on the back of coasters she took from the bar.

In one of the photographs, Antonia and Mom toasted the camera with glasses of red wine. Antonia was laughing so hard she was falling over. The flash glinted off a pendant slipping out of her peasant blouse.

An iron stag with a leaf in its antlers.

I heard the murmur of Mom's voice through the thin

walls as I tried to figure out what it meant, if it even meant anything at all. I crept to my open window, knowing hers would be open as well since the building didn't have air-conditioning. I leaned out, listening carefully. Who could she be calling at one o'clock in the morning? I stretched farther out and caught the last few words.

"Antonia, call me. I think it's starting."

chapter 2
Jo

Saturday

I drove out to my grandparents' farm under a sky the color of bleached bone. Heat wavered off the road, making the trees shimmy. The brown lawns of town gave way to fields of equally brown burned-looking corn and soybeans. My grandparents already lost ten acres of corn, and the stalks stood like forlorn guards with shriveled leaves and papery husks on one side of the winding lane. The pumpkin patches looked thirsty but they might survive. Even then, the harvest might not be enough to pay the necessary bills. The apple orchard was all that was currently standing between them and the last bank loan they were likely to convince anyone to give them, ever.

I loved the farm. I spent my summers here and every

autumn weekend until November. My parents weren't interested, especially Mom, who grew up here and left as soon as she could. Rowan wasn't exactly the big city, but at least there were no barns, no chores, and no squinting up at the sky every morning wondering if the weather was going to destroy your crops. The fact that I loved it did a lot to alleviate the tension between her and my grandparents. They wanted to leave her the thirty-two-and-a-half acres as a family legacy, but she wanted nothing to do with them. I happily spent as much time as I could here, especially since my bratty little brother, Cole, didn't like the farm either.

Nanna was on the porch, her short white hair spiky around her lined face. She wore jeans and sneakers and a faded T-shirt with the farm logo. I was wearing jeans too, and the same T-shirt. This was the only place I ever wore jeans. I usually preferred long, lacy skirts and any blouse with medieval bell sleeves. Not exactly practical on the farm. I even had my hair in two long braids under a pink straw cowboy hat. No one at school would recognize me.

"Jo, you're early, pumpkin." Nanna smiled at me. Her golden retriever, Apple Betty, panted at me, her tail thumping listlessly on the porch floorboards. "Have some lemonade."

I gulped two glasses, the cold juice hitting the back of my throat. It was already humid and gross out. Granddad hoarded *Farmers' Almanac*s like they were gold. He'd gone through every issue and couldn't find a hotter September or October on record.

"I don't think it's going to rain," I said miserably.

She patted my cheek. "Don't you worry on it. Rain comes when it wants to." I'd tried telling my Environmental Science teacher that once, but he'd disagreed. I wanted to see him try and convince my grandmother otherwise. I had to grin at the image. She'd decimate him. "There's my girl," she said approvingly, not knowing what I was smiling at. "Go on and say hello to the old bastard."

"I'm telling Granddad you're calling him names again," I teased.

She snorted. Old Bastard was the name of their goat. He was the oldest goat on the planet. He just refused to die. He was half-blind and he head-butted anything that moved, even if he did miss his target half the time. But he loved Granddad.

"Bring him a glass," Nanna said, handing me another jelly jar of lemonade. I crossed the rut worn into the grass from countless daily walks to the barn. Old Bastard was the only animal they had left, except for Apple Betty, some chickens, and the barn cats.

I could hear Granddad cussing him. "Get outside, you lazy thing," he said.

Old Bastard stayed where he was, chewing on one of the doors. The barn was dark, the air thick with dust and the smell of hay. I'd spent countless summer afternoons in the barn loft, eating Popsicles and reading novels about Anne Boleyn and Eleanor of Aquitaine. My parents were still trying to convince me to go to university and be a history teacher like Mom, but I just wanted to write historical novels, like Phillipa Gregory and Victoria Holt, and run the farm.

"Hi, Granddad." I handed him the glass. At the sound of my voice, Old Bastard made a weird goat sound and charged me. I leaped out of the way, and he got distracted by one of the fences.

Granddad shook his head. "He never did take a shine to you." He wiped his face with a bandana. "Loopy old thing."

I kissed his leathery cheek. His eyes were squintier than usual, and he smelled like cigars. "You've been smoking," I accused.

He shot a guilty glance at the porch of the house, as if Nanna could hear us. "Be a good girl and keep a secret." He slipped me a dollar. He'd been bribing me since I was three years old.

I grinned. "Okay, but you know those are bad for you."

He wagged a finger. "Smoking is bad for *you*. I'm an old man." He wiped his face again. "Hard summer, pumpkin. Hard summer."

I hugged him, feeling useless and sad for him. "I know, Granddad."

"Main well up and quit on us yesterday," he said. "Turned on the hose and nothing came out."

I winced. Wells only ran dry when it was so hot that even the groundwater running under the fields dropped too low for the pump to grab. They had two other wells, but the main one watered the crops and the orchards. Granddad looked about a hundred years old. It was alarming.

He must have caught the worry radiating off me. "We'll get through. We always do. Just have to call a water witch to find us a new well. Trouble is, she's overbooked." He flashed his usual toothy grin. "Go on, Jo-bug, before the Old Bastard makes a run at you again."

Last time he'd caught me, I had a bruise on my butt and couldn't sit comfortably for a week. I went around the other side of the farm fence, wisely keeping it between us. "You're sure?"

"Your grandmother just snuck off to the orchard," he tattled. "You know she's not supposed to climb those ladders alone."

I was crossing the lane toward the fruit orchards when Devin's car rumbled up the driveway, chased by a huge cloud of dust. I blinked at him and Eloise when they climbed out.

"Dev, she got you up at this hour?" They were both decidedly *not* morning people. "Blackmail? Death threats?"

"I am an awesome friend." Devin yawned.

"He really is," Eloise agreed. She was wearing a gingham blouse, nipped in at the waist, and a huge white flower pinned behind her ear. "Plus, I bribed him with caffeine." She handed me a paper cup of iced coffee. "I need your Internet." Devin's computer was in his room and his mom wouldn't let girls up there, even if it was just Eloise or me. Actually, *especially* if it was us. "And backup."

I raised both my eyebrows. "More batty old ladies?"

"Worse."

"All right, give me a minute. I need to go lecture Nanna." We headed toward the apple trees. Both Devin and Eloise worked here during the planting and harvest seasons when there were extra chores to be done. They knew their way around almost as well as I did. The plots of carrots and garlic looked like they might hold on, and there were onions and squash ready to pick.

We found Nanna at the top of a ladder with a basket. The apples were small but they weren't buggy. They'd make decent sauce. This was the oldest part of the orchard. The gnarled trees extended gray branches out like an old-fashioned hoop skirt, trailing leaves and fruit.

"Nanna, Dev and El are here to help me pick apples, so get down from there."

She eyed me sharply. "Tell your granddad I can pick apples without his interference."

"He's too busy smoking his cigars out behind the barn."

She muttered to herself and climbed down off the ladder. She was still muttering as she stalked away. Devin shook his head. "You totally sold your granddad out."

"Hell, yeah, I did. Cigars are right nasty." I climbed over a fence, using the shortcut to the house. "Let's go use the computer and then we can come back and fill up some baskets for them." Eloise was even quieter than usual, chewing on her lower lip. She wasn't wearing her customary red lipstick. Definitely a sign of impending doom.

"Did you tell Dev about the acorn thing?" I asked her.

"Yeah." Devin was the one to answer. "What is it with you two?"

"Hey! How is this my fault, exactly?"

"I don't know," he admitted. "But it usually is."

"I was busy ogling the hot guy, remember?"

"When aren't you?"

"Practice, practice, practice," I agreed.

The farmhouse was painted white with yellow shutters. The inside was cool and dark and smelled like lemons and rosemary. We went upstairs, where I had my own room. It was full of books and posters of Stonehenge and knights in silver armor kneeling before women in velvet dresses. There was a dart board on the back of the door, with a drawing of Henry the Eighth as the target. I was writing a book about him. Devin sprawled on the bed, and Eloise went straight to my desk and booted up my laptop.

"What are we googling?" I asked idly, putting on some music. The harmonized voices of the Medieval Baebes filled the room.

"I'm going to have to introduce you to music made in this millennia," Devin grumbled.

I ignored him and read over Eloise's shoulder. "Lucas Richelieu? Is that the cute guy from the ice cream parlor?"

Eloise nodded grimly.

Devin lifted his head. "This is a boy thing? You said it was important."

"It is," she replied quietly. "He showed up at my place last night. On the roof."

Devin sat up abruptly. "What? Why didn't you call me? Did you call the cops? What the hell?" Devin rarely got this worked up over anything.

"What did your mom say?" I asked.

"I didn't tell her," she admitted.

We both stared at her. Eloise told her mom everything. They were weird that way. "You didn't tell her?"

"I think he was protecting me."

"From what?" Devin demanded.

"Crows."

"Crows," he repeated, baffled.

I tilted my head. "Yeah, that's weird, El."

"I know. But they were dive-bombing us. Lucas gave me this pendant, and then he jumped off the roof. And vanished."

"He vanished."

"Stop repeating everything I say," she muttered, annoyed. She turned back to the computer screen. "There's no Lucas Richelieu anywhere. Certainly not in Rowan, anyway." She spun in the chair. "Something really strange is going on. Mom called Antonia and told her to come home because, and I quote, 'It's starting.' And now she's avoiding me."

"So what do we do?" I asked, sitting on the edge of the bed. "Have you ever googled your aunt?"

She spun around without a word and started typing

furiously. Devin and I got up to lean on the desk on either side of her. We scrolled through pages and pages of links.

"That one." Devin stopped us, tapping the screen. "School yearbook picture."

I whistled. "Did no one in the eighties own mirrors? I mean, seriously."

"She dropped out when she was sixteen," Eloise said. "And then it's like she disappeared. Her cell phone's unlisted, and she changes the number every year. She's never had her own apartment. She just lives in her van and drives around."

Devin looked at her out of the corner of his eye. "Did she gamble or something? Maybe she owed people money."

"Maybe. But for over seventeen years?" Eloise rubbed her temples. "I'm getting a headache." She turned away from the computer. "I'll keep searching later."

"Are you okay?" I asked. "You're a little pale."

"Yeah, it's just the glare off the screen. And stress, I guess."

"You know what solves all problems, including stress?" I asked, slinging my arm over her shoulder when she stood up. "Picking apples."

She snorted.

"I think you're confusing picking apples with chocolate."

• • •

I went to the café the next morning with my laptop and tried to research water witches. I was convinced Granddad was starting to go senile. But after following a few links, I found another name for a water witch: a dowser. Which was really only half-helpful. I didn't fancy calling up some crazy person with a bent wire hanger to walk the fields of the farm, trying to psychically commune with the groundwater. But I read so many testimonials about their accuracy that I phoned the local dowser anyway. Granddad was right; she was fully booked until the first frost, whenever that might be.

"You look organized," a voice like warm chocolate said over my shoulder. "And rather fierce," he added when I tossed the phone aside, frustrated.

I glanced up and immediately had to remind myself not to purr. It was the guy from the party, with the ripped jeans and the great butt. His smile was dark and positively wicked. "Hi."

"Can I sit with you?" Eloise was right, there was something of the rock star about him. He was beautiful, with moody eyes and a sullen mouth.

"Sure." What kind of an idiot would say no to that? It just figured that there wasn't a single person I knew here to see this totally hot guy asking to sit with me.

He raised his eyebrows at my laptop. "School paper?"

"Helping out my grandparents, actually."

"Are they looking for a water witch, then?"

"You know about this stuff?" I asked, surprised.

"Some." He accepted a tall coffee from the waitress, then added three sugars. The music from the speakers behind us was slow and peppery. "What's your name?"

"Jo." I took a sip of my own drink, wondered if he was going to ask me for my phone number or if I should ask for his. Eloise got all flustered around cute guys and blushed and stammered. I didn't have that problem. "You were at the party on Friday night, weren't you?" I didn't mention that I'd followed him into the woods.

He leaned back in his chair, his legs sprawled out. His boots nudged the bottom ruffle of my skirt. "Aye."

Aye. Seriously? Could he be hotter?

Unless he had been looking for his girlfriend at the party.

Not hot.

"I was supposed to meet my cousin," he elaborated. "But I couldn't find her."

Hot again.

"Does she go to school around here?"

"The high school across from the park."

"Rowanwood High. That's where I go." He knew someone from my school. He officially wasn't a stranger anymore, so Eloise's voice nagging in my head to be careful could shut up now.

He drank from his cup, then motioned to my laptop with it. "Found yourself a witch, have you?"

I shook my head. "There's only one dowser in this whole county and apparently she's booked solid."

"Not surprising."

"Not with this heat spell," I agreed. Which was making

the café feel like a jungle. Even the windows were sweating. I hoped my face wasn't shiny or my hair damp.

"I could help you with that," he offered.

I tilted my head. "You could? How?"

His smile was a touch sardonic and more than a touch self-deprecating. It was difficult not to get distracted when a boy smiled like that. "That kind of thing runs in my family."

"Really? What would you need? Those metal rods?" I'd seen them on one of the websites.

He snorted. "Hardly. A branch is all it takes. Apple or willow is best for water witching."

"Apple branches won't be a problem," I told him. "My grandparents have an apple orchard on the outskirts of town. That's where they need to dig a new well because even the rain barrels are empty."

"I could try now if you'd like."

It was a struggle not to pounce eagerly on the opportunity. He was gorgeous, he was sexy, and he was smiling at me. "That would be brilliant, thanks," I said as casually as I could. By which I mean: not even remotely casual.

It felt warmer than usual in the café. And I was thinking all sorts of naughty things. Like whether or not it would be hot enough in the fields that he'd have to take his shirt off. I could just tell by the way the worn cotton clung to him that he had really nice arms. And shoulders. And abs. I shut my laptop and slipped it into my bag, hiding my red cheeks. "My car's just out front."

We walked outside. He was taller than I'd thought, and his eyes were even more mysterious in the bright sunlight. I stopped in front of Granddad's old Buick. It was gray and hideous, and older than I was, but it was all mine. I opened the driver's door and paused. He was still standing on the sidewalk, watching me. "What's wrong?" If I had latte milk foam on my lip, I'd just die.

"You shouldn't let strangers into your car."

I grinned. "Now you sound like my best friends."

"They're right. I'll meet you there."

"Do you have a car?"

He inclined his head. "I'll follow you. Which is your grandparents' farm, in case we get separated?"

"It's Jack Frost Farms, off County Road 7."

"So your last name is Frost?" A faint frown puckered his brow, as if he'd thought it was something else.

"No, my mom's maiden name was Frost. My last name is Blackwell," I explained. "Here, give me your phone number," I suggested, whipping my mobile out of my pocket so fast it nearly flew out of my hand. "And I'll text you mine, so if you get lost I can give you directions." Now I'd have his number. And he'd have mine. *Well played, Jo*, I congratulated myself cheekily. Poor Eloise, how could she not find this sort of thing fun?

"I'll see you there, Jo Blackwell," he said, after giving me his number.

I shivered at the sound of my name on his lips. Then I

just nodded because I couldn't think of anything else to say. I drove away, glancing in my rearview mirror to see if he was following me but I couldn't tell which was his car. It only took about ten minutes to reach the end of town and another five to get to the farm. I passed the Christmas tree lot and Granddad on his tractor a few acres back. The Christmas pine tree crop was part of the reason the farm was named after Jack Frost. Granddad never could resist a pun or any kind of wordplay. It drove Nanna batty.

I texted Eloise once I'd parked the car. ROCK STAR. AT THE FARM!!! I texted Devin the same thing, mostly because it bugged him when I did. I climbed out of the car and leaned against the door. Since it was Sunday, Nanna would be in the back kitchen, baking apple and pumpkin pies to sell at the farmers' market. I made myself turn around to get my knapsack out of the back of the car so it wouldn't look like I was staring at the road, waiting.

When I popped my head back out, he was there. I jumped, startled.

"Easy," he said softly, taking my bag so it didn't drop. He put it on the hood of the car and then rested his arm on the window beside me. He blocked out the sun, which shone so brightly behind him he was a black silhouette.

"I didn't see you," I said lamely.

"A friend was waiting for me. I had him drop me at the end of the lane."

"Oh."

He was really close. I could see the flecks of light gray in his black eyes. I didn't even know irises could come in that color. My breath felt wispy in my chest.

He leaned closer still, his mouth hovering near mine. "Why don't you show me to the dry well, Jo."

I swallowed. "Okay." He pulled back and I felt the ridiculous urge to grab his arms and keep him there. This heat better break soon. It was making me stupid. "This way. The main well's back there behind the barn, but if you need an apple branch we'll have to go to the orchards."

We went down the gravel lane into the apple orchard, the humid heat like water between us. He didn't seem affected, even though he was wearing jeans. I was in a long skirt and tank top, praying I wasn't visibly sweating. My braid hung behind me, bumping my lower back as we walked. His hands were in his pockets. He tossed his hair out of his face.

I took him into the rows of the older trees, the hot air full of the sweet smell of rotting apples. Bees drifted lazily in between the trees. He dropped his gaze to the ground, searching.

"There," he said finally, pointing to a low branch. "We'll have to cut one down. It needs to be a Y shape."

"Sure." I doubled back to the previous row and plucked a hand saw out of a large barrel of assorted tools. I was very aware of him watching me as I reached up and sawed the branch off. I patted the trunk. "Sorry," I whispered. He'd probably think I was barking mad for talking to the trees, but Nanna and Granddad both did too, and I'd picked up the habit. He didn't say anything, just smiled.

"You're handy with a blade," he finally said.

I shrugged one shoulder. "I grew up here." I handed him the branch and he stripped the leaves off. The gray bark shone like silver.

"It'll do," he approved. "In the old stories there's an island of apple groves called Avalon. It's the fruit of love."

"I thought it was temptation."

"That too."

We made our way to the barn and I took him around the back where the well was, its round concrete cover hidden in masses of soapwort and yellow trefoil. He circled it three times.

"Tradition," he explained. "You're supposed to circle wells three times." He put one end of the V in each hand and pointed the straight part of the stick away from him. I grinned. He arched an eyebrow at me. "Are you laughing at me?"

"Just a little."

He nodded. "It's looks a little silly, but this is how it's done." He winked at me. Warmth tickled my belly. "Let's take a walk."

We wandered through the fields, past the shadow of the barn, and among withered stalks of corn. I was in my favorite place with the most beautiful guy I'd ever seen. It felt like we were the only two people in the world with the blinding light and the cicadas. It was strangely romantic. I glanced at him surreptitiously but he was staring at the ground, though I did get a glimpse of a teasing half smile quirking one side of his mouth. I wanted to believe it was for me.

We walked for at least ten minutes, doubling back toward the barn. We were on the border of the pumpkin patch when the branch twitched in his hands. I stopped so suddenly he chuckled.

"Did you do that?" I asked.

"No, that's what dowsing is. The branch points to the ground where there's water." It twitched again. He took another step. The branch dipped down sharply. "There," he said triumphantly.

"Really?" It didn't look like much, just another patch of dusty earth near a small pumpkin struggling to get fat. "Are you sure?"

"Yes." He crouched down and piled a few stones in a mini cairn to mark the spot. He looked up at me through his hair. "You're supposed to leave an offering to the spirit of the well," he drawled. "A piece of your clothing is best."

I turned my head. "Oh, is that so?"

"It's tradition."

I was wearing as little clothing as possible. If I took off my tank top I'd be standing there in my bra.

He sighed dramatically. "I suppose a coin would work as well." He took one out of his pocket and tossed it to me.

I caught it and set it on top of the cairn. "Thank you for this."

He rose to his feet and held out his hand. I took it, feeling shy. I never felt shy around guys. "Now what?" I whispered.

"Now we circle three times," he reminded me. We walked slowly, his fingers woven through mine, the sun hot on our heads. When we finished we just stood there, looking at each other. He looked sad for some reason, and frustrated. Before I could say anything, his gaze moved over my shoulder and a shutter closed over his expression. "Your grandfather?"

I swallowed, turning to look over my shoulder. Granddad cut across the field toward us, his tractor belching dust. "Yes."

"I should go." His hand slipped from mine.

"You don't have to. He'll want to thank you."

He just shook his head. The tractor closed the distance between us.

"You really shouldn't be so trusting, little Jo," he said softly before turning and walking away, the yellowed corn swallowing him.

"Who's that?" Granddad asked, shouting over the tractor engine.

I watched the corn sway as he walked toward the road and realized I still didn't know his name.

chapter 3
Eloise

Monday

Wondering about Lucas and Aunt Antonia and why my mother was being so weird was giving me headaches. And I couldn't help but feel as if I was missing the big picture, whatever that might be. It was like water trickling in a dry river bed, slowly at first, then with greater momentum until mud pushed its way into every crevice, dislodging rocks that seemed solid and heavy. I was full of dislodged stones.

I was remembering things. Little things that didn't seem important at first glance, but *felt* important nonetheless. It was disorienting. And usually I'd talk to Mom about it, but she was the one trying to keep all the stones in place with the sheer force of her stubborn will. I didn't know what was going on; I just knew there were secrets shaking loose.

Like why my aunt lived in her van, why she didn't show up to my grandmother's funeral three summers ago, why pretty much the only photos we had of her were taken in our apartment. Why she insisted on washing all the windows with lavender water and always, always wore her shirts inside out. That one always made me curious, but she just laughed and said she was the scatterbrain in the family.

I was so focused on my thoughts, which felt like a dog chasing its tail inside my head, that I didn't hear the door squeak open. A hand grabbed me suddenly and yanked me into a narrow supply closet.

"What the—Devin?" The bare bulb above us swung on a metal chain. He was holding a book and eating a bag of chips. Light barely seeped under the door. All I could see were broom handles near my head and his white teeth when he smiled.

"You're welcome," he said smugly, barely glancing up.

"Um . . . thank you?" When he didn't move his hand off the doorknob to let me out, I tilted my head. "What's going on?"

"Bianca's coming this way."

"I didn't know I was relegated to hiding in closets now," I grumbled. "She's starting to get on my nerves."

"It's about to get worse."

I hadn't told him about the night of the party. "Why?"

"Graham told her he thought girls with rockabilly hair and tattoos were hot. Ditto for bad reps."

"Is he *trying* to get me killed?" I blinked. "Wait, does that mean my rep suddenly got worse?"

"Bianca said you shoved her and then made a giant bird fly at her head." He snorted. "Drunk girls are so cute," he said sarcastically.

My mouth dropped open. "She shoved *me!*"

"Her lemmings are backing her up. Now that Graham's involved, she wants to prove she's tough. Well, tougher than you anyway."

"That's just great. Is it pistols at dawn, or what?"

"Fistfight under the bridge."

"Get out," I squawked. "I'm not doing that. That's just stupid."

"I know." He motioned to our cramped and dirty surroundings as if they were a palace. "Why do you think I booked the best room for you?"

I sighed when her sulky voice drifted under the door. "Guess we're stuck here for a while."

"If she was a guy, I'd go out there and stuff her in her own locker. But I can't punch a girl." He offered me the bag. "So have a chip."

I crunched gloomily on a handful of salty chips. "I can't punch a girl either, despite my reputation." And despite my family history. My father, before he'd left us when I was a baby, had been violent and angry. Mom had a small scar on her chin that she wouldn't talk about. She assured me that kind of behavior wasn't inherited. But I didn't want to risk it. Bianca had no idea how lucky she was that I was shy and obsessed with self-control. And that Devin was such a great friend.

We were stuck in the supply closet with the brooms for another ten minutes. More memories trickled in, without anything to distract me: the haunted sadness in my aunt's face when she thought I wasn't looking. The small, strange gifts she gave me whenever she saw me: ivy plants, red thread wrapped around a rowan twig, bags of hydrangea-petal pot-pourri that made me sneeze.

But the harder I tried to remember details, the more my head ached.

When the bell rang and the hall cleared, Devin went to his last class. I was glad I was working a shift for Uncle Art at the tattoo parlor after school. I didn't want to go home, where Mom was both avoiding me and watching me with a worried expression.

Bluebird Ink Tattoos was as much a second home to me as Jo's family farm. And at the parlor, no one blinked at my makeup or my clothes. There were girls dressed like me in the waiting room, in the magazines on the tables, sending e-mails on the business website. They had short, curled Bettie Page bangs and wore 1940s and 1950s-style dresses and red high heels with tight capris. Uncle Art was at the drafting table when I came in, the short sleeves of his bowling shirt displaying his heavily tattooed arms as he worked on a sketch. His black hair fell in a curl over his forehead, like a young Elvis Presley's. The only other artist, Lee, was in one of the rooms with a customer. The soft drone of a tattoo needle buzzed under the ever-present music from the speakers and the burble of the aquarium in the window.

"Hey, kiddo," Uncle Art, whose real name was Felipe, said. "Just in time." The phone rang. He looked at it like it was a bomb he couldn't figure out how to diffuse. "Help. It won't stop doing that."

"There's a way to fix that, you know," I said, tossing my knapsack under the desk. I picked up the receiver. "Bluebird Ink, how can I help you?"

I booked an appointment for the man on the other end of the line. People wandered in to look at the framed flash art on the walls and ask questions. I tidied up the desk and sorted through messages and updated the appointment book. I decided coffee was a good idea, and by the time it was finished brewing, Uncle Art was putting away his sketchbook and sniffing the air.

"Coffee. I'm giving you a raise."

I grinned and handed him a cup. It was just before dinnertime, so there was always a lull in the shop. I usually did my homework or took advantage of the Internet. Mom really was going to have to find a way to pay that bill. Only one café in town had free wireless, and it was usually too crowded to hang out for longer than half an hour, and the library closed early most days.

"Cool necklace," Uncle Art said, looking at the iron stag

that I was still wearing around my neck. For some reason, I didn't want to take it off. He frowned. "I've seen that design before."

I went still. "You have?" I asked, trying not to give away how eager I was for him to elaborate. If he was anything like my mom, it would spook him.

He nodded. "Yeah, let me see." He took a closer look. "I definitely tattooed this on someone. I'd forgotten all about it."

"Who?"

He shrugged, grinned. "You know me, kid. I remember art, not people."

He'd always been like that. He wouldn't answer the phone and didn't remember people's names, but he kept very precise documentation of all the tattoos he'd done. He rarely forgot. "Was it this year?" I asked.

"Might have been this summer. A guy, I think." He shrugged and took his cup back to the drafting table.

I opened the large hardcover sketchbook he used for his tattoo record and skimmed through the summer months. There were sketches of dragons and skulls and pinup girls, tigers and butterflies and lilies, but no stags. I flipped past portraits of babies and rock stars and cartoon characters. Nothing. I went farther back, and nearly missed it.

May 1.

It was a very rough outline of a stag with ivy wound around its antlers. It stood out because the other drawings were so detailed, with notes on placement and how long they took. This one didn't have a single word written in the margin, just the picture of the deer. It might not mean anything.

But I didn't believe that for a second.

I photocopied the page and folded the paper in one of my binders before my shift was over. The regular receptionist, Julie, rushed in with a tray of paper cups full of coffee and a box of muffins. "Thanks for covering for me," she said, handing me a cup of hot chocolate. She was adamant that I was too young to drink coffee—but not too young to get tattooed.

"Thanks, Julie."

"Go home and watch bad television." She waved me out. "You earned it."

"Bye, Uncle Art," I called into the back rooms before leaving. The waiting room was starting to fill up with customers. The bells on the door rang cheerfully as I traded the air-conditioned chill of the shop for humid air choked with car exhaust. I crossed the street to walk home along the park so I didn't have to smell the garbage cooking in the bins lining the sidewalk.

The sun was setting slowly in the burning sky, washing the thin clouds with lilac and orange. Cardinals pecked at the ground and chirped from the branches. I wondered if they were the same ones from the weekend. When I was sure there were no crows among them, I edged farther into the park. Grass crunched under my feet.

I went through my favorite grove of maple trees. It hardly seemed large enough to be so quiet and private, but for some reason no one ever came here. The first star of the night twinkled above me through the leaves. A swan flew past, honking indelicately on his way to the pond.

I didn't see the stag until he turned his head to look at me. In the fading light, he was as brown as the trees, and his antlers looked like bare branches. His eyes were dark and wide, hypnotizing. I held my breath. I'd never seen anything so primal in its beauty, so wise. I lifted my hand to touch it. I just couldn't resist finding out if his fur was as soft as it looked. It was the color of caramel. The moment I moved the spell was broken, and he bounded away between the trees into the park. I exhaled wobbily.

"It's good luck to see a stag."

I yelped and whirled around. Lucas stood under a crown of red maple leaves. His leaf-green eyes were serious, alert.

I glared at him accusingly. "You have *got* to stop sneaking up on me!"

He bowed. "Your pardon, my lady."

"And stop that as well."

He smiled quizzically. "Again, your pardon."

"Are you still following me, Lucas?" I reached for my cell phone, just in case.

"Yes," he replied simply.

I blinked, deflated. Weren't stalkers supposed to deny or come up with elaborate excuses? He just watched me patiently. "I would never hurt you," he said. "I'm here to protect you."

"I don't need protection, except maybe from you." Now that the incident with the crows was passed, it seemed silly to have been so frightened. They were just birds. There was no menace to their flocking on my roof. It was just Lucas's fear that had been contagious. "But you can answer a question for me."

"Of course."

"Did you get a tattoo like this?" I held up the pendant.

He shook his head.

"Are you sure? Because some guy got this done on the first of May at the shop where I work."

His friendly expression changed so quickly, my pulse tripped. He closed the distance between us in two quick, angry steps. The dying light glinted off his sword. I noticed a hawk made out of amber trapped inside the hilt. "Who?" he demanded. "Who took this symbol as their own? Who dared on the feast of Beltane?"

"I don't know," I reminded him, easing back. "I'm asking *you*, remember?" I held up the phone. "And I'll dial 911 if you come at me again."

He frowned. "I don't know what that means."

"Then we're even because I don't know what Beltane means either."

"You don't need to be scared of me," he insisted softly. "Be scared of the crow-brothers. Be scared of the swan and the turning of the wheel." He touched my cheek so gently, it was like a snowflake landing, brushing my skin and melting away. "Not me." He bent his head, voice dropping to a husky whisper. "Never me."

We stared at each other for a long, hot moment before I jerked back and let the maples draw a curtain of red and orange leaves between us. I shot across the lawn and the street and onto the crowded sidewalk. I ran all the way home. Mom was working, so I pushed out onto the balcony. I paced the roof, to convince myself there was no danger, no secret, no crow-brothers.

Big mistake.

I didn't even see them appear.

One minute I was alone, and the next . . . not so much. I yelped, my heart leaping into my throat like a disoriented frog. I counted nine of them—five women and four men—all still as glass with black eyes and crow feathers for hair. They wore armor and carried swords of sharpened jet. I swallowed thickly. "Who are you?"

No one answered me; they all just took a step forward, circling me in a sharp silence that made my palms sweat. I turned on my heel, trying to keep them all in sight. I opened my mouth to yell.

"Hel—" I wasn't sure if I was shouting for my mom or for Lucas. It didn't matter, I didn't have the chance. One of them rushed forward, moving so quickly I felt dizzy. The air shifted all around me, and his hand closed over my mouth. I struggled but he only laughed.

"Someone wants to see you."

His hold tightened and he dragged me forward, his crow-brethren laughing in a scratchy, inhuman way that lifted all the hair on my body. Their feathers ruffled. It might have been beautiful if I hadn't been so scared.

He stepped onto the railing, hauling me up next to him. The pavement far below was littered with old gum and candy-bar wrappers. A flock of sparrows lifted from the trees in the park, chirping frantically.

"Let's see if you can fly as well as the whelp boy," he said, as if he was offering me poetry and roses. I thought I saw Lucas, suddenly there behind him, shouting.

And then he pushed me.

I screamed all the way down.

I could imagine, in that moment, my broken body on the pavement below. The last thing I would hear would be my own hysterical screaming and the mocking half caw, half laugh of the crow-people.

I fell for a long time.

There was a hand gripping the back of my shirt, the one Mom embroidered for me, and I didn't know if I should be trying to shake it off or praying it held on tight. I didn't feel like I was dreaming, but I clearly couldn't be awake either.

Especially when I landed.

I didn't break apart into a hundred pieces, I didn't even break my legs, though my ankles felt the impact.

And I wasn't on the sidewalk outside our building. Instead, I was in a long room that looked like it belonged in one of those medieval movies Jo was always making me watch. Candles flickered next to painted oil lamps and beaded floor lamps. Hand-knotted rugs were piled on the dirt floor, and all the furniture was carved out of mahogany and ridiculously ornate. The ceiling was a tapestry of tree roots, hung with lanterns.

People in bustled gowns, leather pants, and jet jewelry drank pale pink liquid from champagne flutes. Their faces were angular and powdered with glitter; some necks were too long, movements too fluid. I really hadn't thought I had such a good imagination.

"The girl, my Lord Strahan." The crows were behind me, each down on one knee, heads bowed.

Strahan wore a lace cravat and silver at his forehead, like a crown. Three women, diaphanous and gray as mist, floated behind him. Everything about them was as pale as pearls: hair, skin, eyes, mouths, clothing. Their tattered gowns undulated in a wind only they could feel. They emanated a glacial sadness that made me shiver.

Strahan was slender and sharp, like a sword. And he was circling me like I was prey. "Dreadful hair," he said. "I'll never understand the modern penchant for cheap fabrics and short hair."

When he reached out to touch my short brown hair, I slapped his hand. I'd seen Mom do it countless times when she tended bar down the street. "Hey, back off."

He paused, as if I'd shocked him. I guess he didn't get

smacked a lot. The crows muttered behind me. The silence stretched, like a thread pulled too taut. Adrenaline fizzed through my blood. I wondered briefly if I was going to be sick on his polished boots. Harp music was soft all around us, incongruous in its gentle lilting.

I really, *really* wanted to wake up now.

He shook his head. "And the pattern of that embroidery is pitiful. Did you really think it was enough to hide you from me? And that tattoo is a pathetic charm." He clicked his tongue. "The glamour that kept you hidden from us is gone, child. Nothing can hide you from me now."

Everyone looked at me, mostly with an odd kind of hunger. There was a girl chained to the wall beside us. She was too thin and looked away when I noticed her. Her wrists were covered in blisters and the translucent wings lifting gently from her spine were mutilated.

Wings.

Because this wasn't weird enough.

She looked terrified, even more so than me. But if this was a dream, and it had to be, I didn't have to just stand around, wringing my hands. I could be brave in a way I might not have been in real life with all those inhuman eyes devouring my every movement.

I bolted for the nearest doorway.

It was stupid. There were too many guards and I knew I'd never make it, but I had to try. Terror had my legs moving before my brain could come up with a better plan.

Strahan just reached a hand out and caught my hair, yanking me to a vicious stop.

"Eloise Hart." His voice was silky, menacing. Beautiful.

And then he smiled, slowly, as if I were a pet monkey who'd amused him. My knees went weak. His entourage laughed, clinking glasses together.

"Lovely," he murmured. "The others broke with such lamentable swiftness. You might be entertaining after all, and I could use the diversion." He stroked my cheek and it tingled, as if I had a sunburn. "And I've such a fondness for diversions." He squeezed, his fingers bruising me. "I'm tired of these games, you see, and I'm tired of Antonia."

"What does this have to do with my aunt?" I suddenly remembered the way she refused to sit with her back to a window or a door, the way she rigged her van with door alarms. Was Strahan the person she was running from? And why?

"You're very like her." There was something in his eyes at odds with his bored tone. "And you'll tell me where she is, little fawn, won't you? And give me what I want."

He yanked the ribbon out of my hair. Welts rose at my nape from the scrape of the material. He looked at the ribbon, dropped it in disgust. "That's not the one."

He was looking for a ribbon? I was being bruised and manhandled and, oh yeah, *abducted*, for a ribbon?

I tried to pull out of his grasp. "Is Lucas here?"

His eyes narrowed suddenly, dark as flint, and I wouldn't

have been surprised if sparks had leaped from his eyelids. He was stunning, all pale hair and lightning. "You would speak the name of a Richelieu whelp to me?"

Chains rattled as the winged girl shuddered. I would have taken a step back if there hadn't been so many crow-guards behind me. I had nowhere to go, and the air felt thin, distant. This wasn't a dream, after all.

It was something else, something much worse.

"You'll lead me to your aunt or she'll come to fetch you," he drawled. "Either way, you are of some use to me. I suggest you remain that way."

"I don't understand."

"No, you wouldn't, would you? But you will, soon enough." He waved a hand dismissively. "Take her away."

• • •

I was taken to a narrow room with a sloped ceiling, also made of braided roots and hung with oil lamps. There was a huge bed, a washstand, and a narrow table with a single candle and a box of parchment and quills. The outer door stayed open. The inner door was thick filigreed metal, like vines curling over themselves. The lock clanged shut. Two of the crow-guards stayed outside, their eyes yellow above sharp noses. A few giggling women joined the guards, clearly tipsy on whatever that pink stuff was they were drinking. They wore matching pink dresses with ornate bustles in silver wire cages.

"She doesn't look like much, does she?" one of them said in an exaggerated whisper. "Her aunt was much prettier."

"*Hsst*, mentioning her. Do you want Himself to hear you?"

She sniffed. "I'm not scared."

Her friend shook her head. Icicles dripped from her hair like a crown. "Then you're as foolish as you are reckless."

"Oh, Poppy, you never let me have any fun. We haven't had a human in ages."

They stumbled away, still bickering. I didn't like the way she'd said *human*, as if it implied some sort of delicacy, like caviar or Belgian chocolate.

Yet another reason I had to get the hell out of here; I didn't want to end up as dessert.

But I still had no idea where I was or how to get home.

I was distracted from the rapid and distinctly downward spiral of my thoughts by some sort of commotion in the hallway. There was scuffing of feet and whimpering. I went to the glittering cage door and looked out. Two men and a woman were dragging the winged girl, her wrists bloody, her feet bruised and dirty. I felt small and scared and sick. They passed by close enough that I could smell her sweat: cotton candy and pond water. I gagged.

The crow-guards advanced suddenly, swinging the heavy wooden outer door shut in my face. I jumped back to avoid getting my fingers and my nose crushed as the fairy girl was muscled into the room next to mine. I pressed my ear to the wall, the silk paper smooth against my skin and patterned with swans holding fish in their beaks.

"Hello?" I called out, wondering how thick the walls were. They felt uneven, like plaster or mud. "Hello? Can you hear me?"

I slid down to sit on the floor in the corner, my mouth close to a swan eye, painted with far too much realistic detail. My mother would have loved it; it was surreal and delicate. I was half-afraid it was going to drop its fish in my lap.

I might have heard a sob, but I wasn't sure. I leaned closer to the swan, could have sworn I felt its warm breath. I blinked, pulled back slightly. The paper was cracked, and if I turned my head at just the right angle, I could make out a tiny glimmer of light, barely bigger than a watermelon seed. "I know you can hear me."

There was a muffled gasp, a pause. I wiped my damp palms on the carpet. "I'm Eloise."

"I know."

I was a little heartened that she'd at least answered me. "What's your name?"

"My speaking-name is Winifreda."

There was a long pause and I would have thought she'd gone away except that I could see small glimpses of her hair, which was knotted and cornflower blue.

"Please talk to me," I tried again.

"I'm not supposed to. We're not allowed to talk to the other displays."

"Displays?" I echoed, insulted. "I'm not some party favor."

"Of course you are," she said softly. "All of us are."

"What? That can't be legal."

I heard a rustle, as if she was shrugging. "He can do as he wishes until Samhain binds him, though it never really does anymore. It's worse now, so close to the holy days. It makes him peevish."

"Peevish?" I thought of the burns and blisters on her pale skin and swallowed. "That's just great. Where are we, anyway? His country house or something?"

"You're at Strahan Hall. They're a traditional family, still keeping to the raths as the ancients did. There aren't many like this. Most have been abandoned."

"Um, can you say that again in English?"

"A fairy rath, under the earth, near Rowanwood Park."

"Rowanwood Park? There aren't any houses in the park." I pressed my eye closer to the gap, saw only a flutter of blood-ied wing.

"We're under the park, in the west hill."

"*In* the hill."

"Of course, where else would a rath be? The fey have always lived close to the earth. Some say we were driven underground while in the old country."

"Oh." Like *I* was the weird one for not thinking people lived inside hills. "Wait, fey?"

"Fae folk," she explained. "Surely you've heard the stories of the Good Neighbors."

"Uh-huh." I had vague recollections of reading Keats's "La Belle Dame sans Merci" in English class last year, about a knight enslaved by a Fae princess. "Do you know how to get out of here?"

Winifreda's voice was small. "You'll never get out of here."

My stomach tumbled. "I have to." I pushed my shoulders back. False confidence was better than none at all, according to Mom, anyway, even if she did deal with drunks and grabby bikers instead of megalomaniac Fae lords. When I sat back, my pendant fell out of my sweater.

Winifreda made a small sound. Light filled the hole when she scrambled away from the wall. "Don't let him see that."

I touched the iron stag, frowned. "Why not?"

"We can't abide iron." I thought of the chains on her wrists, the way Lucas's hand had been blistered when he handed me the pendant. "And he especially cannot stand the Hart insignia."

I slipped the chain off, took a closer look at the spiraling antlers. "This is my family insignia? I didn't even know we had one."

"All the old families do. So you *are* the one," she added in such a soft whisper, I didn't think I'd been meant to hear her. She didn't come back to the wall, and she didn't say anything else.

I wondered what an old family was and what that even meant. I thought about Mom wondering where I was, about Jo and Devin, and about Lucas left behind on the roof. I rubbed the stag pendant and wished it were a magic lamp so I could transport myself home.

chapter 4

Jo

I checked for a message or a text from Hot Guy a hundred times. I checked it so often my chem teacher confiscated my phone until the last bell rang; then I knocked over the janitor in my rush to get it back. Eloise was working and Devin had his nose in a book, so I went back to the café. I was hoping Hot Guy would drop by again. I could pretend to be surprised he was there, pretend I hadn't thought about him all night and all day, pretend I didn't tingle just remembering the way he'd crowded me against the car.

No one was that good at pretending.

I ordered an iced cinnamon latte and tried to read my novel. It was about Eleanor of Aquitaine and dead interesting, but I couldn't stop glancing at the door every time it opened. I was probably being pathetic. I'd never see him again, but until I was too old to even remember my own name, I'd remember the way he held my hand in the fields. Or else I'd run into him in some faraway city, Paris perhaps, on the night before his wedding and he'd weep. Or at least look devastated and kiss me as rain fell around us and the Eiffel Tower lit up the sky. I was still weaving very melodramatic daydreams when a shadow fell over me.

It took me a moment to realize I wasn't imagining him.

He looked down at me, his smile slow and wicked. Butterflies fluttered pleasantly in my belly. "Hello," he said in his whiskey voice, in that strange accent that was faintly British and yet not.

"Hi."

"I was hoping to see you again," he admitted softly.

"Same here." I put my book down. "Do you want to sit?"

He didn't look away from me. "How about a walk in the park? It's rather . . . crowded here."

"Okay."

We stepped out into the late-afternoon heat, but I barely noticed the weight of the humidity this time or even the heat coming off the melting pavement. The trees circled us like dancers, shaking brittle leaves like castanets. And then the world around us receded, faded to meaningless noise and gray shadows until there was nothing but the nearness of his body, the confident, nearly arrogant, way he walked, and the set of his jaw.

"You don't come from Rowan, do you?"

He half smiled. "My family's from the area."

"Oh, yeah. You have a cousin here, right?"

"Yes. And you? Do you live at your grandparents' farm?"

"Not really, but I spend most of my time there. I want to run it once I graduate."

He gave me the once-over, noting my long lace skirt and gypsy-style sleeveless top. "You don't look like a farmer."

I grinned. "I want to write books too."

"Ah, that explains it," he teased. "You have the look about you. They used to say that poets and madmen brought stories from the other worlds."

Was it wrong to just grab him and kiss him?

I restrained myself, but only barely. "What do you want to do? After school?" I slanted him a considering look, just as he'd done to me. "Are you in college?"

"I'm in the family business," he replied, his voice suddenly bland.

"Is is worm farming?" I felt a need to make him smile again. Clearly he felt the same way about the family business as my mother did. "Or degreasing french-fry machines?" I added with mock horror. "Knitting? Making doilies?"

He chuckled. It was a rusty sound, as if he wasn't used to it. "Yes, we're a family of doily makers."

"I'd stick to water witching, then. Much sexier."

"Duly noted."

A crow gave a raucous call from a nearby tree, like a smoker's laugh. He tensed, shooting it a warning glance. He stepped a little closer to me. His arm brushed mine as we wandered toward the pond and the woods behind it. There was no one else around; it was just the two of us, like in Granddad's field. Until three more crows landed on the path in front of us. I frowned, thinking of Eloise's story about the crows.

"That's weird," I said. "They must getting bold because of the drought. Maybe they're hungry."

He snorted. "They are at that.".

A few more crows descended, strutting around us in the grass.

"I'm not sure I like the look of those birds," he said. There was a teasing smile hovering at the corner of his mouth, but his eyes were serious. He slipped his arm around my waist, walking me backward as if we were moving to music only we could hear. He didn't stop until my back rested against a tree and there was nowhere left to go. He pressed against me as if he really did mean to protect me, as if I were something precious.

And when he kissed me, I felt as substantial as sugar. Everything went sweet, went fiery, went sharp as lightning. He wasn't just kissing me, he was tasting me. And I wasn't just kissing him back, I was breathing him into my lungs, into my pores. It was a short kiss, more of a branding than anything else. It shouldn't have affected me like that, shouldn't have made me fist my hands in his shirt or made his breath rough when he pulled away, as if he'd been underwater.

There were crows all around us, perched in the trees and standing in the grass.

He kissed me again, roughly, before casting a dark and hateful glance at the birds.

"I have to go," he said harshly. He looked angry, wild. My lips were still tingling, and I felt as if even my bones were on fire, but he stalked away, without looking back.

• • •

I floated all the way home, stopping only long enough to call Eloise, but she wasn't answering. I sat in my room and grinned at the dark computer screen.

He'd kissed me.

Seriously kissed me.

I was surprised the entire park hadn't caught fire around us. I replayed it in my head, still smiling.

Then I yelped and fell right off my chair.

Because it's not every day your best friend's face flashes onto your monitor.

When it's not even turned on.

"El? Crikey!"

"Crikey? Isn't that Australian, not British?" Cole, my annoying younger brother, paused in my doorway. "And are you talking to yourself, lamebrain?"

"Get lost, git." I reached out and kicked the door shut in his smirking face.

"Jo?"

I froze, looked around my bedroom slowly, wondering where Eloise was hiding. There were posters of castles and *Robin Hood* and *Pride and Prejudice* movies, heaps of clothes on my unmade bed, incense burning from a ceramic dragon, but no Eloise. Even though I swore I'd heard her, as well as seen her. I checked under the bed and then checked my mobile phone, but it was off, the battery drained when it had accidentally turned itself on in my knapsack. I checked my pulse too. Maybe the kiss had shot my temperature into a fever. It was hot enough, however brief. *Focus.*

"Eloise?" I felt like an idiot, talking to my blank screen.

And then I felt positively barmy when her face stared back at me, the screen no longer blank. I knew her freckles and styled hair almost as well as I knew my own face. I'd never seen her that pale before, though.

"How are you *doing* that?" I asked. I was probably looking a little wild and pale myself, come to think of it. "My computer's not even *on*."

"You can hear me?" She looked as if she was going to cry, except that she was smiling too.

"Duh. I can see you too. Is this some kind of trick?" I looked for a projector of some kind.

"You can see me too? It must be the pendant. I was holding it when I said your name." She wiped tears off her face. "How come I can't see you?"

"Okay, if Cole snuck some kind of weird drug in my tea, I'm so going to kill him. A lot."

"Jo, listen, you have to help me." Eloise's voice dropped to a frantic whisper. "I may not have much time."

"You don't even have a curfew. Which leaves us plenty of time for me to get lots of therapy," I added drily.

She shook her head. "I don't even know where I am, except it's somewhere under a hill in west Rowanwood Park."

"You're in the park? So just follow one of the trails back to the lawns. It's not *that* big. And by the way? How are you *doing* this?"

"I don't know!"

"Quit yelling!"

"You're yelling too!"

"Well, you're *freaking me out!*"

We shared a strangled attempt at laughter. We could always make each other laugh, even when we were clearly losing our minds.

"Jo, Lucas was right. I *was* in danger."

"Lucas? He did this to you?" I jumped to my feet. "I'll kill him. Where is he? What'd he do?"

"Nothing. He tried to warn me. Look, it's something to do with my aunt, like we thought, but I don't know what yet. This guy's holding me hostage."

"You've been kidnapped? I'm calling your mom." I reached for the phone. "And the cops. The fire department. I don't know, somebody!"

"Don't!"

I paused. "What? Why the hell not?"

"Because this guy's not . . . normal. He's Fae, Jo, like in all those books and poems you read. His name's Strahan."

"Is this an April Fool's thing? In October? I thought we made a pact last year not to do that anymore." Actually, after the spaghetti incident, our mothers had threatened to ground us until we graduated.

"Jo, I know this is weird, but you gotta believe me." Her lip wobbled, like she was trying not to cry.

"Hey, take it easy," I said. I might be a girl, but I don't do well with crying. That's Devin's department; he just lets people cry and never looks uncomfortable. I was already squirming. I was also going to find this Lucas and kick his ass. He was clearly involved, whatever Eloise might say. "I believe you, El."

I paused, something tickling my brain. I knew something, something important about the Fae. I ran through the poems and novels in my head, then shouted into the monitor. "El!"

She yelped. "What? Don't do that!"

"Don't eat anything. Or drink anything either. At all. I mean it."

"Why not? Isn't it bad enough I'm stuck here, I have to starve too?" Nothing made Eloise crankier than being deprived of food. I'd seen her kiss a piece of chocolate mousse pie once.

"If you eat or drink Fae food, you'll be stuck there forever."

"Oh God," she groaned. "Now all I can think about is mashed potatoes. And olives."

"Gross." I ran a hand through my hair, dislodging the messy braid. "Right. Fae abductions. I'll see what I can do. Then I'll look up the nearest psych ward," I muttered.

• • •

I spent the rest of the evening doing research. I googled things I never thought I'd google, like Fae history and Fae charms, and all the different names they went by: Faery, Fairy, Fey, the Good Neighbors, the Wee Folk. I even googled the topography of Rowanwood Park. Some of the websites made my eyeballs hurt, some were helpful, some were boring as dust. I tried another search on Eloise's aunt but came up empty. I dug out all my English papers and flipped through my books and took notes in a journal with color-coordinated felt-tip pens. I loved researching bits of history or mythological trivia. I even loved reading all of the old fairy poems—just not when my best friend's life might possibly depend on it. Talk about pressure.

The next morning I skipped school and went straight to the public library and found a quiet corner in the back. We often came here to do homework on Sunday afternoons. Well, Eloise did homework. I looked at the cute guys. Like the one standing by the photocopiers right now, his hair long and straight and his jeans frayed at the bottom. He looked a little bit like Hot Guy. Whose name I still didn't know, I realized.

I gathered my books to go say hello, but by the time I stood up, he was gone.

Just as well, I told myself sternly. I had more important things to worry about than flirting, even if I liked flirting as much as Eloise liked strawberry tarts. I forced my attention back to the yellowed books piled all around me. Most of them were old, with folded pages and cellophaned covers.

In the movies, this was so much easier. There was always an old woman who hobbled over to give you the clue you needed the most, even if it didn't make sense at the time. Here, there were only guys throwing spitballs at each other, people studying, a girl talking on her mobile phone, and librarians. And the only old woman we'd seen had pelted us with acorns.

When my journal was half full of little bits of information that might or might not be useful, I decided to take myself off to Rowanwood Park. I was starting to feel overwhelmed and discouraged, and besides, maybe if I could find the hill Eloise was talking about, I'd figure out a way to get her the hell out of it.

'Cause, you know, that made sense.

I really, really wanted to call Devin. And Eloise's mom. If Eloise was missing, wouldn't her mom have called me looking for her?

I reached for my mobile and dialed Eloise's house line. Jasmine answered groggily. " 'Lo?"

"Hi, Ms. Hart," I said. "Sorry to call so early, but is Eloise there?"

"She left me a note saying she was sleeping at your place last night."

Oh. Shit.

"Oh, um, yeah, but she stopped at home to pick up some books," I lied hastily. "I just wanted to remind her not to forget her . . . history homework. Her mobile died."

I could hear Eloise's mom moving around. "Not here." She yawned.

"Okay," I said as cheerfully as I could. "She must be on her way to the library. Bye!" I hung up as fast as I could. Luckily Eloise's mom was never quite coherent in the mornings since she worked so late at night. She probably didn't notice I was lying through my teeth.

Eloise didn't leave that note.

So who did? And why? To put us off her trail? Which meant she was really missing. She'd really been stolen away by the fairies.

I ran all the way to the park.

The wrought-iron doors were open, tall dry grass on either side. The low stone wall that ran along the front of the park was full of people, eating hot dogs, drinking coffee, just sitting in the leaf-shadowed sunlight.

No one had giant glittery wings or ferns for hair.

That was comforting at least.

I went down the path, which was clogged with Rollerbladers and dog walkers, and passed the gazebo where they held outdoor concerts and Shakespearean plays in the summer.

I went every year without fail, usually alone since I couldn't get Eloise or Devin to come with me anymore. They'd grouped together in a strike and would now only meet me for ice cream afterward. Was it my fault they were culturally deficient? How could you not love Ophelia running around in a whalebone corset, tossing flowers, and making mad pronouncements? It was brilliant, plain and simple. I thought of *A Midsummer Night's Dream* all of a sudden and hoped fiercely that no one would come away from our little situation with a donkey's head.

What a weird thing to worry about actually happening.

I made my way toward the west end of the park. The pond glimmered, framed by the banks and sprinkled with wild lilies. A swan floated on the surface and ignored me completely. There were slight rolls and dips in the grass but nothing I'd call a proper hill without a great deal of wishful thinking. I kicked at the weeds, finding nothing but more weeds; no convenient magic door or wooden sign painted with THIS WAY TO YE OLDE FAERY COURTS.

There was, however, a tiny winged fairy lifting out of a hawthorn bush.

I might have thought it was a blue jay or a really big butterfly, something *normal* anyway. But then she turned her head and looked straight at me.

I slid right off my feet and onto my butt, choking on a scream.

It's not that I hadn't believed Eloise. I mean, the trick

with my computer had been pretty unfathomable, but this was something else entirely.

"You're real!" I gaped.

She sniffed. "Of course, I am. You humans don't get any less arrogant, do you?"

"Uh." *Brilliant, Jo*, I thought. I swallowed, forced my brain not to skitter around like a bee at a windowpane. "Where did you come from?"

"I've always been here." She hovered, letting the light breeze lift her up. Part of me was looking for invisible wires. "You must have been Touched, to see me now."

I shook my head as if that would bring order to my thoughts. "Eloise didn't say anything about you being so small. Is she being held captive by a moth-king or something?"

Her lips might have been the color of cotton candy, but they lifted off teeth that were sharp as needles, though still not as sharp as the disdain in her bluebell eyes. "Blast that dodgy old poet," she muttered. "And the bloody Victorians with all their bloody stories."

"The Victorians?"

"Idiots, the lot of them." She paused, glared at me. "You're not a writer, are you?"

"Uh . . ."

She sighed, disgusted. "I always get stuck with you nutters."

I frowned. "Hey." Her wings were so thin and translucent, I could see the glow of sunlight through them, like violet petals. Her hair was a mass of tiny braids. "Um . . . what does this have to do with the Victorians?"

"I was tall and stately before them, wasn't I?" She plucked at her petal skirt. "And I'd never have worn this ridiculous dress. I had proper armor and a sword with opals in the hilt. And then one cursed morning, over a hundred years ago now, I left the rath and some arse of a poet with the Sight saw me. He was so convinced, had believed for so bloody long that fairies were these wee pretty things, that the sheer force of his belief and that of his daft artist friends, eventually shrank me down." She fanned her wings indignantly. "You try finding a sword small enough to be of any use to me."

I was still sitting on the ground, dampness seeping into my skirt. I shivered. "Maybe it's the flu," I said suddenly.

"Don't be stupid, we don't get the flu."

I rubbed at my face, nearly laughed. "Not you, me. Maybe I have a fever. That would explain everything."

She sighed, drifted down to look at me. Even with her impressive wings she was only about a foot long. "This part is so tiresome," she told me. "Could you catch up? I hate having to convince people that they're not crazy. Maybe you are, it's nothing to do with me. And I'm not buzzing about forcing you to convince me you're real, am I?"

"Um, no?"

"Good. Here's the usual list of rational explanations, none of which pertain here: some sort of drug, it was laudanum back when I got caught; illness; hallucination; trickery; or else a vivid dream of some sort. I don't think I've left anything out."

I swallowed, strangely comforted. "Okay. Know anything about Antonia Hart and why one of your lot would have kidnapped my best friend?"

"Did you say Hart?" She paled, cockiness fading slightly. "Blast."

She was gone before I could ask her anything else, but not before I'd seen the look of stark terror on her delicate face.

chapter 5
Eloise

I don't know how long I sat there, waiting. I'd slipped the pendant back under my collar after Jo's voice faded away and that felt like it had been hours ago. The contact bolstered me a little, enough that I didn't feel quite so hysterical. If I knew Jo, she was already researching. I hated that all I could do right now was wait.

I hated it more when the oak door creaked open and then the silver curlicue grate after that. A guard strolled in holding a small trunk, which he dropped on the rug with a thump. "Put this on, little morsel."

I lifted the lid and pulled out a frilly white corset, frilly white petticoats, and a burgundy dress that looked both complicated and revealing. "I don't think so."

He raised an eyebrow, the feather in his hair ruffling over

the black feathers carved into his armor. "Then Lord Strahan will see you naked at his dinner table."

I knew I went pale as milk, then flushed to the color of ripe strawberries. He laughed. "Lord Strahan always gets his way." He nudged me with the tip of his boot. "Want some help, lass?"

I drew back, lifted my chin."I can manage."

"Pity."

I waited until he'd left and shut the heavy door behind him. I was pretty sure the reason the others were leaving me relatively alone wasn't because they didn't want to hurt me, but rather because Strahan wanted to hurt me more. I was starting to feel nauseous. I had to force myself to get up and sort through the clothes. The last thing I wanted was for them to march back in and find me only half-dressed and use that as an excuse to drag me out in my underwear. Or worse.

I was really grateful for all those long dull Victorian movies that Jo loved so much. It was the only reason I was able to vaguely recognize some of the lace and linen piled in a heap on the bed. The lacy pant-things went on first and then the corset—just in case I wasn't already feeling dizzy and light-headed enough. There was a lump that looked like it was stuffed with cotton batting and I assumed it was the bustle so I used the ribbons to tie it around my waist before pulling the dress over my head. The lace clung to the corset, then spilled over the edge into frothy cupcake ribbons and pleats at the bottom. My bare shoulders poked out of peek-a-boo cuts in the fabric. The collar was ruffled with white lace, closed at the throat. There was just enough space to hide my necklace in my cleavage, thanks to the corset. I'd never actually had cleavage before; Jo had all the boobs, I had all the skinny. I thought I'd feel silly in the dress, but it made me stand a little taller.

The doors swung open, clanging against the wall. A guard jerked her head for me to follow her. I swallowed, frozen in place. She paused and turned her head. "Walk or be dragged."

I walked. The hallway was lit with ornate beaded lamps of various sizes. There were crystal bowls filled with lilies everywhere. She wasn't a crow-guard. There were no feathers in her hair, and her armor looked more like a beetle's carapace, shiny black with streaks of green and blue. As she led me back to the main hall, the scent of lilies grew stronger and more cloying.

Exquisite crystal chandeliers glittered overhead, revealing Lord Strahan in a frock coat made entirely of black PVC. Devin's Goth sister would have drooled over it. In fact, she would have loved this whole place, with its overdone glitter and edge. I just wanted our tiny apartment with the cracked Formica counters and radiator that clanked and groaned through the winter.

"Much better," he said, giving me the once-over. "Can't do much about the hair, I suppose, but it's not so ghastly as all that."

I just glared at him. I was so out of my depth it was ridiculous. He kept smiling, like a proud host. His harem of ghostly ladies floated behind him. "You've met my Grey Ladies. Now, do sit down."

His genteel manners were getting to be as creepy as the rest of this nightmare. I sat in the chair he nodded to, mostly because the beetle-girl shoved me down into it. She stood behind me, straight and alert. I knew if I so much as moved a muscle away from the blue brocade cushions, I'd be feeling the tip of one of the daggers hanging from her belt.

"Please let me go," I whispered.

Strahan waved that away as if I were being ridiculous. The Grey Ladies laughed, and it was the sound of ice cracking on a lake, swallowing an unprepared person entirely.

"We've a ball to look forward to," he said. "It's barely a week from Samhain and we must celebrate. Your aunt wouldn't miss it. She'll think to gain her crown back, won't she?"

I'd seen my aunt in ripped jeans, torn T-shirts, and ropes of crystal beads, but never a crown.

"Bring the others in," he said to a man in a starched cravat and holly leaves for hair. I didn't know what to do, so I sat in my chair and tried not to scream. Maybe if I sat quietly enough I could find out what was going on, get some snippet of information that made sense. I wondered where Lucas was and if he knew I was here and why Strahan seemed so infuriated by the mere mention of the Richelieu family. That alone made me want to find every Richelieu in the world and kiss them. With tongue.

The hall bustled with servants and courtiers, the latter lounging about eating sugar-frosted cakes and bowls of chocolate topped with pink whipped cream. There were tables piled with foods of all types: fragrant pastries; honey-painted breads; berries and custards; and crystal tureens boiling with hot chocolate, ginger tea, and that odd pink champagne. My stomach rumbled lightly. It didn't care that I was terrified and held against my will, it only wanted to eat some of those éclairs. I looked away before I started to drool.

The doors at the other end were held open and guards marched in, taking their place, in two perfectly straight lines. The courtiers stopped chattering and a silence slid into every available space, like water, cold and soft and dangerous.

Creature after creature was led into the hall and chained to the wall. Iron touched fairy flesh and the smell of burning mingled with wilting lily. Some walked proudly, some were dragged, wailing. Some were beautiful, some were bizarre; all were bruised or cut or dead-eyed. I shivered, tried to look away, couldn't. He was collecting them like wooden masks or silver beads.

There was a tall, thin woman with birch branches in her hair; a man bleeding what looked like sap; a woman who was half girl, half wren; a white dog with red ears on a choke chain; a mermaid with a peeling fish tail; and Winifreda with her torn wings.

Strahan clucked his tongue. "This won't do," he said blandly. "They're tattered and hardly impressive enough to be enjoyed as entertainment at the ball. I'm known for my collection, after all. Heal them, clean them up, and for God's sake, do something about that fish smell."

Several of the guards nearest to us bowed in unison. A young man began to move through the crowd, setting the corseted courtiers to whispering. Strahan lifted his head like a hunter testing the air before the chase.

"Ah, Eldric," he said, satisfied. "Home at last."

Eldric was about my age, maybe a couple of years older, with a lean and handsome face. He looked human, but with a kind of fierce dignity that was something else entirely. His scuffed boots and ratty jeans didn't fit in at all. In fact, Strahan sniffed once. "You stink of them."

Eldric shrugged. "You were the one who sent me up there." He saw me and stilled, except for the flaring of his eyes, like coal catching fire. "Who's she, then?"

"Who do you think?" Strahan said with a hint of warning and something I couldn't recognize. The Grey Ladies drifted over, stroked Eldric's cheek, swooned and sighed. He ignored them. I had to bite my teeth down to keep them from chattering together. The Grey Ladies weren't any less creepy when they were flirting.

I really didn't recognize my life anymore and I'd been here less than a full day.

"She doesn't look like much," Eldric said. One of the

guards handed him a cup, which he drained and handed back. "Thank you, Malik." When he leaned over me, I smelled honey and wine. There was something not quite tame about him, like a wild dog who might as easily eat from your hand as bite it right off.

"Back off." It would have sounded more impressive if my voice hadn't given out into a pathetic little croak. He smiled insolently. I wanted to punch him.

"She reminds me of that pet ferret I had." He glanced at Strahan. "Before you drowned it."

Strahan didn't look particularly penitent, only nodded at the guards to start leading the captives out. Eldric watched dispassionately, though I did see his jaw clenching.

"Anything?" Strahan asked, so nonchalantly I knew it must be important.

Eldric shrugged again. Everyone else winced, stepped back a little as if they wanted to be unobtrusive. The air crackled. "They're like cattle, huddling together. I'll never understand it."

"That doesn't answer my question."

Eldric pushed his long hair off his face where it kept tangling, lifted by the Grey Ladies' adoring breaths. "Nothing. This one"—he barely glanced at me—"hasn't even been missed yet."

"And Antonia?"

"No trail and none of our scouts have heard anything. Even the Seelie courts aren't sure where she's at."

That made me feel better for my aunt even though white lines of suppressed fury tightened Strahan's mouth. "So near Samhain. She should be here by now."

That did *not* make me feel better.

"And the Richelieu?"

"Not talking. Do they ever?"

"Clearly, you're not being persuasive enough." He smoothed the lace at his cuffs. "You'll be ready." It wasn't a question.

Eldric bowed, but it was all cockiness and condescension. "Yes, Father."

• • •

When I was taken back to my room, every available surface was covered in platters of food and jugs of cider, mead, and peach nectar. There was an entire roasted chicken, herb-encrusted olives, mashed potatoes, roasted carrots, warm bread, jars of blackberry jam, stewed apples, ice cream that didn't melt, cherries floating in some kind of chocolate cream, rice-stuffed grape leaves, spinach pies, chocolate muffins, croissants, and every color of jelly bean imaginable.

My stomach growled so loudly the guard smirked before locking the silver door and leaving the other one open. The smell of so much food was making me want to stuff my face. My mouth felt dry and tasted like an old sock. Nothing a huge spoonful of raspberry coulis wouldn't fix.

And yet Jo had been really adamant that I not eat or

drink anything. At all. Which was totally unfair. I was *hungry*.

And being hungry made me cranky. I kicked at the heavy leg of the four-poster bed and swore. And kicked it again. Looked at the blueberry turnovers. Kicked. Sniffed the vegetable dumplings. Swore. Drooled over a tureen of cucumber soup. Kicked some more.

My toes hurt and I was still hungry.

"Stupid Fae feast," I grumbled, stomping away from the food. "In this stupid Fae hill."

The hallway was clear of guards for the first time since I'd gotten here. I could see the door across the way, also barred, and a few more if I turned my head so that it felt like it was going to pop right off my shoulders.

"Hey," I whisper-yelled. "Anyone?" There was silence, but I caught the faint scrape of movement in the room directly across mine. "Hello?"

First an eye, then half a bony shoulder peeked out. He was sitting on the ground and looked thin enough that a sneeze would break him in half.

"Are you hungry?"

He nodded. He was clearly Fae, so I didn't think a hunk of cheese was going to trap him here. Mmmm, cheese. *Focus, Eloise Hart.*

"I haven't eaten in days," he said, his voice rusty, as if he hadn't spoken in that long as well.

"You don't have food? It's like a banquet here."

"Food is a chain to mortals in this place," he said.

"Don't remind me."

"And summer has blighted our crops so that food is scarce. Strahan saves the best for himself."

"Oh." I took a few soft buns filled with whipped cream and strawberries and rolled them across the floor so they bumped into the bars. He was careful not to touch the iron when he reached out to grab them. He stuffed the food in his mouth, not stopping to chew. There was a smear of whipped cream and strawberry sauce on my thumb. I wiped it on the rug, rubbing so hard my skin chafed.

"What's your name?"

He shook his head, chewed faster. "I can't say, not even to you." His hair was long and braided, the color of honey. Antlers curved out of the braids. One of them was broken, hanging crookedly. It looked really painful.

"Why not?"

"Names have power."

"Um, okay." I thought about Winifreda and how she'd told me her name. She'd called it her speaking-name. "What about your speaking-name?"

"Nicodemus."

Ha, I'd figured something out. Okay, it was a small thing and got me no closer to getting home, but still. "I'm Eloise."

"I know."

"How long have you been here?" I asked, trying to find a comfortable way to sit in a bustle and corset.

He swallowed, peered down the hall nervously. "Three months or so. His bogey-beasts caught me in the fens. I ought to have been more careful, but the harp was singing to me."

"Oh. I don't really know what that means, but it doesn't sound good."

He shook his head. "They've been looking for you, for the Hart girl, for a week now. We were hoping they wouldn't find you."

I made a face. "I was kind of hoping that too." I struggled to ignore the smell of baked apples with cinnamon. "Why did they capture you?"

"I've a way with music," he said. "I was poet-born and I can make the kind of songs Fae like best. I suspect he wants me to play at the ball."

"What is this ball?" If I was kidnapped to go to the Fae equivalent of a high school dance I was so going to kick some ass. "What does it have to do with my aunt? Or me for that matter?"

"It's Samhain," he said as if that explained anything.

"Which is?"

He blinked at me. "Do you not have any schooling?"

I got the impression that I was being called stupid by a violet-eyed fairy poet who played the harp in a swamp. And come to think of it, Lucas had made a comment like that.

"I go to school." I scowled. "And at least I know better than to call girls dumb."

His eyes widened. "I beg your pardon."

"So what's Samhain then? Isn't that some sort of old Celtic legend thing? On Halloween?" Call me dumb, will you.

"Aye, it's the last day of summer."

"Okay." I was thinking really hard, trying to connect the dots before my intelligence was insulted again. "And Strahan wants to get my aunt before Halloween? Or Samhain, whatever. Why? What happens then?" I remembered something about crowns. "My aunt takes over?" I shook my head. "That doesn't make sense, she's just Aunt Antonia. She's not some Fae queen. I think we'd have noticed."

"I wrote a song once about the lovely Antonia." His expression became faraway and dreamy. I'd seen my mom with the same look on her face when she was caught in the middle of a painting. I missed her even more than grilled cheese sandwiches and root beer. "She loved him, you know."

"Strahan? Ew."

He shrugged. "He never lacks female companionship."

I thought of the Grey Ladies and their frigid melancholy, their hunger and pearl-like teeth. "Again, ew." If Strahan had been her first boyfriend, no wonder Antonia took off the way she did.

Every spring.

And came back every autumn.

Damn.

"Are you seriously telling me my aunt is a Fae queen?"

"Of course not, she's as mortal as you are. But she wears the crown, which she stole from Strahan, who would wear it all the year long. It's because of her and the Richelieu that the Seelie courts can still roam free. And because of her, I suppose, that we're here. Every Samhain, it's the same."

I shivered. "What does Seelie mean? I heard Strahan use that word earlier."

"It roughly translates to 'blessed.'" He smiled faintly, looking homesick. "We keep to our own revels. But the Unseelie love only power in both your world and mine. They live for the hunt, and the kill. They want our courts, as well as their own."

"And if I don't want to belong to either?"

"You may not have a choice."

• • •

I must have fallen asleep because the next thing I knew, Eldric was shaking me awake and scowling. "Get up."

I woke suddenly, bolting upright and swinging my fist at the same time. He simply leaned back, avoiding my wild punch. "Someone should teach you how to do that properly."

"Oh, shut up," I muttered. My head felt bleary, as if I'd been sleeping too deeply. I couldn't figure out why I was breathing so lightly until I looked down and realized I was still wearing the corset under my dress. It was quite pretty for an instrument of torture, covered in little pink ribbons and bows.

"Come on," Eldric said, like I was a particularly slow child.

"What?" I blinked up at him. I didn't know how long I'd been staring at my waist. "Why? And where?"

He rolled his eyes, tugged me out of the warm bed. "Just come on. Are you always so difficult?"

"You try being kidnapped by a bunch of storybook weirdos."

"Please, the weirdos are up top."

I just snorted. He yanked on my hand, dragging me until I was walking fast enough for his liking. He probably wasn't taking me somewhere to murder me horribly.

Probably.

The hallway was deserted, lit only with a few oil lamps. The lanterns hanging from the roots were dusty. All the doors were shut and the ground was cold under my bare feet. There wasn't a single window or corridor, no chance of escape. Eldric kept looking over his shoulder, which made me even more nervous than I already was, because whatever he had to be anxious about couldn't bode well for me.

He ducked under an arch like the ones in medieval cathedrals and into a room that quite simply took my breath away. The ceiling-roots were painted silver and hung with crystal and glass lamps. The walls were stone and the floor had white pebbles in narrow paths leading to a fountain in the center with a circle of benches surrounding it. Stone deer and hounds bent their heads to drink.

There were roses everywhere, from tiny buds to fat ripe blossoms, in every shade of cream and pink and red and purple. They climbed trellises, low crumbling garden walls, and up into the silver roots. I turned on my heel to drink it all in.

"It's beautiful," I breathed. It was the most calm I'd felt in days. "I've never seen anything like it."

"It was your aunt's favorite room."

"But she hates roses." She always said they were typical, fake.

He shrugged, but I could tell he was interested.

"Why did you bring me here?"

"I want to know more about Antonia."

"Ask your father."

"I'm asking you."

"Why would I tell you anything?" I trailed my hand through the fountain's water and even though it was full of moss and silver glitter, I seriously considered taking a mouthful. I wondered if that would count as drinking. My throat felt like sandpaper. "Your dad hates her. You probably do too."

"I've never even met her." He was pacing, his boots scattering the pebbles. I envied the fact that he was in comfortable jeans while I had to perch delicately in burgundy silk.

"You want her crown or whatever, right?"

"I just want to know what she's like. Every year it's the same thing, and every year I get sent off on some made-up errand. Not this year."

I raised my eyebrows. And I thought I had parental issues. My dad might live halfway around the world and barely remember he even had a daughter, but at least he never made my voice do that weird squeaky, angry thing. Eldric clearly hated Strahan as much as he might love him. I guess we had something in common, after all.

"Antonia's smart," I said. "And funny. She eats caramels by the ton, and she's going to kick your father's ass."

He snorted. "We'll see."

"She's strong and she's loyal and . . . haunted," I said, realizing it. "I guess I never really got that before now. You guys changed her, stole her life." *Bastards.*

"You sound like Malik."

I recognized the name. It was one of the guards, the one who'd given him the honey wine earlier. He sounded like the one who might not want to drink Antonia's blood as a nightcap. I'd have to try and get closer to him, see if he might help me.

"He would never betray me," Eldric said. I blinked. "Your every thought is written on your face," he explained.

"Crap," I muttered. I'd really have to work on that. "Is he your bodyguard or something?"

"Yes. He's also my taster."

"Your what?"

"He's in charge of my food and drink." He elaborated when I just looked at him blankly. "To make sure nothing is poisoned."

I shivered. "This place sucks," I muttered. I touched the stone deer, rubbed its smooth ear and could have sworn it was warm under my hand. I remembered the stag in the park. "I don't understand any of this."

He nearly smiled. "That's the first step."

"Eldric." I said it softly. "Will you help me get out of here? Please?"

He jerked a hand through his hair, then glared at me so fiercely I swallowed. "Don't make the mistake of trusting me, Eloise. I'm not your friend."

• • •

When I got back to my room, Nicodemus was singing softly. It was such a melancholy sound that it made my eyes burn. There was another sound underneath, a broken sort of moaning from the room next to his.

"What is that?" I asked, pressing against the silver bars. I'd half hoped Eldric would forget to lock it accidentally on purpose. No such luck.

"It's a *ceasg*," he explained, which wasn't an explanation at all.

"A who-what?"

"A mermaid, I think you'd call her. She answers to Cala."

"Is she okay?" It was clear by the sound that she wasn't. It was just as clear that Nicodemus had been singing to soothe her. It made me like him even more.

"She needs water. The dry causes her pain."

"Oh." I might not be able to do much about my own

predicament right now, but that was something I could at
least fix. "Hold on."

I took the jug of water and a basket of figs for Nicodemus
and slid them between the bars, pushing them across the floor.
He stretched as far as he could to get them, the iron singeing
his broken antler. It was oozing sap, green and inflamed. I
winced for him even though he didn't blink. The smell of
burned hair tingled in my nostrils.

If I tilted my head just so, I could just barely see a barred
window between his door and Cala's. I couldn't see her at
all, but I remembered her from the procession in the Hall.
Her hair was all shades of blue and green and silver. She was
quiet now.

Nicodemus smiled his sad, gentle smile. "That was kind of
you." He ate one of the figs. Then he reached up and snapped
off the broken antler, his face going white with pain.

"What are you doing!" Blood and sap ran into his hair.
He tossed the broken antler at me.

"Careful, it's sharp." His violet eyes glittered. "Sharp
enough to cut through silver."

I looked at the silver bars, at the sap-stained antler. It was
soft, like velvet, but the jagged edges did look vicious. "Thank
you. But why did you do that?"

"For giving me food and Cala your water. I would have
no debts between us."

I rolled my eyes. "Is this a guy thing? Who mentioned
debts anyway?"

"It is usually the way between mortals and Faerie."

"Well, whatever. I'm not keeping score. God." I ripped the inside hem of my petticoats and tucked the antler carefully inside. "Will she be okay?"

"They'll move her to one of the fountains for the ball, which will help. After that . . ." He shrugged. "Who can say? It's up to your aunt and yourself, I suppose."

"Great. No pressure or anything."

I moved back into the relative privacy of my room, between the curtained bed and the tables. I didn't want to see those wounded eyes watching me hopefully. How was I supposed to save them all when I couldn't even figure out how to save myself? And anyway, this was their world, wasn't it? Shouldn't they be the ones figuring it all out? I'd hide too if I was my aunt. In fact, I'd hide right now if I thought I could fit under the ornate bed.

And I couldn't even drown my sorrow in chocolate sauce even though there was a huge bowl of it sitting right there next to warm cinnamon waffles. I went over to inhale the steam off cappuccinos, apple pie, pesto bread.

"I'm so hungry."

And now I was talking to myself.

Great.

I gripped the stag pendant so tightly the edges dented my skin. "Jo?" I whispered urgently. "Hey, Jo! Can you hear me?"

"El?" She sounded like she was choking on something. "I'm never going to get used to this. Your face is on my mobile."

"Are you *eating?*"

"Hot dog at the park."

"Damn it, Jo. With pickles?"

"Of course. Sorry. Hey, keep your voice down. People are looking at me like I'm nuts."

"Is my mom worried? Has she called the police?"

"No, you left her a note."

"I did *not.*"

"I know, but there's one there. Apparently you were staying at my place last night. And you will never believe what I saw."

"Wait." I leaned back against the mounds of over-embroidered pillows, frowning. "What do you mean last night? It's been way longer than that."

"Not here. I read that somewhere, actually, that time sometimes runs differently."

"Find anything else out?" It felt so good to hear her voice, so normal. I could almost pretend we were just talking on the phone on a school night, bored with everything. I'd give anything to be bored like that again.

"Well, I met a little fairy with wings."

"*What?*"

"I know, right? Totally bizarre, I mentioned your last name and she got all wiggy and took off."

I chewed on my lower lip. "That could be good, right? Maybe there are other Harts a hell of a lot more powerful than me. What else did you get?"

"Loads. Don't know if any of it's useful or not, though.

I can tell you that if you look through a stone with a hole in it, you can see Fae."

"Yeah, got that one down, I think. Is that what you used?"

"No. She just popped up."

"Okay, *that* can't be good."

"We're not snookered yet. You can use rowan berries and red thread to break a fairy glamour or turn your clothes inside out to be invisible to them. A bunch of stuff like that. And there are these courts apparently, the Seelie and the Unseelie who get all aggro with each other."

"Yeah, they're big on courts here. Oh, and there's some celebration on Halloween when Strahan has to hand over his crown to Antonia so she can take over until spring. And he's obsessed with ribbons. It's just weird."

"That *is* weird. And you're sure you're talking about the same Antonia who can't remember where she put her keys and once lost your mom's motorcycle entirely? Which I still don't get."

"Tell me about it."

"So, which Halloween? Theirs or ours?"

"I never thought of that." I wrinkled my nose. "Why does it feel like I'm going backward, like I know even less than when I started?"

"We'll get you out of there, E. Somehow."

"I know." I tried to sound brave. "Maybe you should start looking for my aunt? I don't want her coming here because they might really hurt her, but she'd know more than we do." An idea struck me. "Can you call my answering machine?"

"What for?" I could hear her dialing and then my mom's message, so curt and familiar it made my chest ache. It was a struggle to sound cheerful. But if time ran differently, I may as well take advantage of it. I so didn't want to come home to cops and my face on a milk carton.

"Hey, Mom, it's me. I'm going to sleep over at Jo's again tonight, to work on a project. I'll see you later, okay?"

There was a click when Jo hung up. "Good idea," she said quietly.

"I'm getting out of here," I told her, shifting when the antler poked me in the thigh. "Tonight."

chapter 6
Jo

I went straight to Eloise's apartment to talk to her mother. I'd promised Eloise I wouldn't call. I didn't say anything about going in person. Eloise sounded like she had some kind of plan and if I knew the Harts at all, her plan would somehow backfire in the most spectacular way. And it wouldn't be her fault, it never was—stuff just happened to them. At her fifth birthday party, the cake got dropped and one of the kids got frosting in her eye and it swelled up with pus. At our first school dance, Eloise's mom was a chaperone and all the boys spent the night crushing on her while the other mothers, mine included, sniffed at her tattoos.

And when a Fae girl the size of a hummingbird talked to you, it was time to get serious.

I ran up to the top floor and pounded on the front door,

panting. "Jaz?" She always let us call her that, even when we were little. I knocked louder.

The door finally opened. Eloise's mom was wearing a black kimono, her hair in a ponytail, black eye shadow still smudged around her eyes. She frowned. "Shouldn't you be in school?" She paused. "Jo, honey, what's wrong?" The blood drained from her face. "El?"

I nodded, biting my lower lip when it trembled.

"Is she hurt? Was there an accident?"

"No, it's . . ." I swallowed, glancing down the hall for nosy neighbors. "Um."

She pulled me inside. Elvis flicked his tail at me from the top of the couch. The apartment smelled like it always did: coffee and oil paints.

"She says she's been kidnapped by the Fae. Strahan or something like that? She said it was about Antonia."

"No. God, no." Jasmine sagged. I leaped forward to catch her. "I'm okay," she said, forcing her shoulders back. Her hands were shaking when she reached for the phone on the table in the hall. She knocked over a basket of keys, barely noticed. "Antonia," she snapped into the receiver. *"Now."* It was all she said. I wasn't any less confused.

"What's going on?" I asked. "Is this even real? I mean, flower fairies? Really?"

She sighed, touched my hair. "Oh, honey. I'm sorry about this. I wish I had time to explain." She rushed toward her bedroom.

"Wait!" I called after her. "What do I do?"

"Absolutely nothing." She paused long enough to shoot me a pointed glance. "I mean it, Jo. This is dangerous. Go home. Or better yet, back to school."

Like hell I'd just wait around while my best friend was in trouble.

She shut her bedroom door and I left, dialing Devin. He answered on the third ring. "Where the hell are you two?" he grumbled. "You both skipped and left me to deal with this pop quiz alone? Where's the love?"

"Meet me at the park, by the pond. One hour." I hung up before he could ask any more questions.

I remembered something about burning thorn trees to release human captives from the Fae. It was a long shot, but I didn't know what else to do. Even if I wasn't sure what a thorn tree was. I went back to the coffeehouse and ordered the biggest mochaccino they had, with extra whipped cream and chocolate sprinkles. And a giant cookie. Knowing Eloise couldn't eat just made me hungrier. I stepped out of the line and called Nanna.

"Nanna," I asked, "what's a thorn tree?"

"Jo?" She sounded confused. Maybe she didn't know what a thorn tree was either. "Aren't you supposed to be in school?"

"I am," I lied. "I have a study hall. And the thorn tree thing is for homework."

"I think a thorn tree is just a hawthorn, dear."

"Oh. Thanks. Nanna?"

"Yeah?"

"What's a hawthorn?"

She laughed. "It's the tree behind the barn that you used to love so much. The one with all the white flowers in spring."

I remembered that tree. It was always full of honeybees and it filled the grass with petals like snow. "Okay, thanks."

I drove out to the farm with the windows rolled down and the music cranked as loud as it would go. I left the car by the barn and climbed over the fence, plastic cup of mochaccino in one hand and a saw in the other. Farm girls knew how to multitask.

The tree grew over the well that had run dry. I'd never noticed before that the gray branches were spiked, like rose stems. I sawed a few branches and then gathered twigs from the ground, wrapping them in twine. A thorn scratched my thumb, drawing blood.

"Jo."

I didn't see him until he spoke, his voice soft as scented smoke. Something about the way he said my name made me feel like blushing, and I never blushed. I also never stood there like a dork, smiling a goofy smile. Damn it, I was already losing my touch. That Strahan had a lot to answer for.

"Are you all right?"

I gave myself a mental kick. "Grand, thanks. You startled me is all. Did my granddad call you about the well? He's been bragging to his friends that I found him a real water-witch."

He just smiled. "Three days in a row," he said. "We're going to have to go on a real date soon."

I couldn't help but remember our brief hot kiss. Something about the way he was looking at my lower lip made me think he was remembering too. "I'd like that." I was going to hell for this—I was supposed to be preparing for a big rescue, not flirting. Oh well, flirting was how I prepared for everything, including exams and dentist appointments, so why should this be any different?

"Gathering firewood?" he asked, raising an eyebrow.

I looked down at my armful of branches. "Um, yeah."

"You're bleeding," he said. "Let me take that from you." He took the bundle and set it on the well cover. "These trees bloom on the first day of May," he remarked, stepping closer to me. "Did you know that?" I shook my head. His lips brushed my ear. "I think I missed you," he said, sounding surprised.

I shivered faintly even as warmth pooled in the oddest places of my body: my belly, the backs of my knees, behind my ears. I tingled and sparkled all over. "I think I missed you too." I turned my head so our mouths were as close as butterfly wings. "And I don't even know your name yet."

"I would have thought you liked a little mystery." His free hand tangled through my hair, loosening my messy braid. I noticed a wicked scar on the inside of his elbow.

"Ouch, what happened to you?" I asked, running my fingers up his forearm, gently brushing the puckered skin. "Did you burn yourself?"

"In a manner of speaking."

I frowned. That wasn't really an answer. "How did it happen?"

"My father," he replied, so softly I almost didn't hear him. I stared at him, aghast.

"What? Seriously?" I wasn't entirely sure what the proper response was. "Your dad's a jerk." Probably not that.

He shrugged. "He's my father."

"What about your mom?"

"I never knew her."

"That totally sucks."

"It is what it is. There's no use weeping over it."

"You should run away." I so wasn't qualified to be giving this sort of advice.

"He'd find me." He sounded very sure.

"So what, you're over eighteen, right? You're legal."

"If only it were that simple."

I didn't know what else to say, so I just leaned down and kissed his scar. "I'm sorry you got hurt."

His breath caught and he tugged on my hair lightly, angling my face back up. His lips descended on mine then, and I forgot everything, even how to breathe. I barely knew him, but it hardly mattered. We were connected somehow; something precious burned between us.

His mouth was cool, like raspberry sherbet. I kissed him desperately, hating any tiny distance that might separate us. I would have crawled right into his shirt with him if I'd been able. He clutched me closer, as if he felt the same way.

His hand tightened in my hair as he deepened the kiss, as he plucked me up and set me on the farm fence. I held on to his shoulders, feeling his lean muscles working under his warm skin.

He pulled back, barely, just as I was beginning to wonder if it was possible to get singed lips from a kiss. "What is it about you, Jo?" he asked, his voice ragged.

I swallowed, my breath trembling in my throat. "What is it about *us*?" I corrected him gently.

"I'm not good for you."

It was a warning.

As if I couldn't already tell he was steeped in secrets and angst. He wore a cloak of solitude and arrogance, but I was beginning to see where it was thin and frayed in spots.

"So?" I kissed him again, a soft nip. "Earnest and true isn't my taste," I murmured. "What about your taste?"

A crooked smile touched his sullen mouth. "I prefer . . . darker."

My pulse danced a complicated jig as muggy white clouds nibbled on the sun. The shadows around us darkened, like bruises. He glanced at the sky. "Storm coming," he said softly, as if he was calculating. "Not tonight, but soon. Too soon."

"Good," I said, taking a sip of my drink to steady myself. "We could use the rain." Secretly, I thought our kiss might have been powerful enough to end the drought.

I reluctantly slid off the fence. "I have to go," I said.

"You should," he agreed, self-mocking in his tone. He reached out and wiped a smear of chocolate from the corner of my mouth with his thumb. "See you soon, Jo." I shivered. Soon was not going to be anywhere soon enough.

But at least this time I was the one to walk away, while he leaned against the fence and watched me, his hands in his pockets.

• • •

I parked in the lot just inside the park, by the swing sets. I would have run all the way to the pond if it wasn't so bloody hot. Or so far away. I hooked the bundle of thorn twigs to my knapsack and slung it over my shoulder, grateful for stamina granted to me by years of helping out in the orchard. It kept me from passing out when the heat clogged my lungs and from collapsing in a nervous breakdown when I thought about what was happening. Nanna said it to me all the time, especially since the rains had stopped: *farm folk keep on.*

By the time I reached the pond, the back of my tank top was soaked in sweat. I guzzled an entire bottle of water and then stuck my wrists in the pond to cool off. The swan was gone. I scanned the grass, the weeds, the wilted dandelions— saw nothing resembling a mouthy Fae dressed like a flower.

Assuming Devin had managed to sneak out of school between classes, he'd be here soon. If nothing else, he was so calm he'd help me feel less crazy. Or I could call Hot Guy and see if he wanted to distract me some more.

I set out the matches I'd packed and then arranged the twigs in a little teepee shape, the way Granddad did when we had summer bonfires. I stuffed crumpled paper in the hollow center and then filled my empty bottle with water from the pond. I carefully soaked the grass around the thorny branches so I wouldn't accidentally set the whole field on fire. I wiped my palms on my skirt.

"Okay, here goes," I muttered, reaching for the box of matches. I lit the hawthorn branches, fanning them with my math binder until the flames caught. They crackled and smoked. I sat back, scanning the grass, the pond, the birch trees. I wasn't sure what I was expecting to see. Which didn't really matter since nothing happened.

Nothing at all.

I coughed on the smoke, deflated. "I was really hoping it would be that easy."

"You ijit," a small, feral voice snapped.

I jumped, lifting my fists in a classic boxer stance.

The flower fairy snorted. "Going to punch a wee thing like me, are you, then?"

I lowered my hands. "You again."

"I prefer 'Isadora' to 'you.'" She circled the tiny bonfire, scowling. "What the bleedin' hell is this?"

"A thorn tree fire."

"Someone's been reading novels." She sighed, her pretty wings fluttering.

"I'm trying to get my friend Eloise out of the hill."

"That won't do it," she replied. "All you've done is made things worse."

I scowled back. "How exactly did I do that?"

"Because now the Fae know you know about them. They know where you are, sitting in this big empty field like a rabbit ready for the stewpot."

I did *not* like that analogy. "Are you cannibals?" I squeaked.

"I eat honey and flowers," she returned, disgusted. "I used to eat the finest braised pork . . ." She trailed off, sighing a little.

"But you didn't eat *people*."

"Don't be daft."

"Are you talking to yourself?" Devin interrupted me. I hadn't heard him coming, and the sudden sound of his voice, after a conversation about cannibalism, made me shriek and leap into the air. I would have fallen right into the pond if he hadn't grabbed me. He was laughing so hard, I still nearly went in.

"No more caffeine for you," he said. He waved his hand in front of his face when the smoke drifted our way. Isadora floated right past his nose and he didn't even blink. "What, it's not hot enough for you?" He shook his head. "Do I even want to know what you're doing?"

I stared at him. Isadora did a somersault.

"Did you not see that?" I asked. Maybe the smoke was making his eyes blurry.

"See what?"

Isadora spun in place like a ballerina, cackling.

"You seriously don't see her?"

"Who?" He looked around. "Eloise?"

"Not exactly." I sat down hard, feeling dejected. My fire hadn't worked. Devin couldn't see Isadora. Eloise was still trapped under some Fae hilltop. "Isadora," I explained glumly. "She looks like a flower fairy from a book of nursery rhymes."

Isadora, in her delicate flower petal skirt, gave me the finger.

"Jo." Devin crouched beside me. "I'm starting to worry about you. Maybe you have sunstroke." He put his hand on my forehead. "We should find some shade."

"Isadora is Fae," I insisted. She perched on the top of his head and danced a jig.

He blinked. "Um . . . what?"

"You heard me."

"Okay, this is weird, even for you." He fished a bottle of water out of his bag. "Drink this." He put his thumb on the inside of my wrist, feeling my pulse. "Feels okay. Where's Eloise?"

"That is definitely a good question. I wish I knew the answer."

He frowned. "What's going on? Do I need to get you to a doctor or something?"

"Eloise is kind of missing."

"Jo."

"Yeah?"

"What the hell are you talking about?"

"It's about Eloise's aunt Antonia, like we thought."

"Gambling debt?" He raised his eyebrows so high his eyes bugged out.

"Worse. And I told Eloise's mom, and she didn't seem all that surprised. She told me to stay out of it."

"Yeah, right."

"Pretty much," I agreed. "So I called you. Because the Fae took Eloise."

Devin exhaled slowly. "Look, it's like a hundred and fifty degrees in the shade, so whatever practical joke you and Eloise have cooked up will have to wait." He wiped more sweat off his face. "If I decide to talk to either of you again."

He walked away. He was remembering the time Eloise and I had dressed up in Lord of the Rings hobbit costumes and crawled in through his window in the middle of the night. He'd thrown a plastic ax at us. Then his mother came in, and we weren't allowed in his house for a year.

But this time I wasn't kidding. I scowled at Isadora. "Well, thanks a lot. Why can't he see you?"

"I'm not your pet, human."

"Well, that's just great." Only I would get the Fae with attitude. "How did you do that anyway?"

"I can choose to be seen, unless the mortal in question has been Touched, as you have. Then it's trickier. Not impossible, mind, just takes more effort."

She'd mentioned that before. "Touched? Touched by who?"

"How should I know? A person, a stray bit of magic; it's of a piece." She danced away from the smoke. "You should put that out," she advised.

"And earlier today? Why'd you take off like that?"

"I had to confirm your story."

"And?"

"And you were telling the truth."

"I know. So now what?"

Her wings moved frantically, a blur of lavender and pink, like candy swirls. Her voice was surprisingly loud.

"Run!"

chapter 7

Eloise

The room was dark and silent, except for the drum currently lodged in my chest pretending to be my heart. I'd put out the oil lamps and I was crouched beside the door, sawing at the silver bars with the broken antler. My hands were sweaty and covered in scrapes. I'd already cut through one end but it didn't make a wide enough opening for me to slip through, even though I was squashed into a corset.

I had no idea where to go once I got free, but I was determined to try anyway. I sawed until my fingers cramped and the antler slipped into a pile of little silver filings. I slid it across the floor, back to Nicodemus for him to find when he woke up. I pushed at the bars until they curled up like vines. There was just enough space to wiggle through if I took off the bustle first. I left on the corset and frilly petticoats, and I was still wearing more clothes then I'd be wearing at home. Every part of me was covered, except for my arms. It wasn't easy, and I was huffing and puffing and covered in more scratches and torn lace by the time I tumbled into the hallway. A single lamp burned, throwing prisms of light from its crystal-beaded fringe.

I still didn't know where I was going but I was headed away from the main hall and Strahan, and that was good enough for me.

I didn't pause, not even to look into the other rooms. I didn't want anyone giving me away, and I couldn't break them all out. I hadn't even had the time to find a way to free Nicodemus or Winifreda. The antler didn't work on iron bars, only silver. I hadn't expected to feel so guilty that I couldn't help them. I should be elated, shouldn't I? It wasn't as if I'd been doing anyone any good all locked up anyway. I didn't have the luxury to rationalize or philosophize. If I got out, maybe I could find a way to get them out as well.

I ran quietly; the hallway felt endless. I passed the rose garden, stumbled into a room filled with snow and ice, backtracked to try another corridor. I was starting to get a little frantic. I could only run for so long before I got caught. Maybe it was silly, but in that moment I wanted to cry even more than when I'd first arrived. I was so close. And it was so unfair. I just wanted to go home.

I shivered in a blast of frigid air, trying to figure out if I'd come from the left archway or the right one. My breath fogged in a white puff in front of me and I frowned. I was nowhere near the winter room. Maybe cold air meant there was a door or a window or some kind of hole in the ceiling, anything. At this point I wasn't going to be picky, even though I could have sworn my corset bones creaked with ice.

And then the Grey Ladies appeared.

"No," I muttered, looking around for someplace to hide. "No, no, no."

I ran and didn't much care if I was going the wrong way. A blue glow followed me, flashing off the gilded mirrors on the walls. I stumbled and they laughed, hair gleaming like pearls. I ended up in a nook, and they blew in behind me, like a sudden snowstorm.

Eldric was leaning in the archway, his black frock coat embroidered with heavy silver thread. One of the Grey Ladies giggled. My teeth chattered.

"Eldric." I tried to catch my breath. Ice pellets scattered across the floor like beads. "Help me."

He just stood there, his expression shuttered.

"Please." When I tried to grab his sleeve, the Grey Ladies swooped in, vicious and unholy in their jealousy. My fingers went blue with cold. They circled me, howling, all floating ragged hems and teeth. The sound was so sharp, so unnatural, that it cracked the mirrors, sending shards of glass everywhere.

"I can't," he said. He sniffed the air. "Is that hawthorn smoke?" He looked furious, furious enough that I stumbled back, right into the arms of a guard. By the time Strahan arrived, Eldric was gone.

Strahan grabbed my arm so hard I immediately felt it bruising. "Well, well, what have we here? So rude to scorn my hospitality."

"Hospitality?" I echoed. "Are you kidding?"

He shrugged pleasantly. His fingers tightened. "Well, if you won't be my guest, I suppose you'll have to be my prisoner."

"What? No!"

"Restrain her," Strahan said mildly.

I really struggled then, even tried to bite him, but the guards fell on me like beetles, like crows on a dead rabbit. They dragged me along as the other captives came to the bars, otherworldly faces crowned with antler, torn wings, animal ears. No one said a single word.

They brought me to the main hall, which was empty except for a few serving girls and house hobs and Winifreda chained to the wall, weeping. There was blood on her gown, on her bruised skin.

"What have you done to her, you asshat?"

Strahan took a handful of my hair, yanked viciously. "You'll not be playing the shrew with me. I've been polite." He shoved me against the wall, closed an iron manacle around my wrist. "But you chose to make things difficult." He sounded like an indulgent, disappointed father. "Remember that."

"Bite me."

Okay, so hardly the smartest thing to say, but a girl could only take so much. I pulled at the chain until my wrist was sore. Strahan only watched, bored.

"I have less pleasant accommodations," he told me smoothly, so close to my ear his breath ruffled my hair. "The oubliette is free. We could forget about you in that dank dungeon in the ground for days, weeks even."

I stopped rattling the chain.

"Better." He waved to serving girls, who hurried forward with trays of food. "To show what a gracious host I am, despite my feral guests."

He left, taking everyone but Winifreda with him. A fire crackled faintly in the hearth, belching more smoke than warmth. Crows perched in the roots and Winifreda hadn't stopped her pitiful weeping. I slid down into a seated position. We were on the edge of a handwoven rug and the stone floor.

And I was chained to the wall in my underwear.

Great.

I huddled into myself, glad I'd dropped the antler so Nicodemus wouldn't be implicated for trying to help me. The platters of food were within reach and about the only distraction from my current predicament. Even the marzipan doves looked delicious, and I hated marzipan.

"Eloise?"

"Yeah?" I literally could not look away from a plate of cheese ravioli.

"You can eat," Winifreda whispered.

"What?" I froze. Excitement at the thought had my mouth filling with saliva. I could almost forget the damp stones, the heavy iron at my wrist. "I thought it would trap me here?"

"It would, yes, but you're already trapped. Strahan laid his hand on you. Food and drink make little difference now."

"Really?" I should be devastated by the news that I was trapped, but hunger was consuming my every thought. I might start composing a love sonnet to the eggplant parmagiana. I didn't wait for a second confirmation. I just gorged myself on anything I could reach: oranges, hot-cross buns, almonds, sugar cookies, baba ganoush, cinnamon biscotti, salty feta cheese, and apricots in jam.

I ate until I felt nauseous and I didn't care. I drank a river of hot chocolate and enough mead to cause my head to feel like it was full of glitter.

I woke up to laughter and the tip of a pink leather boot in my ribs.

"Ouch, hey!" I snapped groggily. I couldn't remember where I was until I sat up and smacked myself in the head with the iron chain. The laughter got louder, and so did my cursing. I rubbed at my cheek, pressing back against the wall, as far from the courtiers as I could get. There were four of them, two women who'd come to taunt me that first night and two men in intricate cravats anchored with jeweled pins. The woman in the vile pink satin had thin black snakes for hair, hissing.

"The little fawn's been naughty," she said.

I scrambled to my feet and glared. It was pretty much all I could do. There were raspberry stains on my petticoats and a smear of chocolate on my elbow.

One of the men held a lace handkerchief soaked in rosewater to his nose. "She smells."

"I wonder how she tastes," his companion drawled. He flicked the ribbon at my neckline.

I slapped his hand away and seriously considered biting his nose. "Get away from me."

He didn't. Instead, he licked my cheek. "I didn't much care for Antonia," he said. "Best hope I find you sweeter."

His hand went back to my chest. I lifted the iron cuff and shoved it at his face until the smell of burning obliterated the smell of rosewater. He leaped back, biting off words in a language I didn't know. I was fairly certain they weren't complimentary.

"Anyone else?" I asked, panting as adrenaline poured into my bloodstream like sugar and champagne. My knees trembled, but at least they were hidden under my petticoats.

It was like that all day.

The courtiers surrounded me, taunted me, called the beetles from under the carpets to crawl over my feet while I tried not to scream. Everyone stared at me. At least I wasn't starving to death on top of it. My stomach had stopped hurting and my throat didn't feel like it was on fire all the time. I only saw Eldric once when he came to whisper something in a woman's ear until she followed him, nibbling his neck.

That night, pretty serving girls and boys in short tunics paraded in from the kitchens with another feast. The lanterns were lit, the lamps dusted, and musicians sat in one corner with silver drums and fiddles carved out of jade and obsidian. The music they made was unlike anything I'd ever heard before, surreal and lovely: lime and lightning, strawberry shortcake, and the forest at night. Pipes were stuffed with flowers and smoked. The Grey Ladies danced until snow fell around them.

And then it all unraveled slowly, like a silk shawl coming apart at the fringes. Couples and threesomes drifted off into the scented shadows, all bare skin and tongues. I didn't consider myself a prude, but there were just some things I didn't need to see. Fae bums were one of them.

I sat with my knees drawn up, trying to make myself as small and invisible as I could. I was dizzy from the smoke. The roots looked like they were moving, slithering, and curling. Eyes from the faces carved into the walls winked at me. The music made me feel loose, like I was a candle melting into nothing. The others circled in an old-fashioned waltz. It was lovely and wrong; feet moved too fast or weren't feet at all; eyes went black from lid to lid, or lavender and silver. It was a long time before the hall cleared and there was only the sweet scent of burning poppies and hobs carrying out empty platters and discarded petticoats.

That was part of the reason why I didn't react when I first saw him. I just didn't think he was real.

Lucas.

He crouched beside me, finger to his lips in warning. His green eyes searched the shadows. "Are you hurt? Can you walk?"

I got to my feet. He caught at the chain to keep it from rattling and it seared his skin. I winced. "Sorry."

He handed me a long key on a red ribbon. "Hurry."

"Hey, Strahan's looking for a ribbon." My hands were suddenly sweaty and clumsy, but I managed to get the cuff unlocked. I massaged my wrist. "Now what?" I asked dubiously. He was utterly alone, no warriors, no guards, just a lone rescuer and his sword.

He smiled at me, sure of himself. "Now we go home."

He took my hand in his and his palm was warm and rough. He blinked at me, bewildered. I blinked back. He took my hands, stared at them as if they weren't doing what they were supposed to do. "Something's wrong." He closed his eyes briefly, as if he was in pain. "You ate."

"So?"

"So, it breaks my magic, what little I have. I can't walk the in-between with you now."

I nodded over at Winifreda. "But she said it wouldn't matter."

He looked at her grimly, then back at me. "She lied." He looked disgusted. "She's one of his."

"What? *What?*"

Winifreda laughed softly, prettily, and rose to her feet. She moved with a languid grace completely at odds with eyes red from crying, and a wretched, wounded expression. She fluttered her wings once and they unfurled, unblemished, soft as satin. Not a single rip or tear, not even a rough patch. She stepped away from the damp wall, shaking her chains free. Her wrists were raw, that much she hadn't been able to avoid.

I just stared at her stammering. "But . . . but . . ."

She called out in the odd lyrical language and the crowguards rushed in, black armor flashing dully.

Lucas stepped partly in front of me, lifting his sword. "Eloise, run."

"Oh right, I'm just going to leave you here," I said. "Besides, I tried running before and it didn't work. At all."

Winifreda shook her hair free, slowly, as if she was in some damn shampoo commercial. I wanted to scratch her eyes right out of her delicate little head. I'd trusted her, felt sorry for her, promised myself that I'd get her out somehow.

"Bitch."

Her eyes flared. "Careful, little morsel."

"What should we do now?" I whispered to Lucas, taking one of the daggers from his belt even though I wasn't sure how to use it.

Winifreda licked her lips. "And the Richelieu whelp. My lord will be well pleased."

"This is bad," I said as the crow-brethren advanced. "This is very, very bad." I brandished the dagger threateningly and nearly took off Lucas's left ear.

"Careful!" He jumped.

"Sorry." I was such an idiot. Only I would totally bungle a perfectly good rescue. Damn those chocolate croissants. Damn food altogether. We pressed our backs to the wall, angled ourselves shoulder to shoulder. Fear had my stomach burning.

"Lucas, you should probably get out of here."

"I won't leave you either."

"I'm sure that's very noble and heroic," I said. "But under the circumstances, it's also stupid. There's no use in you getting caught too."

"No."

"My lord," Winifreda purred as Strahan entered from a back archway, dressed in a silk dressing gown. "A gift for you."

When he saw Lucas and me, his austere face shone with pleasure. It was nearly indecent. He chuckled and it was like cream and honey wine. "Well done, love," he said. "Well done." He took an apple from a basket on the table and bit into it. The crunch was loud, sharp. "Take them."

Lucas fought off two guards with one stroke, took an arm off with another. Black feathers filled the air. I jabbed out with my knife like a temperamental honeybee. Not terribly effective, but at least I didn't get swatted.

We were so badly outnumbered it was ridiculous. I dropped the knife and grabbed the chain instead, swinging it over my head like a lasso. It created a small circle around us, as long as I was careful not to touch Lucas with it, or knock his sword out of his hand.

More guards rushed in, like crows and beetles and fire ants at a picnic.

"I'm so taking more self-defense classes when I get home. The ones at the community center didn't cover this." My corset dug into my ribs. I swung the chain harder, ignoring the twinges in my muscles.

Lucas was bleeding into the handwoven carpets. His tunic was in shreds, his hair damp with sweat. The stones were cold and unyielding at our backs. He dropped to his knees with a grunt of pain, blood staining what was left of his sleeve.

"Hang on," I told him and then leaped forward so I was right behind him, one leg on either side. I swung faster and wider. My shoulders were screaming now, but I gritted my teeth against the pain.

The guards froze, waiting me out. One of them glanced at Strahan for orders. I made sure the chain grazed him, singeing his cheek. "Ha!" They eased back a few more steps. Winifreda was pouting. Strahan didn't look concerned, but not nearly as pleased either.

"You can't keep this up indefinitely," he called out in his cultured tones, sounding vaguely bored. I hated that he was right. I knew I couldn't keep my arm up much longer, and then they'd swarm us. They might not kill me. I wasn't much good as a hostage if I was dead, after all; but I had no doubt I'd end up in some dark hole with rats and spiders. And I didn't know what they'd do to Lucas, run him through or torture him. There was definitely a score to settle there.

"You let him go," I said, sweat dripping down the side of my face. "You let him go free and I'll put this down."

He shook his head, leaned against a table. "My dear girl, you're in no position to give orders."

I kept the chain moving, though the arc was sagging. "I might be tired, Strahan," I said with as much haughty disdain as I could manage. "But I bet I can reach that pretty face of yours before they take me down."

"Not with a sword through your throat."

"Maybe not, but I wouldn't be much leverage then, would I? Come Samhain you won't have a single advantage." Apparently fear and fatigue was making me shoot my mouth off.

Lucas groaned. "Eloise, leave me."

I ignored him.

Strahan lifted an eyebrow. "I must say you are proving more interesting even than I first thought."

Winifreda sniffed. "She was pitifully easy to fool."

"Be that as it may." He tossed the apple core away. "Enough of these games." He motioned to the guards choking the hall. "These men will die for me. Now put down that silly toy."

My arm was starting to go numb, and I was out of options.

"Get the hell away from my niece."

I didn't know where she came from. She was just suddenly there, regal in a green velvet gown with red cardinals circling over her head.

"Aunt Antonia!" I faltered, suddenly just a normal girl again, in frilly white skirts swinging a chain over her head and feeling stupid. She glanced at me, smiled faintly. There were iron bangles around her wrists and an iron torc necklace at her throat. Her tattoo of ivy leaves wound its way down her left arm, like mine.

"Antonia," Strahan said and there were so many emotions in that one word I couldn't begin to decipher them all. Winifreda glanced at him, frowning. "You have something of mine."

"That old thing," Antonia scoffed. "I tossed it away years ago. Did you really think I'd want to be reminded of you?"

"You had better be lying, woman."

She nearly smiled. "So that's your weakness," she said. "The ribbon."

He snarled, advanced.

"You're not to go near Eloise again." Antonia stepped closer to me. "Ever."

The chain clanged when I dropped it. Lucas pushed himself stiffly to his feet, using his sword to hold himself up.

"Antonia," I babbled with relief. "I'm so sorry. I ate the food. It's totally my fault."

"This is *not* your fault," she said gently before lifting her hand and slapping me right in the chest, pressing the medallion into my skin. "Go home, Eloise."

chapter 8
Jo

"Run!"

Isadora sounded frantic, but she was so small that a stray cat or an angry pigeon might be enough to worry her. I looked over my shoulder, wondering how long Devin was going to stay mad at me.

And then it made perfect sense why Isadora was freaking.

Perfect sense.

My feet were moving before my brain had caught up. There was a buzzing in the air, menacing and strange. It sent tingles across the back of my neck.

Apparently, Isadora wasn't mates with the other Fae. Especially not the tiny flower Fae riding the back of wasps and hornets and screeching at us. They sat in saddles embroidered with sequins, the wasps obeying their every signal.

Their arrows looked more like silver needles than any feathered and sharpened arrow I'd ever seen. One of them sliced the air near my ear.

"Shite!"

"Don't let them hit you," Isadora warned.

"Well, duh!"

I ducked and ran faster, legs pumping madly until my calves felt like rocks and my lungs were filled with molten lava. Devin was just up ahead, totally oblivious to the swarm of angry Fae coming up right behind him.

"Dev!" I hollered. "Move it!"

He turned on one scuffed Converse and rolled his eyes. "What now?" He blinked, blinked again. "What the f—"

I grabbed his sleeve and dragged him along with me.

"What the hell are those things?" Needles gleamed in the grass by our feet.

I yanked harder. "Run away now. Talk later."

The wasps were quick and there were enough of them to make me anxious, even without their demented riders. Fear sat like a lump of dry bread in my throat, choking me. An arrow pinched into the back of my arm. "Ouch! Bollocks!" I pulled it out, tossed it aside.

Isadora was sweaty and furious and very unfairylike. "You have to run faster."

"I can't! I don't have wings, in case you hadn't noticed!" I panted, and then swore when another arrow bit into my elbow. "Those things *hurt*."

Devin swatted one off the back of his neck. "Wasps hate water," he said, opening his knapsack, scattering loose change and chocolate bar wrappers as he searched for a bottle of water. He jogged backward, squeezing the plastic bottle so the water squirted out. One of the wasps lost control of its wet wings, a lime green fairy somersaulted in midair with a similar problem. The rest just moved into some kind of formation, like they were some military insect battalion.

"Now you've made them mad!"

"Shit! Shit!" He threw the bottle at them and then went back to running as fast as he could.

"Get inside somewhere," Isadora said before tossing insults behind her. "Son of gopher dung! Goat tick!" She dove behind a garbage can to avoid being hit. "I need my bloody sword!"

"Eloise's apartment," I wheezed, forgetting to use the British term "flat." We passed the playground. "It's closest."

People were looking at us as if we were insane, which we probably were. All they saw were two teenagers running and waving their arms at nothing. Eyes narrowed disapprovingly and the word "drugs" was muttered more than once. My shoulders were beginning to make me feel like a hedgehog. And I was light-headed, a little faint. Devin was a weird gray-green color, even with his dark skin.

"I feel funny," he slurred. I squeezed his hand. My tongue felt too thick in my mouth and it was hard to talk.

We hurled ourselves across the street, ducking into the

alley toward the side doors, since they were closest. I'd never noticed how heavy they were. Devin tried to pull on the handle and lost his balance. Isadora shot straight up the wall of windows until she found an open one and disappeared inside.

He slumped against the wall, shaking. "I don't feel so good, Jo."

"Me neither," I croaked. "We'll be okay." I kept repeating it because it had to be true. "We'll be okay."

We both hung from the door handle, trying to use gravity to make us heavier. Dropping like a stone was about the only power either of us had at the moment. The door creaked open. Wasps came around the corner, their savage riders spotting us with high-pitched war whoops.

We tipped over like dominoes, me into Devin and Devin through the narrow doorway. Needles clattered into the window. Devin grunted, trying to pull me inside. The heavy door swung shut on our legs. I was so tired, I was seeing double.

In fact, I was so tired, I was seeing two of Hot Guy.

He bent down and scooped me up against his chest. I let my arms dangle, like I was floating. "You're so pretty," I mumbled.

"And you're a fool," he said darkly. "You stink of hawthorn smoke."

He stepped sideways, and suddenly we weren't in an alley sticky with spilled garbage and thick with arrows anymore.

We were in a small room with a ceiling of dangling tree roots and lanterns. The only light came from those lanterns, candles flickering, their light filtering through jewel-colored glass. There was a carved bed piled with blankets and hung with blue velvet curtains, and an old-fashioned hutch filled with books. The heavy wooden door was bolted shut.

I was safe, cradled in the arms of a moody, beautiful boy. His heart thundered loudly against my ear. He let me go and I slid down his body. His T-shirt had turned into a black medieval-style tunic edged with blue embroidery somewhere along the way. And I was now wearing a matching blue velvet dress, like ice over a stormy lake. It had long bell sleeves and silver ribbons. My hair was wrapped in a pearl snood. I touched the silver bracelets on my wrists, confused.

"Fae glamour," he whispered. He stood very still, like a dog expecting to get kicked.

"You're Fae," I said, details suddenly fitting together like puzzle pieces. The water witching, what he knew about hawthorn trees, the fact that he kept appearing out of nowhere. The way his kisses made me feel as if I were falling. "Is that where I am? In Faerie? Where's Devin? And did you cure me?" I pushed up my sleeves. There were little scratches and pinpricks on my skin, but I didn't feel sick or lethargic anymore. "Those arrows made me feel funky."

"Elf-shot," he explained. "I can only cure you as long as you're here. You'd need salt in your world. But this is my own small corner of the world, where no one can intrude, not even my father."

"And Devin?" I pressed. "Is he here too?" It didn't seem likely, unless he was under the bed.

"No."

I gaped at him. "He's still at the flat getting attacked?" I grabbed his hand. "Take me back! Right now!"

"So you can die too?" His voice was harsh.

I felt all the blood drain out of my head. "Devin can't die."

"He might not. If he's strong enough."

"Take me back!" I punched his shoulder for emphasis.

"We still have time," he said, gripping my wrist tightly when I went to punch him again. "Time runs differently here. A few more minutes here will be less than seconds for him."

"Do you promise?"

He inclined his head. "Would it matter if I did?"

"Of course it would." He was different here. Which was the real him? Hot Guy? Or the one I'd walked the fields with? Or this one?

His eyes glittered. "Then yes, I promise."

I released a breath I hadn't realized I was holding. "Okay."

"You could stay," he suggested. "With me."

"Am I trapped here?"

He shook his head. His expression was cold and haughty, but there was something else in his eyes, something that hurt to look at.

I wondered suddenly if Eloise was here. After all, how many doors to the Fae world were there in Rowan? I tried to whirl around to get to the door, but he was still holding my wrist. He didn't let go, even when I tugged.

"I can't protect you out there," he said.

"Who are you really?" I whispered. We were close enough that I could see the odd gray flecks in his eyes, the angle of his sideburns along his jaw. I thought he was going to kiss me again, but he just dropped my arm abruptly. He didn't say anything, but his eyes were so dark and intense that my mouth went dry. He rolled up his sleeve, showing a tattoo of a leaping stag with ivy in its antlers. I'd seen that same design on Eloise's medallion.

"I don't understand," I said. "What does that mean?"

"It means I'm a Hart." He smiled, but it was sharp and derisive. He jerked his sleeve back down. "Like your friend Eloise."

"I . . . You know Eloise?" I asked, head spinning. "Is she here?"

I went for the door again. I managed to pull it open a few inches before he was behind me, slamming it shut. I pulled and he pushed. He was stronger than me. It was infuriating. I turned around to glare at him. His arm was extended, palm flat against the door right by my head.

I suddenly wondered, for the first time, if I should be afraid of him.

My pulse stuttered in my throat. He smiled again, just

as mocking. Only I couldn't tell if he was mocking me or himself.

"You're in a rath under the ground," he said, caging me with his body even though he wasn't even touching me. "If you go through that door, you'll end up buried in earth or in another rath. I can guarantee they won't look kindly on the intrusion. You wouldn't like the reception."

My head was starting to spin. "This is insane." I glanced down at my gown again. "I feel like I'm in one of Devin's fantasy novels, or a Dungeons and Dragons game or something."

He crowded me. "This isn't a storybook," he said menacingly. He blinked, and I was wearing my regular clothes, my long skirt smeared with dirt, my hair a dusty, sweaty tangle. He wore his torn jeans again, his scuffed boots. He leaned in so that I had to look up to meet his eyes. They were inscrutable. His hair fell forward, veiling us from the soft light.

"I'm not afraid of you," I said evenly. My heart was pounding, but it wasn't fear I was feeling. Not exactly.

"Then you really are a fool." He pushed away, his hands dropping to his sides. "My name is Eldric Strahan," he said.

My eyes widened until they hurt. "Shite." Not exactly my most poetic of responses.

"You've heard of our illustrious family," he drawled, and bowed. It was a horrible, polite, sophisticated movement. It was graceful and sarcastic, and it made me want to kick him.

"Don't do that," I said quietly.

He straightened. "You should hate me."

"Why? You just saved my life."

"My father stole your friend away."

"Did you help him?"

"No." His sullen mouth crooked with a sad smile. "But I didn't hinder him either."

"So you can make up for it by helping us now," I insisted. "Come back with me. Help us break Eloise out."

"Or you could stay with me." His arm slipped around my waist, drawing me against him. His voice caressed me, struck sparks of longing in my belly. "We could run away," he murmured, brushing his lips lightly over my temple to my ear. "We could go anywhere, be anyone. Let them fight their battles without us." His teeth bit gently down on my earlobe. I shivered, clutching at his arms.

"We could go to Provence and live on a lavender farm and eat brioche every morning." I turned my head so I was smiling against his lips as I wove another daydream. "Or to Scotland and live in a castle with ghosts and sheep." I'd be lying if I said I wasn't tempted.

"Exactly," he said, and kissed me so slowly it made me want to cry. Our breaths mingled, became one. "Anything you want, Jo."

"I just want you," I returned softly. Then I forced myself to step back. It was the hardest thing I'd ever done. "But I can't."

He closed his eyes for a long, painful moment. When he opened them again they were stark and hollow. Something inside me broke. I bit my lip hard enough to taste blood, forcing myself not to throw myself at him.

"You want to go back," he said flatly.

"You know it's not that simple."

"It is. If you won't stay here with me, and you won't run away with me, then this is good-bye."

I felt cold all over. "No."

"It has to be." He turned his head away, his hair blocking his expression.

"Eldric, please."

He flinched at his name. But when he tossed his hair off his face, he was smiling. I hated that smile. "I could refuse to bring you back," he said.

I looked at him steadily. "You won't."

"How can you trust me still?" he asked furiously.

"Do you trust me?"

He remained stubbornly silent.

"You do," I told him. "I know you do. For the same reason I trust you." I didn't tell him I loved him. But I wanted to. "What about Devin?" I asked. "Can you rescue him too? Please?"

He nodded sharply and then took my hand. He didn't say anything, didn't stroke my wrist with his thumb, didn't even look at me. He stepped back and fell away into nothing, pulling me with him. It was like the sudden drop of a roller coaster, the feeling that there's nothing under you and you might fall forever.

We landed in Eloise's rooftop garden, with the sun glaring down on us. He vanished again and reappeared in the next second, dropping a weak and cursing Devin beside me. I felt the venom of the arrows running through me again, pressing on me like rocks. It didn't hurt nearly as much as the long, silent look Eldric gave me before he disappeared.

chapter 9
Eloise

I landed on our couch.

My mother was just coming out of the kitchen when she saw me fall out of nowhere, followed by a boy dressed like King Arthur. She made a sound like *"yaaargl!"* and then threw her cup right into the air. She didn't even blink when hot tea rained over her. Elvis yowled and tore off.

I struggled to sit up, trapped by yards of petticoats. Lucas groaned as he tried to free his knee, which was jammed under an end table. Mom just stood there, lips trembling. I launched myself at her, and she came to her senses just in time to catch me. We staggered clumsily, but she didn't let go. "I'm murdering that rat bastard Strahan and you're grounded forever." She pulled away, surveying me closely. "Did he hurt you?" She looked into my eyes like a doctor, ran her hands over my shoulders and down my arms. "Oh, look at your wrists. I *will* kill him."

Lucas took a step back. Mom could be scary at the best of times with her tattoos and tight jeans, but she was really, *really* scary when she was angry.

"It's nothing. Antonia came and sent us home somehow." I hugged her again. "Where is she?"

Mom frowned, wiping tea off her face. "I don't know. I still can't reach her. I was just about to call one of her weird friends. They always know more than they should."

"You mean, she's not here?" I spun around to Lucas, agitated as a wet cat. "She's not here!"

He tugged his coat back into place. "Strahan has her."

Mom paled. "What do you mean, Strahan has her?" She sank weakly into a chair. "This is not good."

"So she's stuck there?" I asked Lucas. "We have to get her back."

Mom gave me the evil eye before she went to put the kettle on. I knew she was making rose hip tea. Crises of any kind were tamed with rose hip tea. "You aren't going anywhere, young lady."

I rolled my eyes. "I don't think you can really effectively ground a girl who was just chained to a wall."

The kettle nearly toppled out of her hand. "What?"

Oops. Probably shouldn't have mentioned that. Parents had such a habit of overreacting. Lucas was poking around the apartment, looking at our books and art and family photos.

"You are so like her," he whispered, staring at Mom. "Like the queen. I never even knew she had a twin," he added. "Until recently."

"She made a bargain, a long time ago, so no one would know and use me in her place. And when Eloise was born, she set a glamour on her so she would be invisible to the Fae. But glamours only last so long before the magic runs out."

"And it started to fade just this past week," I said softly, remembering what Strahan had said. "And I started remembering things."

"Yes," Lucas agreed. "We looked for ages before I saw you eating ice cream. We've been searching for you since we unexpectedly caught scent of your bloodline. We thought you might be Antonia's."

"She's mine," Mom said fiercely. "So you can all back off. Now."

"It's a little late for that." I hugged a cow-shaped cushion to my chest just because it was soft and familiar. It was the one I used as a pillow when I wasn't feeling well. "And you have *so* been keeping secrets. I might be really mad at you for that later." Right now I was too glad to be out of Strahan's Hall.

Mom measured dried tea into the pot, added boiling water. Her hands were shaking, even though she was trying to look so calm. "And who are you, by the way?" she asked Lucas, trying to change the subject.

"Oh, I forgot," I said. "Lucas Richelieu, this is my mom, Jasmine Hart. Lucas went to Strahan's rath to rescue me."

She looked at him steadily. "You get chocolate cake."

I nudged him, smiling. "That means she likes you. She doesn't make it for just anyone. Even on my birthday, I have to beg."

He bowed, polite as the out-of-time gentleman he appeared to be. Never mind that there was blood on his hands and his collar was torn.

"Richelieu?" Mom said. "Sounds familiar. What are you? Deer? Dog? Badger?"

"We are from the Hawk clan, distant cousin to your own Deer people."

"They're not my people."

"You'd be surprised."

I sat up straighter. "Hey. A hawk chased away my bully in the park."

Mom frowned. "You have a bully?"

I waved that away. "So not a big deal right now."

"I wish you weren't so afraid of yourself," she said quietly. "Anger's not a bad thing, El. It has energy; it can give you the power to change things."

"Or break things." I looked at her faded scar. "You're the one who says physical violence isn't about being angry, it's about feeling out of control." After Mom got away from Dad, she read every book in the self-help section of the library. "I don't want to be like Dad."

"Oh, honey," she said, smiling a little. "You're nothing like that. *He's* not even like that anymore. You have your own voice. You need to use it. Too soft isn't any better than too hard."

"Even without a voice, the hound-people would have smelled you, even though they wouldn't have known what precisely it was they were scenting because of your glamours. We couldn't be sure until the magic faded, and hawks have keen instincts. But Antonia would have wanted you to be safe. It's likely her doing." He looked away, his ears red. Come to think of it, the hawk had feathers the same color as Lucas's hair: like dark tea.

I was so relieved to be home again it barely fazed me that Lucas might possibly turn into a hawk sometimes. I just circled the living room, touching the crowded paintings, the DVD towers, the computer on a table made out of an old door and two sawhorses covered in silk flowers. I noticed details I'd never noticed before. The pattern on my shirt, which Strahan had pointed out, was everywhere; stitched on a pillow, painted on a river rock on the windowsill, even hanging from the ceiling cleverly disguised in a wind chime made of driftwood and red berries. Even the ivy plants in clay pots meant something more—the plant in the stag's antlers on the medallion was ivy, and so was my tattoo. And I knew it had to mean something. I was nearly as disoriented as I'd been landing under a hill full of the Fae.

"Why ivy?" I asked quietly.

"Ivy can break glamours," Lucas replied.

"So is that why mine broke?"

"No, ivy used that way would have broken others' glamours against you. It's why you recognized those crow-brothers."

"Oh." I shivered. Lucas pulled off the jacket he wore over his tunic and settled it over my shoulders. I blushed. It was a dumb reaction. Probably posttraumatic stress or something.

"Come and sit down," Mom said quietly.

"Mom, what about Antonia?"

"We'll get her out," she promised me fiercely. "But you're not going back there. I'll figure something out."

"Mom."

"End of discussion, Eloise Hart."

Lucas wouldn't sit down until we were both seated, so I curled back up on the couch and pulled the afghan over me. Elvis had apparently forgiven our entrance enough to come back and hop up on top of the television to watch me with sleepy eyes.

"So what's the plan, Mom?" I asked after she'd added extra honey to my cup.

She wiped honey off her thumb. "I guess I shouldn't have expected to keep this from you forever." She sighed. "You know your aunt. Her taste in men has never been good, even when we were your age—*especially* when we were your age. She met this guy, and for months before our sixteenth birthday, he was all she talked about. She stopped going to class, stopped dance classes and doing homework. All she wanted to do was write these really awful poems about him." She grimaced and I nearly smiled. Bad art of any kind was an affront to her, always had been.

"So, she had a crush," I said. "Jo has crushes all the time. It's like her superpower."

"Not like this. She didn't even bother showing up to our birthday party, and didn't come back for three whole days. And then she wouldn't talk about what had happened, not even to me. I could tell something was wrong though, something bad." She stared at the geode collection in the cabinet, not seeing them. "That's when it really started. She'd disappear every spring, come back every autumn. No amount of arguing would get her to tell me where she went or why. She'd only say it was safer that way, for her and for me, for the whole family. When you were born, she told me a little more, but not much. We were both so young."

The apartment was too quiet—no music, no television, just Mom's haunted voice. I flicked on the fan to help move the stifling air.

"I didn't believe her at first, of course. But then I saw things, impossible things. Out of the corner of my eye mostly, never clearly or for long enough to really figure out what I was looking at." She seemed older and more tired than I'd ever seen her, even when she spent weeks working on an art show. "He's been searching for her all these years, and every summer she hides out because that's when he has the most power. She can hold her own again come fall, but not before. I'm still not sure how it all works, only that he's cruel and not to be crossed."

"He's causing this drought," Lucas said quietly. "We knew it would come to this."

"She promised me you'd be safe," Mom said to me, choking back a sob.

I felt like I should defend Antonia. "She did get me back here, even knowing it would trap her there."

Lucas leaned forward, his elbows on his knees. "You know that my people and I will do all we can to safeguard Antonia and the entire Hart line."

"Yeah," I said, tired. "What's with that anyway?"

"It is our bond."

I raised an eyebrow. "That's not really an answer."

"It has always been so. The Deer people and the Hounds and the Hawks have ever been as one in this matter."

I lifted the medallion. "Deer people."

He nodded. "Long ago your people knew how to shapeshift into the deer. Fae don't forget, only humans do."

Mom's foot tapped. "Antonia said a Richelieu helped her escape once."

He nodded modestly. "We did, yes. It's how I had the token to give to Eloise, how I knew to find her and warn her."

"Yeah, thanks for that by the way. Guess I should have listened." I yawned, the soft couch and blanket exerting their power over me. "I thought you were crazy that night in the parking lot."

Mom stroked my hair, fussed with the blanket. "Why don't you sleep a little?"

I smothered another yawn.

"Can't. Too much . . . to . . . do . . ."

I was asleep before I'd even finished protesting.

• • •

I shouldn't be asleep in Strahan's Hall. Someone would hurt me. It wasn't safe. My wrists hurt. I was bruised and scared and I didn't know what else they'd do to me. He was laughing. The Grey Ladies were there too. My teeth chattered in the cold.

"Shhh," someone whispered to me.

A hand touched my hair. I jerked awake, blinking blearily. I didn't know where I was and my heart was going too fast.

"I won't let anyone hurt you," Lucas said.

I was stretched out with my head on his knee. I didn't think I'd been asleep for very long, at least not long enough to drool on myself. The afternoon light streaming through the window made his hair the color of honey. He looked tired.

"You should sleep too," I whispered.

"I have to stand guard," he replied. He was still stroking my hair. It felt nice, and I suddenly wanted to stretch like a lazy cat. Fatigue smeared the lines of the room, making them soft and hazy.

"Thank you for coming to get me."

His fingertips brushed my cheek. "You're welcome. I've been looking for you for months, even before the glamour wore off, only I didn't know it. I caught a glimpse of you somehow. I couldn't let Strahan have you," he whispered. "Even if there wasn't war on the horizon."

I smiled shyly. "Do you miss home?"

He tipped his head back, resting it on the cushion. "Yes."

"Tell me about it," I asked. "I'd like to think that if there are worlds under the hills, they're not all like Strahan's. Because that's just creepy."

"He wasn't always as he is now," Lucas admitted reluctantly. "When he first wed your aunt, he was a good king. Selfish and arrogant perhaps, but that's nothing new, nothing that can't be got around." He sighed, stretching one arm along the back of the couch. "He's a brother of sorts to us. Bird-brother, if you will."

My eyebrows rose. "The crows too?"

He nodded. "Not all crows are like the ones you saw. They're uncanny because they have the wisdom of death, but they don't usually bring it themselves."

"So you can't tell good Fae from bad?"

"Not any more than you can tell good humans from evil, at a glance."

His hand stilled in my hair, fingers warm on my skin. I could see his scars. "And your rath?"

"We have a rath, but we much prefer the treetops." His mouth quirked in a bright smile that made me catch my breath. In this light, when he wasn't covered in iron-blisters and blood, I could see the Fae beauty of him. It wasn't unearthly or darkly seductive like Strahan's. Lucas's shadows didn't conceal cruelty or secrets; they were only there because he shone so brightly. "And our house is built on a hilltop, where we can see the sky for miles."

"I thought raths were *under* hills?" I asked, confused.

"They are, but Faery is much more than hill-hidden raths. It's an entire world to itself. The raths are doorways and crossroads, where we can be in both worlds at once."

I rubbed my forehead. "You know, this is getting more and more confusing."

"Parents used to teach mortal children," he said. "I can't think why they've stopped."

I mock glared at him. "You're not going to call me uneducated again, are you?"

He flashed a grin. "No."

He leaned down again, looking at me the way he had in the grove with the stag. He was going to kiss me. This time I wasn't going to run away. I met his pale eyes, licked my lips. Soon there was only a breath between us.

And then before our mouths could meet, there was a scratching at the window. Elvis grumbled, annoyed with yet another interruption. I frowned at Lucas, who jerked his head up, alert. "What is that?" I asked.

He was on his feet, reaching for his sword. "I don't know."

chapter 10
Jo

When we finally got the window open, I pulled myself in on my hands and knees. I think Devin might have been hooked onto my foot. I felt like lead all over, so it was hard to tell. My vision was blurry but not so blurry that I couldn't make out Eloise's worried face.

"El!" I slurred. "You're back!" I blinked. "Are you wearing vanilla frosting?"

She made a face at her petticoats. "Don't ask." She frowned when I just lay there. "What's wrong with her?" she asked Lucas.

He crouched down next to her and peered at me. He plucked a needle out of my butt.

"Hey! Ouch!"

"Elf-shot," he answered grimly. "The boy too."

"Who are you calling 'boy'?" Devin muttered, drooling on his chin.

"This kind of poison works quickly."

"Poison!" Eloise grabbed me, as if that would help. I squeaked. She didn't let go. She reached out and squeezed Devin's hand. He rolled his head toward her, eyes too bright.

"They could be disoriented for days if we don't do something right away," Lucas continued. "Some never really lose the ability to see the Fae afterward and it can make them mad. If they survive."

I wasn't fully listening to his uplifting speech. I was too busy trying to figure out what it was I was forgetting to remember. And my mouth tasted like a combination of soap and burned coriander. I rubbed my tongue sluggishly on my sleeve.

"We need salt," he said. "As much as you've got."

That's what I was trying to remember. Eldric said we needed salt.

Eldric.

I think I whimpered.

Lucas was standing up to follow Jaz when I kicked him in the shin. It was feeble but unexpected. Lucas tripped and fell right over.

"Lucas!"

I frowned at Eloise when she fussed over him. "He did this to you."

"He tried to rescue me."

"Oh. I still don't like him." There were three of him now, all wavering. "You either," I told the others.

Devin lay very still beside me. I wanted to close my eyes and sleep for about a hundred years except that Eloise's mom came back with a box of table salt and suddenly I was on fire. They threw handfuls at us, packing it into our pinprick wounds, even making us gargle with it. It was like being rubbed with hot coals.

"Bollocks!" I squirmed. "Get off!"

Eloise's eyes were suspiciously moist. "She's back!" Her voice cracked.

"Don't you dare cry." I brushed salt out of my nose. She hugged me so hard her corset dug into my ribs. She helped me sit up, propped me against the leg of the kitchen table, and then did the same with Devin. I felt like a rag doll.

Lucas bowed to me warily. "Josephine."

I narrowed my eyes at him. "Call me that again and I'll wallop you." I spat a length of hair out of my mouth. The rest hung bedraggled down my back. "I feel like shite. Hi, Jaz."

She shook her head, but she was smiling. "You might be grounded too, young lady. I distinctly recall telling you to go home and do nothing." She handed Devin and me cups of tea.

Devin grimaced but drank it. "Why do girls have to drink boiled flowers all the time?"

I snickered, meeting Eloise's grin with my own. I felt

utterly knackered and giddy with relief that neither of us was dead. "Nice outfit."

"Shut up." She grabbed the afghan and wrapped it around herself, blushing. There was salt all over the floor, down my shirt, in my bra, and possibly even in my underwear.

"Thanks," I said to Lucas. "You saved us," I admitted. And now I was conscious enough to feel the hole Eldric had left in my chest.

Lucas bowed again. Elvis gave a yowl that had us all jumping.

"What now?" Eloise turned toward the window, paused, rubbed her eyes. "Um, anyone else see that?"

Isadora floated on the other side of the glass, knocking with a perfect tiny fist.

"Oh, right," I said. "Everyone, meet Isadora. Let her in, would you? And make sure the cat doesn't eat her."

Jaz blew a breath, riffling her bangs. "There isn't enough rose hip tea in the world," she muttered.

• • •

"This totally sucks." I was dangerously close to pouting. Hearing Eloise's story and being used as a pincushion did nothing for my temper. And her aunt might be flaky, but I *liked* her. She'd been the one to introduce us to David Bowie and Kate Bush and the *Pride and Prejudice* miniseries when Jaz had been lending us the Sex Pistols and the Smiths.

They'd had the best fight that night, until the neighbors complained about the loud music.

Isadora was currently perched on a lampshade, well out of reach of Elvis, who couldn't be convinced to release his claws from the sofa. His ears were flat against his head. Lucas was watching her as well, eyes wide.

"Isadora," he said. "I thought you were just a story to scare children."

My fairy friend was a bogeyman? Cool. I couldn't help but feel a little proud. She didn't particularly look proud though, just thoroughly disgruntled.

"I'd rather not discuss it," she said crossly. I nudged Devin to get his feet off the coffee table before Jaz freaked out when she got around to noticing. And she *would* notice eventually, Fae apocalypse notwithstanding.

"What's going on with you two?" I asked.

Isadora gave a long-suffering sigh, folded her arms over her chest, and refused to elaborate. Fortunately, Lucas didn't have any such compunctions.

"Isadora was Lady of her ancestral rath," he explained. "Until she was transformed and could hold it no longer."

"She was shrunk," I explained for the others. She glared at me and I shrugged. "Well, you were. You said so yourself."

"By who?" Devin asked. "Evil sorcerer? Troll king? Man, this is just like D&D."

I snorted. "Not quite."

"What then?"

"A poet."

Silence.

"A *poet?*"

I nodded. "Apparently he 'believed' her into being wee."

Devin wiped cookie crumbs off his shirt and sprawled back into his chair. "I *told* you English class was bad for my health."

Lucas and Isadora were still staring at each other.

"There's more to this, isn't there?" Eloise asked. She'd changed into her favorite flannel pajama bottoms, but there was something else different about her. She seemed brighter somehow, more sure of herself. It was kind of nice to see. It wasn't like she'd ever been a pushover, not the way people thought she was. But she was guarded and now the walls were cracking a little.

I had the opposite problem: no walls, no filter, and it didn't feel as if fairy poison had magically changed that.

And I missed Eldric.

I knew I needed to tell the others about him but I couldn't, not quite yet. I wanted to keep him untainted for just a little longer. They would never understand. They would hate him. And I wouldn't. Couldn't.

"No one's even seen Isadora for nearly a century," Lucas said.

"Well, I had to go away, didn't I? Only milksop poets could see me or children inclined to pull off my wings for their butterfly collection. And the rath . . . well, I could hardly defend it, could I?" She kicked at the tassels on the lamp. "My own people turned on me, blamed me. Still blame me." Her eyes were like bluebells shivering in a cold wind. "They're the ones chased us out of the park."

My mouth dropped. "Your own people did this to us? Harsh."

She looked almost embarrassed. "They got caught by that old poet too. He refused to see a family hall, only some ridiculous forget-me-not queen in her bower with servants drinking from acorn cups."

Lucas frowned. "One poet shouldn't have been enough to change you for so long."

"It's not her fault," I said. She might be on the cranky side but I considered her a friend, and when my friends were mad at someone, I was mad at them too. I couldn't help myself. It was probably a good thing Eloise and Devin were so even-tempered. And that neither of them dated much.

Isadora glanced at Lucas, at me. "It *was* my fault," she said crossly. "I loved him, didn't I? Told him my true name one night, even though I knew better. And that gave him the power to do this." She motioned with disgust at her tiny figure. "And my people were angry that a poet bested me, leaving them undefended. It's how Strahan was able to claim our rath as his own." Isadora spat at the mention of his name. The cat spat back. "They've a right to be angry."

Eloise leaned forward. "Wait, just wait . . . Strahan's rath is actually yours?"

She nodded. "And lovely it was, before his mangy beasts fouled it up."

"So can you get us in?"

Isadora nodded once, slowly. "I suppose so. There's a secret door, under the pond, that he still hasn't found."

Eloise nearly clapped her hands, she was that excited. "That's it, then!"

"No," Jaz snapped suddenly from the hall. "Absolutely not."

"We can't just leave Aunt Antonia there!" Eloise exclaimed hotly. Isadora and Lucas watched them curiously. Devin and I, having more experience with this sort of thing, leaned back and tried to stay out of the way.

"She'll be fine for a few days. *I* will find a way to get her out," Jaz said between her teeth. "She's my sister and you are my seventeen-year-old daughter. I can get in easily enough closer to Samhain."

Lucas nodded. "The doors would open then for someone from Antonia's bloodline."

"She showed me how. No!" She cut off Eloise's protests and questions, stared hard at both Devin and me. She looked even fiercer than usual. "You are all absolutely forbidden. Do you hear me?" She checked her watch, cursed. "Now, I have to go to work because I can't afford to get fired on top of everything else. You will all stay safely inside this apartment.

Do I make myself clear?" She paused. "I said, *do I make myself clear?*"

We nodded. We were lying. She stalked off, the front door shutting firmly behind her. Eloise stared after her for a long time before turning back to us, looking every bit as unyielding as her mother.

"We need a plan," she said. "Because we're going. Tonight if we have to."

She marched into the kitchen, wiping at her eyes. Lucas and Devin both watched her go, twitching to follow. I darted after her before either of them could move.

She was staring unseeingly into the fridge. I linked my arm through hers.

"Okay, so forget about boys for a minute," I said.

She pretended to recoil in shock, forced a watery smile. "Did *you* just say forget about *boys?*"

"Ha-ha. Seriously." I reached in the fridge for cheese and lettuce to make sandwiches since we were standing there anyway.

"It is serious," she agreed. "I've never known you to pass up a good flirt."

"I do have some self-control, you know." I thought about Eldric. Maybe self-control wasn't the right word. "You're really okay, right?" I asked. "I'm a little tired to beat up Fae lords, but I could give it a try."

"I'm okay. You?"

I lifted one shoulder, let it fall. "Sure. Mad as a March hare but fine."

"I feel like I got you all messed up into this."

"Oh please, that's what best friends do." I poked through the cupboards. "Where's your mother's stash of PMS chocolate?"

"Behind the dried lentils. But it's for emergencies."

"Hello?" I pointed at her. "Kidnapped." Then at myself. "Shot."

"Good point. Give me a piece of that."

I rolled my neck. "I hurt all over. Elf darts, my ass. I'm getting myself a water gun full of holy water."

"We're not after vampires."

We stared at each other in horror.

"Oh God," she groaned. "You don't think they could be real too, do you?"

I shuddered. "Eat another pickle and let's forget we ever had this discussion."

"Deal." She chewed enthusiastically.

"I changed my mind. I want to talk boys." She didn't look remotely surprised. "Lucas is into you." She was nearly as red as the tomato she was slicing. I poked her. Hard. "You're blushing."

"I was kidnapped, remember? I'm just tired."

"No deal. Tired does not equal embarrassed blushing. Spill."

"We nearly kissed." She opened a jar of pickles. "I'm sure it was just the stress."

"Mm-hmm."

"You know, adrenaline. Or Fae magic."

"Wow." I grinned. "You're really bad at this."

"At what?" she asked, confused.

"Crushing on boys."

"I bow to the master."

"As well you should." I leaned my hip against the counter. "He's nice enough, I guess, since this isn't his fault, after all." And if anything, Eldric probably carried more blame. "He's just a little too perfect. Wholesome."

"Oh right." Eloise snorted, sounding like her old self. "'Cause you only date outlaw bikers," she added sarcastically. "I forgot." She passed me another piece of chocolate. We chewed contentedly for a while, pretending everything was normal.

Finally, I couldn't avoid it any longer. "I have something to tell you." I couldn't quite look at her. "You know Hot Guy? From the party in the woods?"

"Yeah, what about him?"

"We're sort of . . . I don't know, together? Or we were. Are. It's complicated."

"That was fast."

I shifted uncomfortably. "I guess so." I shifted again. "The thing is . . . his name is Eldric."

She blinked. "That's not funny."

"I know."

"*Jo*," she burst out. "He was in the rath. He's Strahan's son."

"I know that too. Well, *now* I do." The chocolate suddenly

tasted like dust in my mouth. "I just found out. I know it's freaky, but he did save Devin and me. How else do you think we got on the roof?"

"Do you have any idea what they do to people in that rath? To other Fae even?"

"He's not all bad," I insisted stubbornly.

"He watched them chain me to a wall."

"Well, he's not all good either," I admitted. "But I know him better than you do. He's had a rough go. He hates his dad as much as you hate yours. He needs to see there's another way."

"It's not that simple."

"He just needs a chance."

"There's too much at stake, Jo."

"I know that," I said stiffly. "I'm not talking with my hormones here. I l—"

"Don't." She stared at me as if I'd grown a second head right there in her kitchen. "Don't say what I think you're going to say."

"I was just going to say I *like* him." Maybe I loved him too, but it had been only three days. She'd never get it.

She took a deep breath, released it carefully. "I'm not sure I can talk about this right now."

"But—" We always told each other everything. There were dark circles under her eyes, so I snapped my jaws shut.

"Jo. Seriously. Drop it." She shook herself, as if she were

covered in spiders. "I need a minute." She ignored the others and went straight to her bedroom.

I ate the rest of the chocolate and felt like the worst friend in the world.

chapter 11
Eloise

I felt betrayed.

Maybe it was stupid. Jo had tried so hard to rescue me that she'd nearly been killed. I felt horrible about the bloody pinpricks all over her, about the way Devin slumped on the couch as if he'd just recovered from the plague. I should forgive them anything instantly.

But Eldric? Seriously?

So now I felt betrayed *and* guilty.

I changed out of my pajamas, because despite what Mom said, I was going to rescue Antonia. Tonight. I knew the only reason Mom wasn't trying to find a way in right this second was because she was worried about me, and because she needed backup and she wasn't sure where to find it. If something happened to Aunt Antonia, she'd never get over it. I couldn't help but picture Nicodemus's oozing broken antler and hear Cala's pain-racked moaning. And Strahan didn't even hate them, not the way he hated Antonia.

Going back to the rath was demented. I was fully aware of that.

It was also my only option.

I couldn't be passive anymore. I had to stand up. Mom said it herself: I had a voice. Even if this wasn't exactly what she had in mind. And I, at least, had backup.

I put on dark jeans and a T-shirt with a decal of an angry punk-haired fairy on it because it seemed appropriate. I clipped my lucky red flower behind my ear, the one painted with glitter, and added a coat of matching red lipstick. I might not have a sword like Lucas's or chain mail, but this was my personal armor. And it helped me feel less vulnerable than petticoats or flannel.

Until I glanced in the mirror that hung inside my closet door. My bed was unmade, the covers bunched around the shape of a sleeping girl. Not just any sleeping girl.

Me.

It was my face, my freckles, my exact hairstyle.

But my eyes, when they snapped open, were all wrong. They were entirely black from lid to lid.

When I whirled around to look directly, I wasn't looking at myself anymore.

My features melted away as I watched, my nose turning bulbous, my teeth sharp and rotted. A raspy laugh made the hair on the back of my neck stand straight up. A glance in the mirror showed two of me again. It was disorienting.

The creature scrambled out of the bed, my hair turning into a red hat, faded to pink at the edges. He smelled like old vegetable peelings and roses. I staggered out of reach, knocking my lamp off my desk. It fell with a clatter.

"Um, guys?" I backed out of the doorway, tripped over Elvis, and crashed into the wall. "We have a problem!"

The thing leaped at me. I kicked out, landing a glancing blow. It was enough to knock him back slightly so I could scuttle out of the way again. Lucas was already leaping over the back of the couch, drawing his sword. Devin grabbed my mom's brass statue of a pig, hefting it like a weapon. Jo threw one of her shoes.

"What is it?" I asked, kicking again.

"A bogan," Lucas replied grimly, swinging his sword. The bogan gnashed its teeth.

"And a Redcap at that," Isadora said, shooting up to hover near the ceiling. "They like to pull the wings off butter-flies." She fluttered her pretty wings, well out of reach. "Nasty things."

"Little bite," the Redcap whined, scrabbling for me. "I was promised blood to fix my cap; it's ever so faded."

"And they like to dye their caps with human blood," Isadora added helpfully.

I looked at his stained cap in horror. Jo gagged. Lucas sliced at him until he howled.

"Use your own blood," Devin muttered, smashing the statue down.

The Redcap slumped dizzily and then began to weep. "Just an old bogan, I am. Fast asleep, not hurting anyone." His tears were fat and glittered like diamonds. He looked sad and pitiful.

"Don't fall for his tricks," Lucas warned.

"Wasn't going to," Jo snorted. She threw her other shoe. It left a black scuff on the wall. The Redcap snarled at her. When Lucas's sword came down toward his head, he faded away. We were silent except for the rasping of our breaths and Elvis's hysterical hissing.

"Why did that thing look like me in the mirror?" I asked. "And how long was it in my room?"

"All night probably," Lucas said. "It's a changeling, meant to buy Strahan some time. He was supposed to fool your mother so she wouldn't know you were missing and come searching."

"Like Jaz would ever think that gross goblin thing was Eloise," Jo said incredulously. "And anyway, she told me there was a note."

"Another trick," Isadora said. "The note's long turned to leaves and acorns I'm sure."

"Its reflection in the mirror looked just like me." I shuddered. "And it was in my bed." I shuddered again. "I'm sleeping on the floor from now on."

Lucas reached down to help me to my feet. His hand stayed protectively on my elbow.

"We can't stay here," he said, his sword still in his hand. He looked just like a boy who could turn into a fierce hawk now. "Antonia sent you here and Isadora's folk followed your friends. There's too much magic. And with the changeling, it's a trail a drunk cluricaun could follow."

I took that to mean we were too easy to find. I didn't ask what a cluricaun was. I honestly didn't want to know.

"Eloise needs to eat," Devin said quietly. He knew me so well. I couldn't function if I was hungry. Which contributed to my pathetic lack of self-control in the rath.

"And sleep, I reckon," Lucas added.

"We can't stay here, and we can't go home," Jo said. "Mine and Dev's parents wouldn't know what to do if Isadora showed up, never mind a Redcap. So let's go to the diner and grab some food and come up with a plan."

The elevator smelled like wet dog, as usual. I could never figure that out. Dogs weren't even allowed in the building. The muscle in Lucas's jaw clenched spasmodically.

"What's wrong?" I asked. "Are you claustrophobic?"

"Iron," he said, his skin suddenly a sickly gray. "It's worse in confined spaces, without a view of the sky." He nearly shoved an old woman to the ground in his rush to get out when we reached the ground floor. He steadied her, muttering embarrassed apologies. She blinked at his sword. She didn't even see Isadora darting like a hummingbird out the revolving doors.

"School play," Jo explained quickly before the woman could call the police. "You need to be less conspicuous," she told Lucas.

His sword suddenly shimmered out of sight. I could only see it if I concentrated really hard. It gave me a headache.

When we stepped outside, the heat folded us in its fist and squeezed. Jo lifted her thick hair off her neck. "How's Strahan doing this again?"

"He's holding on to summer tightly," Lucas replied.

"I hope that makes sense later," Jo said, sighing as the air-conditioned air of the diner slapped away the muggy humidity. It was mostly empty, with only an old man at the counter drinking a lemonade. It was too late for lunch and too early for dinner. We piled into the back booth, like any group of students skipping class. The red vinyl of the seats stuck to the back of my arms. Isadora perched on the old table jukebox. It didn't work, but it was the perfect size for her. The waitress didn't even glance her way. I found it hard not to stare. She was so different from the others.

"I vote we eat first and plan nefarious deeds later," Jo said, scanning the menu.

I was all for that. Not only did I need to eat at least two cheeseburgers and a root beer float, but I needed to clear my head. Too much had happened and I hadn't had a minute to myself to process it. Food made everything better. I ate all of my French fries and half of Jo's. She let me because she knew I was still mad about Eldric.

We ordered slices of chocolate cake for each of us and then finally it was time.

"Okay, so we need a plan," I said.

"Are you sure?" Lucas raised his eyebrows. "Didn't your mam forbid you to go?"

I made a face. "What, where you come from you always do what your parents tell you to?"

"Where do you come from anyway?" Jo asked.

"The Richelieu belong to the Seelie courts," he said. "And Talia's court under that."

" 'Cause that's clear. What the bollocks is a Seelie court? Or a Talia for that matter?"

"The Fae are divided into raths and halls, mostly held by clans with familial associations. A hall is just part of a rath. There are the Seelie—who can be kind, the Unseelie—who can also be kind, but always at a price. And it's never one you can pay. And then there are the solitaries, and the rogues and hermits, with no particular affiliation. Talia is the Bird queen."

"So Strahan is Unseelie?"

"Not exactly," Lucas said.

Isadora snorted. "He's a git."

"Maybe so, but he didn't used to be Unseelie. The crown changed him and then the Unseelie pledged to him."

"And where does my aunt fit in?" I wondered aloud. "Since she's not Fae?"

"She isn't Fae-born, but she was a king's consort. Fae-human matches are fairly common, actually. Most of us aren't pureblood, since Fae can't reproduce," he explained. "My own Da had me with a human. And Antonia has treaties with the

Seelie. They have no love for Strahan; even Talia exiled him, much good it did."

"Treaties?" Jo said dubiously. "I knew I should have taken government classes this year."

"I expect they'll help," Lucas continued. "If *you* ask them," he added to me.

"What, like make a formal speech or something? No way."

Jo patted my knee. "Breathe, El."

"You know I hate public speaking." My voice squeaked. It was ridiculous to be nervous about being the center of attention when we'd just fought off a Redcap who wanted my blood for his fashion accessories, but try telling my heart rate that.

"Can I do it for her?" Jo asked.

"I'm afraid not. Since this matter involves Antonia, the request must be made by a member of the Hart family."

"Of course it does," I muttered. "So, what, I just waltz in there and ask for help?"

"More or less. I ought to warn you though, not all will look fondly on you."

"Why not?" Jo was clearly offended. "She's fab."

"She's mortal. They will dislike you on principle."

I flopped back onto the cushions. "Well, great."

"Dude." Devin shook his head. "Chill. Do you even know how to talk to girls?"

Lucas cleared his throat. "They dislike Strahan even more than your aunt, and that is to your advantage."

I nodded slowly. "The enemy of my enemy is my friend, or whatever that saying is." I tapped my fingers on my knees, trying to get my brain to work properly again. I looked at Isadora, who scowled back at me suspiciously.

"What?"

"What about your people?" I asked. "They hate Strahan too, right?"

"They hate me more."

I chewed on my lower lip. "Could you convince them to work with us against him?"

"Perhaps," she said doubtfully.

"You could reclaim your rath," I suggested. "You know, once we depose Strahan."

Her eyes glittered. Lucas winced, touched my arm. "Rath politics are notoriously vicious, Eloise. You don't want to get involved."

"Probably not, but I already *am* involved. And I'll do what I have to do to make sure Antonia's okay. She might not have a few days, despite what my mom wants to think."

"She has two days, until Samhain."

Devin stared at him. "Until who-what?"

"The New Year. It's when Strahan has to cede to Antonia."

"Halloween," I added for Devin's benefit.

"Figures," he said tiredly. "This is straight out of some Halloween movie anyway."

"But Antonia will be okay until then?" I wanted Lucas to repeat that part. "Are you sure?"

"Yes. She'll not be comfortable, but they can't do each other any real harm except on Samhain and Beltane. The first of May," he explained before I could ask.

Isadora was pacing the rim of the jukebox now, her skirts shimmering.

"Will you show us the secret door into the rath?" I asked her. She stared at me for a long time before nodding once, sharply. Lucas sighed. "Jo will go with you and Lucas will take me to the Seelie courts."

Jo bared her teeth. "I am so going to flick one of those fairies right in the head."

"Maybe not the best negotiation tactic," I pointed out.

"You're not going alone," Devin said, rolling his eyes. "Please, like I'd leave you two on your own. That's how catastrophes happen. You know, plagues, locusts, floods."

Jo made a face, but neither of us could actually contradict him. Especially not now. "Thanks," she said finally.

"But maybe we should go with Eloise first," Devin added. "Then sneak in through the pond. I don't like that you'll be alone in some other realm. You don't even read fantasy novels. How will you get by? I have training." He winked, trying to lighten the tension.

"Playing Dungeons and Dragons is not training," Jo teased.

"And she won't be alone," Lucas said, affronted. "I'll be her guard and guide. Besides, if I brought two other mortals, they'd never listen to us. Half of them would want to dance you to death."

We stared at him. "Sorry?" I asked.

He shrugged, almost looking embarrassed. "It's what we do."

"And you want to go off with him?" Devin asked me.

"I trust him," I said apologetically.

"Some Fae are trustworthy," Jo agreed pointedly. Very, very pointedly. I ignored her and jerked my hand through my hair, making it stick up. "You guys, are you sure about this? It could be dangerous."

"Blah, blah, blah," she said.

I tossed an olive from Lucas's plate at Jo. She ducked and it hit Devin in the eye. "Hey!"

"We'll need rest first," Lucas suggested.

"I don't want to sleep. I want to save my aunt."

"It's no use going in ragged. You haven't slept and your friends were just dosed with Fae poison."

Unfortunately, he was right. I hadn't slept properly since Sunday. I slipped my phone out of my pocket when it vibrated. "Text message from my mom," I told the others, as I sent a quick text back. "I'm now supposed to text her every hour so she knows I'm all right." I grimaced. "She's so going to kill me."

"Look on the bright side." Isadora shrugged. "You might not survive this rescue anyway." We all stared at her until she blinked. "What now?"

"Ignore her," Jo said. "She's cranky."

"We need supplies too, right?" I suggested. "Food and

water for sure." Lucas smiled at me approvingly. It was nice, but a little distracting. Jo might have thought him too wholesome, but he was handsome, in a chiseled, knightly kind of way. "Believe me when I tell you, you do *not* want to eat food from the Fae. You were right about that, Jo."

"And salt," she added. "Lots of it."

"And iron too. Nails and whatever else we can find."

"Weapons," Devin suggested quietly.

"I'll protect Eloise with my life," Lucas protested.

Jo waggled her eyebrows at me and I felt my cheeks go pink. "Still," I agreed with Devin, "better safe than sorry. I have a Swiss Army Knife; that's about it."

"I have a baseball bat," Jo said. I blinked at her. Jo enjoyed sports the way Elvis enjoyed a cold bath. "It's Cole's," she admitted. "He won't miss it. It's in his locker at school. Where do we sleep?" she added. "If none of us can go home?"

"Bus station?" Devin suggested. "My uncle works the ticket booth. He'll pretend not to notice us, if we're quiet."

"Good idea," I said. "We'll meet at the bus station tonight, and in the morning, Lucas and I will go to the courts. And Jo and Dev and Isadora and her people will meet us at the pond. Deal?"

"Before dusk," Lucas warned. "We count our days beginning at sundown, Samhain particularly. And we're stronger during the in-between times—dusk, midnight, and dawn."

We hung around, not really wanting to leave, until the

waitress needed our booth for another group. I looked at Jo and Devin, bickering over the last bite of cake.

I was afraid for them, afraid enough to understand a little of what my mom was feeling.

chapter 12
Jo

We were completely knackered, but it made sense to split up and get supplies before meeting at the bus station to sleep on the benches. Devin called his sister and had her meet us the café. I ordered a latte and turned my back on the table where Eldric and I had bumped into each other. While we waited for Devin's sister, Aysha, I left a message for my parents, telling them I'd be spending the week at the farm, and one for my grandparents telling them I was home. Isadora sat on the dashboard of the car and muttered complaints.

Aysha drove up in Devin's car. "He promised to lend me his car for the rest of the month if I did this," she said to me. She was wearing her full Goth gear, down to black velvet, even in the heat. "I want witnesses."

"Yeah, yeah," Devin said, pulling a bulky green garbage bag out of the backseat.

Aysha shook her head. "You're such a geek."

"Thanks, Twilight."

"How many times do I have to tell you I'm not into vampires?" She sped off, tires squealing.

"What's that?" I asked.

"Shields." He showed me a corner of painted plywood before stashing the bag in the trunk of the Buick. "You know, for elf arrows."

"Dev, that's brilliant."

He shrugged. "They're the practice ones from that medieval fair you dragged us to this summer. And I got something for you too," he told Isadora. He handed her a sword about the length of my finger through the open window. Her face brightened, as if he'd given her a hundred red roses.

"A sword," she said breathlessly.

"It's not really sharp, but we can probably fix that." He shrugged at my questioning glance. "I took it off one of my old D&D figurines."

"I'll never make fun of you for those again," I vowed solemnly.

"I want that in writing."

"You're brilliant, Dev, really."

"We're not just your eye candy, you know." He winked at me.

Isadora was doing some sort of intricate dance with the

sword, ignoring us completely. She was looking at the sword as if she might like to kiss it.

Our next stop was the grocery store for salt. I popped into the toy store next door as well. The fashion dolls were in the back, with an entire wall of clothes and accessories. Maybe it was silly, but I wanted to do something nice for Isadora. She was trying to help us, after all, and I felt bad for her, forced into a skirt like a limp tutu. I picked out miniature combat boots from an army figurine and a plaid mini-kilt. And if she complained, I'd come back and buy her the Little Bo-Peep milkmaid costume, complete with clogs and wooden pails.

When I gave them to her she grinned. "You might make up for that ijit poet, after all." She dipped down behind the seats, and when she emerged, she looked more like the type of person she was: tough, confident, and arrogant. Then she did a somersault and ruined the image. "Well?" She hooked her sword on her belt. "Best get this over with."

• • •

It didn't go well.

Devin and I huddled behind one of his makeshift shields. Elf arrows bit into the wood with alarming frequency. Isadora hovered over my shoulder, muttering under her breath. An unwary sparrow caught a dart to the wing and tumbled sluggishly into the grass.

We were getting nowhere.

"I told you this wouldn't work," Isadora said as Devin lobbed rocks at the bushes where the furious flower Fae were hiding. One of them squeaked, tumbling heels over head. The volley paused, then resumed with increasing ferocity.

"This is daft." I huddled closer to the shield. The sun was hot on my head, making me sweaty and cranky. "Don't you lot have some sort of truce symbol? Like the white flag?" I fished a crumpled tissue out of my pocket hopefully.

"How is that disgusting thing supposed to help us? Honestly, humans."

"Oh, shut up, Tinkerbell."

She narrowed her eyes at me. I narrowed mine right back. "Do something," I insisted.

She huffed out a breath, clearly put out at having to ask for anything, including help. "Fine," she snapped. "For all the good it will do us."

I'd have maybe had more sympathy for her if there weren't poisoned arrows aimed at my head. "Just do it," I hissed.

"This is embarrassing," she muttered, digging in the grass. It was so long in spots, she disappeared altogether. Devin blinked sweat out of his eyes and lobbed another rock. Isadora finally emerged just as I was about to threaten to step on her. She was holding small white flowers, like daisies; and she was scowling.

"Bleedin' poets and their pretty stories," she was saying to herself before she called to the others in another language entirely and tossed the feathery stemmed flowers over the top of the shield. "Chamomile," she explained to us. "Meant to promote peace. We used to drink the tea during treaty negotiations, but that ijit poet was all about the pretty blossoms, wasn't he?"

It took only a moment before the bows were lowered, albeit slowly and suspiciously. A Fae clad entirely in ivy hovered above the lilac bushes.

"We will hear your plea," he said arrogantly.

"Sod off," Isadora called out, perched on top of the shield and looking annoyed. "I've no intention of begging. And to think we were lovers once," she added under her breath.

I took the chamomile, brown and wilted as it was, and waved it around before peeking over the plywood. Devin was tense beside me, pocket knife in his hand. "We have a proposition," I offered.

The ivy-man sneered. "We don't make deals with mortals. We know better than to trust such a thing."

"Yeah, yeah, you don't like us. I get it," I said, standing slowly.

"Jo," Devin said warningly. He angled himself to try and shield me.

I stumbled. "Quit shoving me."

"I'm trying to help you," he argued.

Isadora rolled her eyes. "You two mind?"

I faced the Fae who were perched on the branches like exotic flowers. I held Devin's hand behind the shield for courage. There were a lot of needles glittering among them, and I remembered the sluggish burn of that Fae drug in my blood. I wasn't eager to experience it again. "We're taking Strahan down."

There was a pause and then disbelieving laughter. "You're mad as a box of frogs."

"We're going to do it," I insisted. "And Isadora is going to reclaim the rath."

It was kind of eerie having that many candy-colored eyes staring at us. Isadora lifted her chin defiantly. "That's right," she said. "Now, would you rather pout like ill-tempered brats or are you ready to go home?"

He drifted closer. "What makes you think you can defeat him now, after all this time?"

"We've allies now," she replied. "And Antonia's niece on our side."

He was joined by the rest, fairies clad in rose petals, violets, brambles, and clovers. They were armed to the teeth; angry, wary, but clearly interested.

"The Samhain ball is in less than two days. We've the tides on our side." She motioned to the brittle grass, the wilting flowers. "The land herself would have us succeed. King of Summer, isn't he? And summer is grand, but it's only one of many seasons."

I thought of the dried-up wells in the parched fields and the heat baking the streets and my grandparents worrying over bills and lost crops.

Isadora and the others were speaking in their own

language, shaking their heads and shouting but eventually gripping forearms the way warriors always do in medieval movies. She turned toward me, nodded once. "It's done."

The Fae from her clan drifted away on their hornet-steeds and Devin and I sprawled in the grass, catching our breath. Tiny, angry Fae were exhausting.

Isadora hopped from grass tip to grass tip. "It's not time for sleep yet, you two. Lazy sods, come on. We've blood to spill!" She waved her sword around.

"Just give me a minute," I said sleepily, watching the clouds drift overhead. They were dark around the edges. Eldric had promised a storm. Was that really only this morning? No wonder I was so exhausted. For once the heat felt pleasant, like a soft blanket. Devin started to snore beside me. Isadora was put out. She had a sword again and she clearly wanted to use it. She hacked at the weeds, grinning manically.

"Eldric," I whispered. I pushed up on my elbows, waiting. "Eldric."

Nothing happened. I wasn't sure what I was expecting, that he'd come striding out of trees or appear next to me in the grass. He'd said good-bye. I sighed. "Isadora?"

"Aye?"

"If I called your name and you were inside the rath, could you hear me?"

"Only if you used my *true* name."

"Which is?"

"None of your business," she scowled. "Fae don't give out their true names, not to anyone."

"Oh." Come to think of it, I'd read that somewhere. And that meant even though I finally knew Eldric's name, I didn't know his *true* name. And he'd broken up with me before we'd even had a chance to figure out if we wanted to be together in the first place.

Now that the adrenaline was wearing off, I just felt tired and despondent. I got up and wandered toward the birch grove on the edges of the field, letting Devin sleep and Isadora practice her swordplay.

The shadows were dark and welcoming, but the birch trees glowed like candlesticks in the shafts of sunlight filtering through the leaves. It was peaceful and quiet here. I could barely hear the sound of birds or Devin snoring. The white branches swayed in a wind, which didn't touch the grass or the pond's surface. It smelled green. It made me smile, made a musical hum build in the back of my throat. I turned in a circle, arms out, letting the sun dapple my face.

"Jo!" I thought Isadora might be saying my name, but it was so quiet I could barely hear her. The trees danced around me.

"Jo!" Her little voice was annoying, like a fly buzzing around my head. I swatted it away, hummed louder. Birch was so slender and pretty. I'd never noticed before.

"*Jo!*" I squinted. For some reason I could barely see on the other side of the trees. The sun was too bright in the field and painfully hot. It was nicer in the grove. I turned away from Devin and Isadora and their frantic waving.

"Josephine Alice Blackwell."

It was Devin that time. The use of my full name made me start. I could see him a little clearer.

He didn't look happy.

He was trying to get inside the grove, but the wind was tossing the trees too violently. He was avoiding the branches like they were elf arrows. His voice was muffled. I frowned. "What?"

"Don't let them touch you!" he yelled.

I looked back because Isadora was now trying to stab the nearest birch with her sword. It was like the use of my full name had woken me up. Jo was apparently just my speaking-name. And if Devin hadn't known my middle name I would still be trying to dance with the birch trees.

Because they weren't birch trees.

They were tall, skeletal old women with ragged white dresses and ragged white hair. Their eyes were too black, arms too long, fingers extended.

"Don't let them touch you!" Devin repeated.

Easier said than done.

I was in the heart of the grove and they slapped at me with their long arms, branches dragging this way and that, trying to catch in my hair, trying to claw at my chest. The hot wind seared my nostrils. I jumped as if we were playing double-Dutch jump rope. I ducked and weaved and sweated through my shirt. My throat burned, my legs muscles ached.

I wished fervently for Granddad's handsaw.

The birch women kept swatting at me and my dance became frantic. I didn't know how long I could keep it up. I somersaulted to avoid getting poked in the eye.

"Keep going!" Devin yelled, trying to reach my hand. "You're so close."

It didn't look close, and it sure as hell didn't feel close.

"On your left!" Isadora shouted. I jerked out of the way. The leaves rattled like a hiss. Sweat and dirt ground into the pinpricks left by the arrows. I inched forward, using the most foul language I could come up with. When I reached the edge of the grove, it was like crawling out of a trench. Devin grabbed my shoulders and pulled me the last of the way out. I was panting, my lungs screaming, sweat soaking my hair and stinging my eyes

"What the hell just happened?" I croaked. Devin opened a water bottle and thrust it at me. I guzzled it so greedily and so quickly that I gave myself the hiccups.

Isadora snapped a curse at the birch trees and they shook their branches at her menacingly and then subsided.

"Seriously, what the hell, woman?" I said.

"Those aren't regular birch trees."

I rolled over to glare at her. "You think?"

"It's the One with the White Hand," she explained, hovering well out of reach. "They are usually solitary. Groves like these are rare."

"Don't I feel special."

"And as Samhain approaches, everyone stirs."

"Great. Why couldn't I let them touch me?" I groaned, trying to sit up. My legs felt like marmalade.

"If they touch your head, you go mad."

I blinked, horrified.

"And if they touch your heart, you die."

I shivered, crawling farther away from the woods and into the field.

I'd never look at a birch tree the same way again.

chapter 13
Eloise

Lucas and I wandered through the park while he told me about his home, about people that turned into birds and deer and otters, and tunnels of silver under the ground.

"So, if I'm part of the Deer clan, does that mean I'm Fae too?" I frowned. "Because I don't feel particularly deerlike."

The sun gilded his profile. "Your Fae blood is very diluted," he said. "It's a curiosity more than a strength. We value history and bloodlines. That's why Antonia was chosen. Strahan likely thought she had just enough of a connection that the courts would follow her. It's tricky with mortals. We need them, but we don't *want* to need them."

"You need them? Why?"

"To vary the bloodlines, to have children. Some Fae think of humans only as animals, and it galls them to be dependent on them in any way."

"What about you?" I asked quietly. "What do you think about humans?" I was almost afraid of his answer. He wanted Strahan deposed. I could be a means to an end, whatever Jo might say about how he looked at me.

He was looking at me like that now. It made me warm all over. "I'm pledged to you, Eloise."

"Oh." I tried not to sound disappointed.

"But even if I weren't," he said, "I would still be at your side." He took my hand. "I want to show you something."

I let him pull me along. His fingers entwined in mine, grounded me when I was so tired I felt like I could drift away. I might as well be pollen. He found a secluded stretch of lawn and winked at me.

Just before he leaped up into the air, transforming into a hawk.

His chest was white, with brown wing feathers darkening at the tips. His eyes were green, even from a distance. His talons looked as deadly as the sword he wielded in human form. He soared above me and I watched him spellbound as he drifted on invisible pockets of air. He was beautiful, magical. And the splendor of it washed away some of the fear and fatigue clinging to me like mud.

He let out a shrill, piercing cry that shivered over the treetops. He widened his circles until he was right on the edge of the woods, a brown speck in the distance. He dropped, gave another cry, and flew back my way.

When he landed in the grass, shimmering back into the

brown-haired boy I knew, he wasn't alone. He grinned, taking my hand again and turning me in a slow circle as if he were waltzing. Birds filled the sky, settling on branches and benches. There were cardinals, like the ones that had watched my mom and me on the roof. Blue jays perched next to sparrows and yellow finches. Hummingbirds darted; pigeons cooed. A heron glided past on his way to the pond, gray-blue feathers the color of water.

"I've never seen anything like it," I whispered. A chickadee landed on my arm and watched me with curious eyes. I laughed. "Are they all Fae?" I asked, astounded.

"No, but I can speak to them. Otherwise, they'd never share the sky with a hawk."

"Why not?" The chickadee hopped down my arm to my wrist.

"They might think I was hungry."

"You'd *eat* them?" The chickadee flew off, insulted.

Lucas laughed. "I prefer hamburgers," he said.

"Does it hurt? When you change, I mean."

He shook his head. "No."

At some silent, secret signal, the birds all lifted into the air and flew away. Feathers drifted to the grass like multicolored snow.

I beamed at Lucas. "Thank you."

He bowed. "Simple joys can arm you for battle better than any weapon can." He glanced at the sun, sinking behind the town. "We should go," he said.

We walked through the streets, and Lucas put his arm around me. It probably shouldn't have made me so happy, considering what was happening all around us, but it did. It was simple, like any boy who liked a girl.

We got to the bus station just before dusk. Clouds gathered, dark as pewter and edged with fire from the last of the sunlight. Lucas glamoured his sword away so no one paid much attention to us. Well, not as much anyway. He was still handsome, with a smile that could sell toothpaste to the toothless. I bought us coffees and we found seats in the back. There was one bus out of town leaving at seven and after that it would be mostly deserted. I texted my mom again, then leaned back against the hard plastic seat.

I rested my head on his shoulder and closed my eyes. "Are you really a hundred and eighty-seven years old?" I asked.

I felt him smile into my hair. "Yes."

"That's pervy."

He kissed my temple. "I'm about nineteen by your reckoning. Time runs differently for us, remember?"

"You were the hawk at the party, weren't you?" I drifted off before he could answer me.

I woke up a little while later. Lucas's arm was still around my shoulder. I kept falling asleep on him. At this rate he'd get a complex that I thought he was boring. I looked up at him through my lashes. "Don't you sleep?"

He just angled his head, leaning down. I could see the hawk in him, the alertness, the absolute focus on me and me alone. I shifted so we were closer. My breath was frayed and there was heat lightning flashing through me. I swallowed, parting my lips.

And then the others arrived.

"I'm beginning to dislike your friends." Lucas smiled against my mouth. Our lips were touching and we still weren't kissing.

"Me too," I murmured back.

We pulled away as Devin set down a large garbage bag. Jo dropped onto the seat across from me. She was ragged, covered in dirt, with her hair in knots.

"What happened to you?" I asked when she didn't bother to wink at me or waggle her eyebrows suggestively because she'd caught Lucas and me nose to nose.

"A birch tree tried to bitch-slap me." She looked a little shell-shocked.

I blinked at her, then at Devin. He just nodded. "Blimey," I said, using her favorite word. A ghost of a smile touched her lips. I handed her the rest of my coffee. "Here. Clearly you need this more than I do."

"The veil is thinning," Isadora said, marching along the backs of the chairs. Lucas nodded like that made perfect sense. I glanced at him quizzically.

"The closer to Samhain, the farther the Fae can roam," he explained. "And the easier it is for mortals to see them."

"I do *not* like birch trees anymore," Jo muttered. "If I find one on the farm, I'm chopping it down for firewood." She rubbed her arms. "That was *not* fun." She set down the empty cup, wiping her mouth with the back of her scratched hand. "I'm going to get some air," she said.

"I'll come with you," Devin said automatically.

She smiled wearily at him. "You don't have to. I'll be right outside; you can watch me protectively through the window." She wandered out, still rubbing her arms. She went around the corner to where her car was parked in the alley and sat on the hood. Her hair trailed behind her, the ruffles of her skirt torn. She looked sad.

Devin and I exchanged a worried glance. I wanted to go join her, but I knew better than anyone that sometimes *not* talking was the best cure. So I stayed where I was, in an uncomfortable plastic chair, worrying. Time trickled.

"This is the part of the book I always want to skip through," Devin admitted, rubbing his face. "The boring rest-until-you're-strong-enough-and-freak-yourself-right-out-while-you're-at-it part."

"You don't look freaked out," I assured him.

He snorted. "Of course I don't; I am coolness personified."

"If you say so." I grinned. "Is that why you're tapping your foot like a deranged hummingbird?"

He opened one eye. "Where's the love, Hart? Where's the love?"

We sat back and tried to get comfortable for the long wait. He was right; this part was almost worse than being attacked. The constant waiting, the sizzle of adrenaline in the belly.

"Eloise." Lucas stood slowly. "Eldric Strahan is talking to your friend."

Eldric was sprawled on the hood of Jo's car, the sunlight on his face making him look younger than he had in the rath, surrounded by the Grey Ladies. It warmed him, made him seem more human, more vulnerable. I still wanted to go out there and kick him, though.

Jo looked wretched as it was, but something about her glowed when he was beside her. Even I could see that. "Leave them," I said reluctantly. "But watch him."

Isadora floated innocently away, toward the door.

"Don't let her see you," I said.

"Teach Grandma to suck eggs, mortal," she shot back. "I'm going to check on her, then go meet the others. We have maneuvers to discuss."

"You know Eldric?" I asked Lucas.

"Of course," he replied tightly. "How could I not? He's Strahan's son. He's not to be trusted."

I sighed, hearing him echo my own thoughts. Eldric had been benignly ambivalent about my capture and hadn't lifted a finger to stop the Grey Ladies from giving me away. But he hadn't hurt me either.

And Jo had good instincts, I felt obliged to admit, if only to myself. She'd never let him hurt Devin or me, no matter how much she wanted to make out with him. Devin was still frowning out the window, but not at Jo. "Storm's coming."

He climbed up on a chair and turned up the volume on

the television hanging in the corner. "Hey, Doug," he called out to his uncle, over the heads of passengers lining up for the last bus. "Change it to the weather channel, would you?" His uncle fiddled with the remote, aiming through the plastic partition of his booth. The channels changed and changed again until he found the right one.

"Residents of Rowan and surrounding areas should take immediate shelter," the newscaster said in strident, professional tones. "We repeat, a tornado warning is in effect for Rowan and surrounding counties. Active weather is imminent, producing strong and damaging winds, hail, and danger from flying debris. Take immediate shelter in a basement or a room with no windows."

"But there's not even any wind," I said. The trees were still, and even the litter on the curb didn't skitter across the pavement. The quiet was eerie, actually.

"Not yet," Lucas said grimly. "But look at the clouds."

I looked again. The clouds charged toward us, not just black, not just green, but shaped like horses and stags blowing fire from their nostrils. The sky cracked and broke open.

"Get Jo. *Now.*"

chapter 14
Jo

"I tried to stay away."

Eldric climbed up to sit next to me on the hood of my car. The metal was hot and he winced, though that could have been because of the iron. He was careful not to brush any bare skin over the hood. I didn't turn my head to look at him. I couldn't bear to see his beautiful brooding face looking distant or cold. I wanted to remember him smiling wickedly, kissing me.

His voice changed. "What happened to you?"

I pushed tangled hair off my shoulder. "The One with the White Hand."

He cursed softly, under his breath. "I told you this was dangerous."

"I know."

He leaned back against the window. "You should put rowan berries and salt in your pockets, for safekeeping."

"I'll keep it in mind." I wished he would go away. It hurt to have him so close and so far at the same time.

"You'd do well to stay away from me."

"Yes, you've said that already." Was it really necessary to break my heart all over again? I rubbed my breastbone, as if that would help. "You came to me. Did you have something else to say?"

"Yes. I—" He cut himself off with a frustrated sound. He jerked a hand through his hair. "You don't get it." His voice was raw. "You can't belong to Antonia and Eloise Hart and belong to me."

"Then how about I belong to myself?" Though the truth was I did want to belong to him. Or at least have us belong to each other.

"You don't get it," he said again.

"Maybe not," I agreed. "But neither do you. You're not your father, Eldric. And you can love him and defy him at the same time." I smiled but there was no humor in it. "I'm proof of that, with you," I added softly.

"I don't know what you have planned, though I'm sure it's something reckless and insane, but my father can never know about you. About us."

"You said there is no us," I replied evenly. "So you don't need to be afraid that I'll embarrass you." I bit the inside of my cheek. Farm girls don't cry, I reminded myself.

He swore again, took me by the shoulders and forcibly

yanked me around so that I was facing him. His curious gray-flecked black eyes blazed. "I'm not ashamed of you, you daft cow. I *love* you."

I blinked rapidly, choked out a laugh. "I think I love you too, you tosspot." I reached up to touch the ends of his hair. "Because you're so romantic."

He lowered his forehead to mine. "God, Jo. Don't become a part of this, please. Let me hide you where you'll be safe. You could die."

"So could El and Dev. And you." I kissed him lightly, barely a brush of lips. "And we've had this conversation," I reminded him, running my hands up his arms, just because I could. His muscles moved under my fingertips.

"You are the most infuriating person I've ever known." He said it softly, like poetry.

"Right back at you, handsome."

"My father can't ever know that we've even spoken. Do you understand?"

"Are you that frightened of him?" I asked.

"Of what he could do to you? Yes," he said grimly. "Especially if he thinks there's something between us. Promise me, Jo. Whatever happens, don't attract his attention."

"Okay, but we're going—"

He cut me off with a deep kiss. It turned sudden and desperate, heated so quickly I had to grab his shirt to steady myself. Our hair tangled together. His lips were clever, wicked. I was like chocolate melting in the sun.

"I can't know," he finally rasped. "Don't tell me."

We kissed again, until the pressure in the honey-thick air around us changed. My ears popped. I pulled away, looking around. The air was tinged with green, as if we were in a cloudy aquarium full of algae. Dark clouds boiled in the west, where the last of the sunlight set them on fire. The air tingled and it wasn't just because I could still feel Eldric's kiss on my lips.

"This is tornado weather," I said, scrambling off the car.

He slid to his feet as well, his hair lifting in a hot wind that flared and died just as suddenly. He studied the sky, a faint frown between his brows.

"That's not just a tornado." He went stark, sharp. "Get inside."

"What?" I made a fist, though I doubted I could punch a rogue Unseelie Fae in the face with much success. I may as well start practicing.

"That's the Host." He stepped in front of me, his arm protectively across my body.

I stared up at the clouds as they pressed toward us. At a second glance, there were horses striking lightning from the sky with their hooves. They were the blue purple of a fresh bruise. An enormous black stag kept pace, fire blowing out of its nostrils. Thunder rattled under its hooves. Their riders held up spears and swords, all etched with silver. They were black and gray and white and indigo, all the colors of the worst storm you've ever seen. The kind that breaks houses and people, that opens the earth and overflows rivers.

"I'm guessing the Host is bad?" I asked as the wind picked up again. Litter flew across the street, pushed up against parked cars. I shaded my eyes from the stinging dust. Devin pounded his fist on the window beside us, trying to get us to come inside.

"The Host are Unseelie. And this is a hunting party of sorts. Samhain revels where they pluck unsuspecting mortals off the streets." He eased me toward the bus station, so I was partly hidden from view by the overhanging roof. "You need to get inside," he said again. The storm churned and growled, sounding like a train bearing down on us. The wind was pinning us down. I was starting to feel like a heroine in a Victorian melodrama, with the villain twirling his storm-black mustache. We tucked our heads and pushed against the wall of heat and debris. "Before they see you. Before my father finds out."

"They know your father?" I shouted over the wind and thunder.

His smile was frosty. "They're my uncles. Family isn't just about blood in Faerie; it's about allegiances."

"Well, your family sucks." I gasped as the roof of a convenience store began to tear off like an orange peel. A pop can hit me in the kneecap. The garbage bin on the sidewalk skidded toward us. Rain began to slice through the green air, like needles.

The Host galloped closer and closer. A bicycle crashed into a car. The windshield shattered, scattering glass like shards of ice. Trees bent double; a maple sapling in a concrete planter snapped. Ghostly rabid dogs howled between the wind-horses and fire-stags.

Devin struggled against the weight of the storm to open the door. My hair was whipping around so that I could hardly see. The door finally opened, but barely. Devin pulled, Eldric pushed, and I popped through, scraping my elbow on the handle. A clay flowerpot filled with wilting geraniums hit the window, cracking it. Someone inside screamed.

The Host was passing over us now, laughing and singing a strange, morbid song I tried not to listen to. One of the dogs trailing behind snapped his head down, eyes blazing. He caught sight of Eldric and howled, changing his course so quickly he created a backdraft that slammed the door shut, nearly severing my arm.

Eldric was on the other side. I pulled on the handle even as Devin pulled on me.

"You need to get under a chair," he yelled. "Before the window gives out."

"But he's alone out there!"

The Fae dog bore down on Eldric, jaws wide, teeth flashing. He was the size of a pony, with shaggy black fur that swirled like rain clouds. He barked and thunder shook the sky, pushed Eldric's hair back.

A young girl stared outside with rapt attention. "Doggy!"

"Sara, get down." Her father tucked her under his coat. The rain slammed into the roof so hard it shivered.

"Jo!" Devin shoved me and I flew a few feet away from the door. "Now!"

The storm was so thick I couldn't even see Eldric anymore. It was just dust and electricity and debris hitting the windows like bullets. We ran, covering our heads. Eloise and Lucas were crammed inside the coffee booth, behind the shelter of the counter. The nearest chairs already had people curled under them. Devin and I skidded across the polished floor, aiming ourselves for the back corner where at least there was no glass.

"In here!" Devin's uncle shouted, crouched near the opening to the ticket booth.

Devin slid in on his side, as if he were playing baseball. He was still gripping my hand, pulling me along behind him. My skirt wrapped around the metal legs of a bench and wedged there. I jerked out of his grasp. Momentum pushed him into his uncle. I yanked as hard as I could but the fabric wouldn't release.

I was stuck.

The windows shattered.

I curled into myself as time slowed down. Devin yelled my name. Glass flew in every direction. Jagged shards shot toward me. I tried to tuck my head under my elbows.

And then suddenly Eldric was there. He stretched over me, sheltering me from the rain of glass. He was using his body as a shield. His cheek was tucked next to mine, his eyes fierce. The bus station shook, belched more glass and broken chairs, and then was still.

The Host had passed, taking the storm with them.

I turned my face slightly, toward Eldric. "I thought the dog got you," I gasped, hugging him tightly.

"He used to be my pet," Eldric replied, smiling grimly. He reached down and ripped the hem of my skirt free. "When I was little."

"You're okay? Are you okay?" I sat up, searching his back and hair for glass, for bleeding gashes. His shirt was ripped, the back of his knee bled, but he looked mostly unharmed. "Thank you," I said, kissing him hard. "You keep saving me." I kissed him again. "Are you going to let me save you back?"

"Jo!" The others ran toward us before he could answer. Eloise slid to a stop, gaping at Eldric.

"You saved her," she said, sounding shocked and teary. Lucas was beside her, expression impassive but sword in his hand.

"Eldric," he said.

Eldric flicked him a glance. "Lucas." He tipped my chin up. "I guess this is good-bye again." He smiled at me once sadly and vanished.

chapter 15

Eloise

I texted my mom as soon as we were able to climb out of the ruined bus station. I knew she was at work, worried. The tornado skipped her street altogether, and the apartment. I didn't tell her I wasn't there. I texted her again just as Lucas and I were leaving. We'd decided not to wait until dawn, knowing the Host were roaming so close. And Mom would get home from the bar at around three a.m. and tie me to my bed if I so much as twitched toward the door. It was best to get it over and done with.

Jo lent us her car and I followed Lucas's directions. "I can't believe we're driving to Faeryland or whatever you call it," I said. "That's just weird."

"There's a doorway just out of town, by the woods. It's the fastest way to get there," he replied, slightly abashed.

The streets narrowed, giving way to brown gardens and then brown fields, the corn withered on the stalks.

I pulled the car over when Lucas pointed to a narrow field. I got out and coughed on a mouthful of dust kicked up by the tires. The tornado had done nothing to break the heat wave the way they usually did. The Host were to blame for that.

The woods were a little cooler, which only meant it would take a full five minutes to broil, instead of two. It was quiet except for the twigs and pinecones crunching under my feet. Lucas had the uncanny ability of avoiding them. The creek had narrowed to a faint trickle.

"Are you ready, Eloise?"

"No." He looked concerned. I tried to smile. "But I'm not going to get any readier, if that's even a word."

He pulled out a wreath woven of ivy leaves, rowan berries, and red ribbons from his pack and set it carefully on my hair. "There." He pointed to a clearing of wilting flowers. Bees hummed lazily. A circle of mushrooms dotted the brittle grass.

"I don't see anything."

"A fairy ring," he explained, taking my hand, his fingers tangling with mine.

I dug in my heels. "Wait."

"It won't hurt a bit." He was grinning, excited about going home.

"That's what they all say."

"Just come on." He tugged until I followed. He was the first to step into the circle, and then I joined him, screwing my eyes tightly shut. I felt a moment of vertigo, a slap of hot wind in my face. I opened my eyes slowly: mushrooms in the grass, trees, pollen hazing the air.

"It didn't work." I was both relieved and disappointed.

Lucas laughed. "Of course it worked." He drew in a deep breath. "The very air is sweet."

It did smell nice, a combination of honey and apples, but it was hardly proof that we'd stepped between worlds. A rabbit darted past us, shaking the bushes. Lucas was still holding my hand. "Shh. Look."

I followed his shining gaze, and my heart could have stopped entirely and I wouldn't even have noticed. I'd walked into a poem or a painting, dripping impossible colors and pure light that made me feel nearly melancholy. The trees, even the dry dirt, were made somehow holy for being the canvas of such a moment.

They moved quietly between the birches and the cedars, women and men, pale as mist, dark as chestnut. They wore silks and lace and velvets, layered petticoats, jeweled cameos, tailored frock coats. Hair was braided, jeweled, dark as jet beads, pink as peonies. They wore piles of flowers, and their features were delicate and wounded, right out of some pre-Raphaelite painting. Red deer walked between them, silent and strong. A woman in a blue gown with silk ruffles rode on the back of a giant white stag, antlers hung with flowers.

Hounds trotted peacefully along with the deer, neither concerned with the other. The moon touched them with silver
fingers.

I was following without even realizing it. A branch
snapped under my foot. I froze. My breath felt like thunder
crashing everywhere.

The parade stopped, each to a one turning to pin us with
his or her otherworldly eyes. One of the dogs, easily large
enough to bite my arm off at the shoulder, growled. One of
the deer vanished, running swiftly between the trees. I felt
Lucas coming up beside me.

"Come along," he whispered. We were led through the
forest, alongside the river. It was thin here as well, but not as
thin as the one back home. I tried not to jerk when a deer
sniffed me, hot breath on my neck. She nibbled at the collar
of my T-shirt.

"Meg." Lucas sighed.

The deer made a rather human-sounding snort before
she shimmered and melted into a girl. I nearly swallowed my
tongue. "So this is her," she said, totally uncaring of the fact
that she was naked. "Why'd you bring her?"

"Why wouldn't I? Eloise is one of your folk."

Meg shrugged. "You know how some of them feel about
Antonia."

Their conversation was doing nothing for my confidence.
I pushed my shoulders back stubbornly.

"Just go on, Meg," Lucas said, exasperated. It was the

same tone Jo used with her little brother. "I've enough to worry about."

"I thought you weren't worried," I muttered at him.

"I lied."

"Great." I jumped when a black dog shoved his wet nose into my palm. I didn't know if I should pet him—was he really a dog or a prince in black silk? What was the etiquette here?

"You too, Niall," Lucas said fondly. He watched the dog bound away. "Now he'll race Meg to see who will be the first to reach Mag Mell with the tale."

"Who's Mag Mell?" It seemed easier to focus on that than on the serenely graceful Fae all around us.

"Not who, but what," he said, presenting it to me with a proud flourish. It was a mansion of gleaming black stone with silverwork in every gable, window, and balcony. It had towers and turrets and massive wild rosebushes all around it, like a moat.

"This is your *house?*" I gaped. I could only imagine what he thought of our secondhand couch, which sagged in the center, and the worn rugs, but he only shrugged, arrogantly unimpressed.

"Oh man," I said as we entered the marble foyer, and the mirrors reflected my jeans and scuffed boots. "I'm not sure about this." All of Bianca's insults concerning my tacky poor taste and hillbilly fashion poked at me.

Lucas took me past beautiful rooms filled with carved

wooden furniture and crystal chandeliers to a cavernous hall not unlike Strahan's. There weren't any chains on these walls though, only portraits. But there was a door in the very back corner with iron bars.

"Lucas." A tall woman with blond hair glided toward us. Her corset made her waist impossible. She was as elegant as a champagne flute. "You've returned."

"Mother." He greeted her with a kiss on each cheek. "Father. May I present Eloise Hart. Eloise, Ronan and Imogen Richelieu."

His mother lifted her chin coolly. "Charmed, I'm sure."

Lucas clapped forearms with a man I would have recognized as his father even without an introduction. They had the same moss-green eyes, the same chiseled chin.

"So this is the girl." He appraised me with a cheerful smile. I couldn't help but like him, even with the broadsword at his shoulder and the wicked scar on his chin. His velvet coat was the color of milk chocolate, or hawk feathers.

"It's nice to meet you, Mr. . . . uh . . . Lord and Lady Richelieu?" It came out as a question. Miss Manners so never covered this. If he turned into a hawk, I would be at a total loss.

"As pretty as your aunt." He raised an eyebrow. "And as fiery?"

"She protected me from Strahan," Lucas told them, explaining my trick with the chain. My shoulder still twinged at the memory.

"We've come about my aunt," I said quietly.

"Of course you have." His smiled dimmed, but he offered

his arm very graciously. I took it, feeling only a little foolish. "But first, some refreshment."

We sat at a mahogany table so long it was lit by four separate crystal chandeliers. Bowls of dandelion greens and pomegranate seeds and fresh breads and cheeses were brought on a silver tray.

"Aren't you eating?" Imogen asked.

No way in hell was I going to make that mistake again. Finding a polite way of saying that would take some doing. And the way she looked at me, she knew it too. It was a test of sorts, to see how well I could navigate their customs. If I couldn't resist freshly baked bread, how was I going to bring down Strahan? And that bread did smell good.

"Um . . . I brought you delicacies from my world," I said, putting out ginger cookies and a jar of almond butter. "I'd be honored to share them with you."

Lucas nodded proudly. I stifled a sigh of relief as he bit into the first cookie. Imogen inclined her head. I felt some of the tension leave my shoulders.

"I need your help," I said after a moment. "That is, I think we can help each other."

"And how do you propose to help us, little girl?" Ronan asked, amused.

"Strahan has captured my aunt."

"We know."

"She gave herself up to rescue Eloise and myself," Lucas said quietly. "I owe her a life-debt."

Imogen closed her eyes briefly. When she opened them

again, they were hard. "I remember your aunt at your age. She was trouble then and is trouble now."

I scowled. "Hey, from what I've heard, she's been keeping Strahan controlled half the year without help from any of you. Don't you blame her for your weird politics."

"Eloise," Lucas whispered.

"Yeah, okay." I knew it was stupid to lose my temper, especially after years of carefully controlling it. "Look, I'm going to free my aunt and take out Strahan. I'd like your help."

Ronan watched me so intently I wanted to squirm.

Lucas broke the stare. "I mean to help her."

"Lucas, no."

"Mother, I have to. I owe it to her and to Antonia."

"What do you want from us?" Ronan asked.

"Information, warriors, weapons, anyone you think might be on our side. Anything at all, really."

He leaned back in his chair. "Samhain is near."

"Which is why your help would be so appreciated."

"Very well." He nodded. "Since our son owes you a life-debt. And I'd rather like to stick a sword in Strahan's eye myself."

"Oh, Ronan." Imogen sighed.

• • •

Meg was the one who came to get me. I was in the courtyard, sweating. The sun baked the stones and the roses were scorched around the edges. Her long brown hair hung in four braids, bumping against her hips. Her dress was faintly medieval in style and looked way more comfortable than the bustles and stays of Strahan's court.

"Where's Lucas?" I asked her.

"With his mam," she answered, dropping down on the bench beside me. She smelled like pine needles.

"Oh. She doesn't like me."

"You've the right of it there."

At least she wasn't heaping on false flattery or watching me carefully as if I were poisonous, the way Imogen did. In fact, Meg was swinging her bare feet, like she didn't have a care in the world. I couldn't help but remember her shifting from a deer to a girl. She turned her face to the sun. "I'll be glad for summer's end," she said.

"Are you going to fight too?"

She shrugged, not opening her eyes. "Of course. This is my home and I'll not sit idly and let Strahan have it, not now that we might have a chance to finally best him. It's bad enough his selfishness is cooking the fields and forests."

"You don't sound scared," I remarked enviously.

She shrugged again, but this time opened her eyes. "Are you?" I nodded. "Well, only a fool wouldn't be frightened." She grinned. I couldn't tell if she was calling herself a fool. I felt better though; her calm was more comforting than Lucas's swearing valiantly to protect me. I didn't want him to die for me.

"We'd best be off," Meg declared, leaping to her feet

with a grace that was all deer bounding through twilight forests.

I was considerably slower in moving. "Where are we going?"

"To see Mother Hazel, of course."

"Of course," I said drily.

She chuckled. "I like you."

"Oh." I blinked. "Um, I like you too."

"Good. It's dull as dishwater around here with all of us fretting and wailing. This change will do us good, I reckon." She headed down the stone pathway, waiting for me to catch up. I looked at the mansion but didn't see Lucas pressed against any of the windows in warning.

"Mother Hazel is the midwife," Meg explained. "She's a little dusty to be sure, but wise as crackernuts." I was trying to decipher that last analogy when she elaborated, waiting for me to follow her under an oak bough with leaves crispy enough to rattle at our passing, like loose teeth. "Hazelnuts, you'd say. Eat those with red salmon and you'll be wise beyond your ken."

"I could use a little wisdom."

"That's why Ronan's having me take you to her. She knows all sorts of delicious secrets and little trickeries. You'll need both if you mean to win."

"Oh, I mean to win."

"Good." She threw herself into the green shadows of the forest, landing as a deer, muscles bunching under sleek fur. I didn't hear the other deer, but all of a sudden, I was surrounded. The black eyes were clever, clear; the hooves fast as rain falling.

Meg nudged me with her nose, circled me, then nudged me again in my lower back this time. I stumbled a few steps at the push. The other deer began to run, and after a few more nudges, I joined them. I felt wild and free, running and jumping over logs until there was nothing but my breath, and the deer like a red glow between the white birches. The birch thickened, gave way to more gnarled oaks. The heat slicked my skin and I didn't care, I just kept running until I was laughing out loud for no reason at all. I stopped in a clearing, and Meg bowed her head, her gaze bright. I felt better than I had in days.

"Thank you," I murmured as they melted away deeper into the woods, leaving me standing in front of a whitewashed cottage with a thatched roof and a red door. There was a stone chimney but no smoke; it was simply too sweltering out, even for an old woman. The doors and windows were wide open, the fenced garden a mess of herbs and flowers. Several cats prowled the top of the garden gate like sleek-eyed sentries. I went up the path, the grass growing yellow between the stepping-stones.

"Hello?" I knocked lightly on the open door. The inside was one large room, the hearth opposite, a spinning wheel under the window, and glass lanterns and bunches of herbs hanging from the rafters.

"Looking for me, are you, girl?"

I jumped, whirled. "Oh, sorry." The midwife was behind me, wearing a red dress and a long apron over an ample figure. Her hair was white and fell nearly to her ankles.

"Bless me, a mortal girl," she said. "It's been an age, and make no mistake." She ushered me farther inside. "How queer girls dress now. I'll never get used to it."

I sat down on a worn bench. There were birdcages everywhere but not a single bird. Instead they were filled with curiosities like painted clay eggs, a chunk of amber, a fossil. Strands of beads hung from nails in the wall, and there was a basket of yarn at her feet.

"I remember that look," she murmured. "I wore it for months after I was first brought here as a wet nurse."

"I thought you were a midwife?"

"I was both, which is why they took me from my village. The Richelieu boy needed me. That was nearly two hundred years ago." I goggled. She chuckled. "Aye, you do well to stare. Not many mortals survive this place."

"How did you?"

"I had talents that I could trade for protection and information. And I always had the Sight, even back home. I just found more ways to use it here."

"I guess Ronan thought you could help me?" I said hesitantly. "He sent me."

"Bless me, you're *that* girl." She nodded to herself, head bobbing like a bird pecking at seed. "Of course, of course."

She stuffed her pipe full of dried herbs and lit it, the spicy smoke curling around her like a shawl.

"So you'll help me?"

"If I can. What have you got to trade, then?"

"Trade?" I asked, confused.

Her eyes went hard. "Aye. Nothing's without price, dearie, especially in this place."

Fortunately my mother was a champion bargainer. I wasn't afraid of a little haggling; it ran clearer in me than deer blood. "Well, as a favor to you," I said, widening my eyes innocently, "I suppose I could give you a taste of home."

"Could you, now?" She chewed on the end of her pipe.

I nodded confidently even as I frantically ran over the contents of my bag, figuring out what I could spare and what she might want. I'd already parted with some of my food rations, and I had no idea how long I might be here, even if it was only a day back at home. I didn't think she'd much care for notebooks or chewing gum or toothpaste. She'd been a village midwife in the early eighteen hundreds. Ireland, by the sound of her accent. Tea. I'd stashed a box, along with some hot chocolate. That might work too, but I'd rather give away the tea so I'd start with that.

"I have some lovely Earl Grey tea," I offered. "How long's it been since you had real proper tea?"

She puffed away, eyes twinkling. "Oh, you're a clever one, you are. Still. Tea's a mean trade for what you'll get from me."

I sighed. "How about hot chocolate, which you can heat over your fire with cream?"

The pipe came out of her mouth. "I've not had a pot of chocolate for nearly a hundred years. How the fine ladies used to drink it every morning, and the smell was enough to drive me to distraction when I attended them."

I nodded smugly. A love of chocolate I could understand. I could work with that. "A fair trade, then?"

"Aye, lass."

I handed over the packets in my bag. She handled them reverently, putting them in a wooden box that she locked with the key she wore around her neck.

"I need to know about Strahan and Antonia," I said, watching a spider spin a web in the corner of a window. There was no wind outside, just sun and unbearable heat. I wiped my forehead. "Anything you can remember, anything at all. I have to find a way to stop him."

She nodded to the trees outside, leaves hanging limply. "He has a lot to answer for." She puffed on her pipe. "His greed has changed him. He doesn't seem to care that our wells are drying up, the crops smoldering in the fields. He still eats like a king in his stolen hall."

"Do you know him? Can you help me?"

"Better, I can show you." She added more herbs to her pipe and a generous handful to the brazier on the table. Smoke thickened the already thick air. I coughed.

"What is this stuff?" I fanned my face. It smelled sweet now, less spicy than before.

"Don't fight it," she said calmly as a coughing fit strangled my throat. "Just take deep, slow breaths and look into the candle." She slid a beeswax taper, clearly hand dipped, in front of me.

The blue center of the flame widened, stretched, wavered.

"What's happening?" I croaked, feeling odd, vague, and focused all at the same time. So much for learning from my mistakes—I'd fallen for Winifreda's deceptions and now I'd done the same with Ronan and this woman, who was drugging me for her own nefarious purposes. I wondered if it was poison, like the elf darts. But when I couldn't hold my breath any longer, instinct had me hauling more drugged smoke into my lungs. My eyelids went heavy, drooped. I cursed my naive stupidity.

I was so going to wake up dead.

chapter 16

1984

Twilight fell soft as blue silk, covering everything: the tree-tops, the peony bushes, the streetlights flickering dimly. The night smelled of earth and rain, and she waited impatiently for midnight to bloom.

It was perfect.

"Toni, you can't be serious." Jasmine scowled from where she stood in the shadows of the front porch. The house behind her was quiet and dark. She wore a pair of pajamas, spattered with paint. She and Antonia wore the same face—identical pert noses, wide mouths—except for their expressions, one impatient, one hurt.

"Don't you dare tell Mom and Dad," Antonia said,

shrugging into her jacket. Her long skirt foamed over pointy-toed boots; a lace bow held back her long brown hair. Jaz's hair had been recently dyed black, the bangs teased.

She tapped her fingers, hands planted firmly on her hips. "Antonia, you barely know him."

She shrugged crossly. "I love him, he loves me. It's romantic."

"You're sixteen," Jasmine said. "It's illegal."

"Don't be such a wuss." She scanned the deserted road, the dark shadows pooling under every tree. The wind moved slowly through the gardens. "Can't you just be happy for me?"

"I don't understand why you're doing this."

"Because it's exciting. Because he's gorgeous and sophisticated and elegant."

"And old."

"Not *that* old."

"Are you sure? I mean, really sure?" Worry softened her voice, her stance. "Is he worth it?"

"He's better than this stupid little town. He's seen things, Jaz, done things. You'd never believe me."

Jasmine felt hurt, and just as annoyed as her twin sister. "I want my sister back, Toni. I don't even know who you are anymore."

Antonia forced herself to look away from the road. Her bag was heavy over her shoulder, filled with the last of her baby-sitting money, sweaters, and her Walkman. She just wanted an adventure, to get away from this small town and small people. But sisters were sisters, and Jasmine was a part of her, even if right now she was linked to the boring part that Antonia wanted to forget. Jaz would understand eventually; she always came around.

Antonia hugged her briefly. "You know I hate it here," she whispered.

Jasmine blinked back tears. "I know."

"Look, it'll be fun. I'll call when I can."

Jasmine hugged her tight. "Be careful."

"I'm always careful."

She snorted. "Are not."

Antonia shrugged, grinning at the sound of a motorcycle approaching. "Whatever." She whirled, excitement thrumming through her entire body. "He's here."

Jasmine took a step back, feeling as if she'd already lost her, as if she was growing hazier as the motorcycle drew closer. Jasmine already felt as if she was missing something vital, her arm, her eyes, part of her breath. The Antonia she knew as well as she knew herself faded a little more.

Antonia flung her a look over her shoulder, then paused.

She knew what Jasmine was feeling, wanted to relieve them both of the bitter weight. She lifted the pendant she wore on a long silver chain around her neck. Strahan had given it to her, teased her that it was a good luck charm when she wondered at the crowned swan with a little silver fish in its mouth.

"Here," she said, pressing it into Jasmine's hand before running down the porch steps without another word and flinging herself on the back of the bike. It was sleek, blue as the twilight, growling softly. She was already laughing when he took off, her hands digging into his hips. The wind pulled her hair, ruffled her twisted skirts, and blew away the last of her doubts and nerves.

When he went through the gates into the park, where motorbikes were forbidden, it only added to the sense of adventure and secrecy. The grass was like spilled ink, the trees as slender as writing quills. He brought her deep into the dark woods, to the edge of the pond where they first met, when she was walking off her temper after another fight with her parents. This was where he proposed. The swan was there that night too, glowing like the moon on the still water. Frogs sang at her arrival.

Strahan tossed his helmet off, gave her that slow, arrogant grin that warmed her belly. "Antonia."

He tilted her head back for a deep kiss, his tongue touching hers. This part, at least she understood. It was simple enough, in a way that her mysterious, enigmatic boyfriend never was. She kissed him back until they were both loose and trembling.

"Not yet," he murmured against her lips. "We have to do this right."

She shivered, suddenly cold when he stepped away.

"Did you bring your vows?" he asked.

She nodded. They were folded in her jacket pocket, next to her breath mints. She didn't want to wake up after her first night with a guy, her husband no less, with morning breath. She'd been dreaming about this for weeks now, down to every detail: the white silk slip she'd stolen from her mother for a nightgown, the strawberry perfume she dabbed behind her ears and knees, the silver ring she'd bought off a street vendor. She'd spent so much time writing Antonia Strahan on her binders, she was going to fail math and history. But she was sixteen now; she didn't have to go back to school if she didn't want to, didn't have to go home and be grounded. She was almost an adult now and soon to be a wife too.

The idea made her giggle. It would be such a romantic story to tell her friends, the ones who weren't too mundane to enjoy it, the way her sister was. Especially this part, the little ceremony in the park where they first met, with roses and starlight. It was a custom in his family, he said, to speak vows alone before the public ceremony. They'd go to city hall tomorrow instead of classes and get all the paperwork done there. She'd already forged her mom's signature on a letter of consent.

He spread a scarf on the ground, then laid out a black glass bottle and a silver cup. He took her hand, his features stark in the shadows. "Are you ready?"

She nodded, her fingers tightening. "Of course."

"Then follow me, beloved."

He led her to the center of a small field, where the grass

grew taller in the middle, and greener, even under the pale moonlight.

"Oh, it's beautiful." She couldn't help but imagine herself in a white gown, with a beaded veil. The light was odd suddenly, like ice crystals melting, shining. Before she could question it, the ground tilted.

"Easy," Strahan murmured, bracing her. She blinked until she stopped seeing spots.

"What's going on?" She gripped his arm tightly enough to make her knuckles ache. The field had given way to a long hall, the ceiling made of woven tree roots, jeweled lamps burning in every corner. The fire crackled, scenting the air with smoke and warming cider.

"Don't be afraid," he told her. His calm presence at her side was the only reason she didn't give in to the hysteria bubbling in her throat and chest. She noticed the throngs of finely dressed people all staring at her with a mixture of smiles and scowls. She wasn't sure which made her more nervous.

"I don't understand."

"These are my people."

She saw wings like blue butterflies', silver ones like Luna moths', multicolored ones she couldn't even have imagined, all unfurling from the slender backs of men and women with pupilless eyes and skin like fire opals. There were others, too tall or small and wrinkled, some with ferns for hair, or too many ribs; others looked as human as she did until on closer inspection they were shining in some mysterious way.

Strahan himself was suddenly more than the university student who used to drink black coffee and meet her after school to take her to the movies.

He was brighter, darker, more. Part of her was drawn to the pulse of power; another part was repelled. She wondered briefly if she ought to have listened to her sister.

But then he looked at her, touched his lips briefly to hers, and none of it mattered, not even the strange ghostly girls who poked at her with frigid fingers.

"Don't mind them; they can be a little jealous."

"Where are we?" she whispered.

"In my home. These are the Fae, my family."

She wasn't sure if she should laugh, if this was some sort of intricately wrought practical joke. "Fae? Like in the poems?" she finally asked.

He smiled faintly. "Yes, of a sort. And I'm the king of the Swans."

"Really?"

He kissed her knuckles. "Really. And when we are married, you will be queen."

"Queen? But I have classes." She immediately felt foolish for saying that out loud. This was an education she would never get anywhere else. She could memorize dates and the customs of other cultures from dry textbooks or she could observe them for herself. As a queen. "Do I have to wear a tiara?"

He chuckled. "Not if you don't want to."

"But I could?"

"Yes."

"Weird."

"My lord." A man with a long white braid approached them and bowed. He wore a lace cravat and a velvet coat long enough to brush his boot tops. She coveted it immediately. "All is ready."

The crowd parted before them as Strahan took her to the end of the hall to a marble table in front of the crackling hearth. Women in Victorian gowns moved aside, their hems sweeping the carpets. On the table was a black glass bottle, a silver cup, and hawthorn branches, dainty white flowers clinging prettily. It was as if she were moving through a dream; the colors changed, the light haloing shadows like velvet. Silence fell softly. Antonia shifted nervously from foot to foot. A house hob in a red vest handed Strahan the chalice.

"Strawberry wine," he murmured in her ear. "For May eve."

She knew she should be more frightened, should ask more questions, but she felt light as cobwebs. It was kind of nice.

His eyes burned into hers. "Did you bring the vows I gave you?"

She nodded, pulling them out of her pocket. He turned to the courtiers for a moment, suddenly regal. "I present to you Antonia Hart, soon to be my consort. Our union will bring fruitfulness and abundance to this court for seven long years."

There were smiles, clapping. Antonia lowered her voice. "Why me?"

"Because I love you." She shivered, his voice touching her all over. "And you belong to this place more than you know."

"I do? How?"

"Your great-great-great-grandmother had a lover from the Deer house; it's why your branch of the family has the last name you do: Hart. 'Hart' is just an old word for deer, beloved."

She didn't know if it was true, but it was a lovely story and not as dull as most family trees. A lady in a tight corset sprinkled them with hawthorn petals. The vows were said and seemed to echo gently from one end of the hall to the other.

"By the May moon and the hawthorn, I crown you." A silver-dusted crown of hawthorn branches was placed on Strahan's brow.

"By harvest moon and deathcap mushroom, I crown you." A wreath of red berries was set on Antonia's hair.

There were other words spoken in a haunting language she didn't recognize as a red velvet ribbon was wound around their wrists, binding them together. She repeated the words, growing more pliant, melting, coming apart like warm wax. When he offered her the wine, she drank even though it made her light-headed. It was sweet on her tongue, and when he kissed her, sweeter still. It was like fire and summer rain.

When they broke apart, the ceiling hung heavy with flowers and leaves of every description.

• • •

1991

Seven years later brought another celebration to the rath. Antonia had grown accustomed to the travel between worlds and was so fiercely in love that even stepping into Fae didn't faze her for very long.

There were changes of course, most obvious being Strahan's clipped tones as tension mounted within him. The Seelie courts noticed, watched him carefully. He wasn't the first to cling to the crown when his seven years came knocking. It was custom, after all, for the king of the Seelie courts to pass the crown to another; at least the sacrificial death was no longer required. Everyone agreed he'd acted as a good and proper ruler.

Antonia walked toward the main hall, holding another kind of secret entirely in her belly. She'd never taken on the custom of corset and bustle; still, she wore a fine velvet dress and wished her sister could see her now. She'd tried to convince Jasmine to join her under the hill but with no success. At least, between the two of them, they'd been able to construct the illusion that she was a wild child with restless feet, rather than an abducted or vanished daughter.

She found Strahan brooding in his chair, his hair mussed. There were tight lines around his mouth. He hadn't aged, looked virtually the same as the boy who brought her iced cappuccinos on hot summer days when she was sixteen. She tried to find that boy in him now, but it was a struggle.

It made her sad to think of it. She hoped her news would bring him some measure of joy.

"Strahan."

He barely looked at her. The Grey Ladies showed their skeletal teeth snidely, hovering behind his chair, blowing cold air through his hair.

"Strahan," she repeated.

"What?" he asked crossly, coldly.

She might have shivered if she hadn't already learned not to show weakness in the hall. "The guests are arriving."

"Guests," he spat. "Vultures." But he straightened in his chair, his eyes hot and arrogant. The silver hawthorn crown was on his brow, glinting in the lamplight. She didn't know why it suddenly made her nervous and uncomfortable to see it. She made her expression blankly polite and stood behind him to welcome the representatives of other Fae courts, mostly royalty and a few advisers.

There were Deer girls and packs of dogs, some of whom shifted into princes and princesses. There were ladies in corsets slit to allow a fan of glittery wings, small hobs with fine sequined cravats, water fey, and the frail Winifreda, who always watched Strahan hungrily. He confided in her, lately sending her on private errands he would not speak of. The other kings and queens sent their own trusted people to Antonia, with long letters full of concern. She fed them into the fire and never mentioned them, though they stayed with her.

There was honey wine in every cup, and a small, gnarled

man with cloven hands was beating the ceremonial drum. Above the rath, twilight fell. Inside, it was all soft lamplight and rising tempers.

"It's time," the representative from the Bluebird clan said firmly, her violet skin shimmering.

Strahan remained in his seat. The Swan house stood at his back, white feathers tied to their hair. "About that," he said softly.

"You've had your seven years."

He lifted one shoulder negligently, let it fall. There were mutters, agitated whispers. He lifted his chin. "Do you deny I've done right by my rule?"

A Deer woman shook her head, the pelt cloak over her shoulder finely brushed. "We cannot and do not deny that. But you know the way it's done. The king must make way for another, or the land will not flourish. Our own queen gave up her crown to another, just last moon."

He snorted. "The power over the Deer clan hardly compares to that over all the Seelie courts combined. There is still so much I would do, *could* do, with a little more time."

The Beetle queen, Cartimandua, wearing a shiny black bustle dress like a carapace, nodded. "I agree, the tradition is antiquated and does us no honor."

It escaped no one's notice that she was in the sixth year of her reign. The seven-year time span was only enforced over the high king or queen, but many of the houses followed a similar pattern.

Ronan set his cup down. He had a grim mouth and a powerful wife at his side. The dogs in the hall lifted their heads, scenting the charged air. "Strahan, it's not your decision to make. It's too much power to have for long; we all agreed on this, centuries ago."

"Seven years," Strahan mocked. "Barely a moment."

"Then take it up with the council. But the fact remains, the crown is no longer yours."

The Grey Ladies wailed, and ice crackled over the lamps, freezing the honey wine in the cups. The dogs growled in reply. The hawk on Ronan's shoulder flapped his wings and shifted into Ronan's son. Lucas drew his sword. Strahan only looked amused.

Antonia put her hand on his arm. The muscles were tense as bowstrings. "You still have the Swan house and all your allies. Why not rest now?"

He looked down his nose at her with a kind of condescension he'd never shown her before. "You are too mortal to understand."

She drew back, stung. "I haven't been too mortal to live as your wife."

He tried to make his heart cold against her. There was too much at stake and she wouldn't stand by him; he could see that already. With his hands full of power, he could do so much for the courts. What could he do with love? Write sonnets and play the lapdog until he grew into a doddering old man. He'd seen it happen, could see it happen easily enough.

At least with the Grey Ladies and Winifreda, the rules were simple; there was no danger of growing muddled with desire. Mortals never fared well in Faery; he'd been an impulsive fool to marry Antonia, for all that she'd done him proud in the last seven years.

"Don't be tiresome," he told her, barely glancing at her. He didn't have to look to feel the hurt emanating off her. One of the wolfhounds tucked his nose into her palm. She'd always been a favorite with the hounds and the hawks; small wonder Ronan was glaring at him.

"Step down, Strahan."

"No."

"Then I call council," Ronan declared.

Strahan raised an eyebrow imperiously, though in the private chambers of his chest, his heart lurched. "That will take some time," he said calmly.

Ronan nodded, unsurprised. "We expected this might happen. You stink of greed and fear." Winifreda bared her teeth. The dogs answered in kind, with warning growls that filled the hall like a swarm of bees. "I've already alerted the council," he added grimly. He withdrew a silver branch hung with bells and shook it once. Strahan paled slightly but didn't otherwise react.

The first to arrive was Cu, a grizzled wolfhound, tall as Ronan's shoulder. Silence greeted him. When he shifted, it was into a tall, lanky old man with white hair to his elbows. His eyes were husky blue, piercing. The Hound clan bowed, and even the actual dogs rolled briefly on their backs, exposing their bellies. Other houses were headed by old Cu as well: Fox and Wolf and Coyote.

Next came the stag king, Kern, his antlers emerging from a human face and wreathed with oak and holly. The Deer girls looked shyly at him through their lashes, and Sava the Deer Queen inclined her head.

Talia wore a cloak of many feathers, and Lunae arrived in a cloud of butterflies and bumblebees. The most ancient of them all gathered rarely. The other monarchs, even the high ones of both Seelie and Unseelie courts preferred not to catch their attention. Their justice was sharp and sliced through all other magics and oath.

The gathered courtiers pressed against the silk-papered walls, trying to stay unnoticed and yet still be able to hear the goings-on. The council hadn't been called in its entirety in nearly two hundred years.

Cu was the first to speak. "Who has called us?"

They knew very well who had called them, but traditions died hard among them.

Ronan stepped forward, Lucas eager at his side, brimming with injured honor. "Ronan of the house of Talia," he declared. "The high king refuses to relinquish the summer crown."

Strahan stood, unrepentant, the Grey Ladies sighing around him. "I can do more," he said simply. "I will do more."

Kern folded his bare arms, muscles bulging. "Perhaps. But not at this time."

Strahan's eyes flickered like the blue center of a particularly violent flame. "I won't bow to you. And even you lot haven't the power to take my crown from me."

Kern's voice was soft, nearly gravelly. "You'd make the land suffer for your ambitions?"

"For the good of the courts."

Talia sniffed disdainfully. "For the good of your ego, you mean."

He drew himself up and power sparked around him like fireflies. "You are in my court now, where I am king."

Behind him, with the hawthorn crown at his brow dripping with ice, stood the houses of Crow, Swan, and Beetle. The Deer, Hound, and the rest of the winged houses stood near the council. The remainder pressed themselves farther against the walls, inching toward the arched doors.

He flicked his wrist once. The Grey Ladies widened their mouths to form caves of dark and cold. Frost seared the walls, the gowns, the lamps, even the antlers of the stag king. Snow and wind whipped through the hall. The battle was swift and bloody. Claws and beaks and teeth joined the other weapons. The deer kicked out flashing hooves. Blood dripped into the drifts of snow. Roots cracked under the pressure of ice.

Strahan had enough of the high king still in him to engender loyalty, even when logic and tradition might have told them differently. Beneath the sudden winter, roses bloomed.

The council stood grim-mouthed, and Strahan laughed softly though sweat sheened his neck. Antonia shifted uncertainly between the two, surrounded by snapping dogs trying to protect her, sensing her secret.

Cu growled, hackles rising. "Enough."

Strahan turned his sword in his hand. The lace at his throat fluttered. "I can keep this up indefinitely."

Kern's antlers nearly touched the ceiling roots. "We shall see."

Something unspoken passed among the council. When Cu nodded once, light poured out of them, bleaching the edges in the hall, setting fire to the shadows.

Strahan threw his arm up to shield his face. "Trickery," he called to his armed followers. "Didn't I tell you?"

But the light touched everything, seeped through silk and skin, muscles and bones, corsets and cravats. There was no escaping, no hiding.

"The Swan belongs to my court," Talia declared, her voice deadly. "And I do not support the House of Strahan. Stand aside," she added, staring at him.

"I will not."

"So be it."

The council raised their left hands as one. The light flared like a bonfire traveling through the air. The Grey Ladies writhed. The Crow queen spat, her silver and jet beads sparkling. The hawthorn crown burned Strahan's forehead, and he thought he could smell his hair singeing, but he refused to take it off. He wouldn't allow them the satisfaction.

Antonia, on the other hand, had dropped to her knees and

was clawing at her wreath. Under the impossible light and snow, he saw the sleek branches turning to silver, the berries into carved garnet beads.

"No," Strahan shouted furiously. "No, damn your eyes!"

Cu wasn't sympathetic. "You chose, High King. We cannot separate you utterly from your reign, but justice would have your queen gifted too. From Beltane to Samhain, you may rule, though few may follow." He continued smoothly. "From Samhain to Beltane, Antonia will rule freely. You, however, are bound to this rath, Strahan, and to your oaths."

In Rowanwood Park, the pond boiled for a brief moment, the tiger lilies on the banks shedding burning petals and smoke.

chapter 17

Eloise

Present day

When I came back to my surroundings, the midwife was still rocking in her chair, smoking her pipe. I felt as if I'd been dreaming for days, but the liquid in Mother Hazel's cup was still steaming. She nodded at me. "Got what you came for, did you?"

I knew my eyes were bright with excitement. "Thank you, Mother Hazel," I said, using her honorific title. She totally deserved it. I was practically buzzing with energy, with the need to do what must be done.

"Easy, girl," she soothed, chair creaking. "You'll wear yourself out before you even get started. That's the trick to Fae magic: not using it."

"That doesn't make any sense."

She grinned. One of her back teeth was missing. "Aye, lass."

I shook my head but I was smiling. I felt too glad to worry about it, as if I'd been eating champagne-soaked strawberries. I practically leaped to my feet. "I think I know what Antonia needs," I said. "I saw it. I have to go." I rushed back in. "Thank you," I called again before rushing back out.

It was hot as an oven, but I barely noticed the heat for the first time in days. I ran between the trees, following a narrow trail back to Mag Mell. Brittle leaves crumbled under my feet. The animals were listless in the woods, drowsy as they poked their heads out to watch me pass. A hare wiggled her nose at me, and I was nearly certain she could turn herself into a girl. I thought of Nicodemus, of Cala suffering for water. I'd be able to help them as well. I was practically laughing as I emerged onto manicured lawns with hedges trimmed into curious faces, half-animal, half-human. Shriveled berries covered the flagstone walkways. The mansion towers rose into the bleached-bone sky. It was so hot and dry, like the desert. I wouldn't have been surprised to see a flying carpet or a genie's lamp.

I found Lucas pacing between two hedges, one shaped like an old wolfhound I now recognized as Cu, and the other like a blue jay, complete with blue-and-white flowers, though a bit wilted. He was frowning, kicking pebbles. I knew that look, I'd seen it on Jo often enough. "Are you pouting?"

He looked up sharply. "Eloise."

I grinned. "Lucas."

He tilted his head, nostrils flaring. "You've been to see Mother Hazel, then."

I skipped like a schoolgirl and I didn't even feel dumb doing it. "I feel great."

"I see that."

I fell against him, laughing, out of breath. He was close, so close I could see the crinkle lines at his eyes when he smiled. He looked into my eyes for a long time, the pale green irises searching. I smiled tentatively. His palm stroked down my spine.

Then his gaze slid sideways. "You can come out, Meg."

Meg strolled out of the bushes, unrepentant. There were brown-edged leaves in her hair. "Imogen's done with you?"

"For the moment. You know how she is, she worries." He looked down at me. "We should go back. You'll have to make your formal declaration."

My euphoria faded a little. "I have to get back, now that I know what I'm looking for. Besides, they already agreed to help me, didn't they?"

"I know, but they're a traditional lot, especially now. The other Seelie courts gathered while you were visiting Mother Hazel. You'll have to stand before them."

I dug in my heels. "I don't want to." Crowds were bad

enough, Fae crowds had my throat tightening up. Lucas and Meg exchanged a glance. Their hands gripped my elbows.

"Come along, Eloise," Meg said simply.

My feet left trenches in the dust. "You two are bossier than Jo," I complained.

Meg was completely unruffled, as usual. "The quicker you do this, the quicker you can go home. Besides, we haven't the time for nerves."

"Easy for you to say," I muttered. "You can let go, wardens," I added. "I'm coming, I'm coming."

Meg half grinned. "You have Deer blood, Eloise. We're fleet of foot. I ought to know."

They didn't let go until we were in the marble foyer. Blown glass oil lamps caught the sheen of the sun through the windows. We could hear the murmur of voices in the ballroom. I wiped my hands on my jeans. "So what do I have to do exactly?"

"Just stand on the dais and make a formal call for aid." Lucas squeezed my hand.

Conversations faded when we entered; I in my worn T-shirt, Meg in her russet dress, Lucas in a frock coat fit for a prince, which I suppose, in a way, he was. Ronan and Imogen were near the front. There were folks from every house: hawk, hound, deer, fox, wolf, bear, rabbit, horse, cat, mouse, horse people and mer-people, house hobs and winged sprites.

All staring at me.

If I could be undone by this, how could I hope to free my

aunt and Strahan's other captives? No one seemed to understand I was less scared when that crow pushed me off the
roof than I was right now. That, at least, was quick. This
moment, however, already felt like it stretched until next
winter.

My mouth was dry and I desperately wanted a sip from
the water bottle in my knapsack. Instead, I took a step forward, and another, until I reached Ronan.

Imogen looked at me disdainfully. "You don't mean to
wear that, do you?"

"Mother." Lucas sighed.

Ronan motioned to the dais, which looked like a little
stage, filled with huge potted ferns and rugs. I climbed the
stairs slowly. From my new vantage point, I could see that
in addition to the mahogany tables and fainting couches,
there were spears, swords, and quivers of delicately carved
arrows. Among the corsets and breeches, there were also
bright armor, grim mouths, excited eyes. I couldn't forget that
although all I wanted to do was rescue my friends, these Fae
courts wanted to depose Strahan once and for all. And with
the faint whiff of hope provided by my offer, they meant to
do just that.

They were starving, their crops blighted, their numbers
thinned as Strahan gathered captives for his exhibits. This
was so much bigger than me and my family. Even a few mem-
bers of the Unseelie courts had come and stood ready to hear
my speech. I suddenly wished I'd taken debating class. Just

a formality, I reminded myself. Ronan had already agreed to help me, and preparations were already under way.

I didn't even attempt to smile. My mouth was so dry my lips would have stuck to my teeth. The only sound was the rhythmic bang of the smithy's hammer from somewhere beyond the back kitchen. I knew I was already bright red as I cleared my throat. Lucas nodded encouragingly.

"I'm Antonia Hart's niece," I said. My voice wobbled a little. "You all know what Strahan is doing to this place and to your courts." I spoke louder. I really hated this. "He's been capturing your people and displaying them as curiosities." My wrists were still bruised, and I held them up as proof. "And now he's captured my aunt, and I mean to rescue her."

A short, grizzled man who looked just like what I imagined a dwarf would look like, spat on the ground. A house hob scowled and hurried in with a cleaning rag. "Why should we risk ourselves for Antonia? She's been nothing but trouble." There were shouts of agreement. My temper warmed, remembering Mother Hazel's vision.

"Antonia was just a girl when Strahan dragged her into your politics," I shouted over the din. Anger made my voice strong. My mother would be proud. "And Strahan's the one who refused to give up his crown, not her. She's had to flee for half the year to keep herself safe and your court safe as well. How long do you think you'll last as free houses if Strahan binds my aunt come tomorrow night?"

Everyone assumed that Antonia had kept on the run during Strahan's summer reign because she had to keep herself and the handfast ribbon out of his reach.

But I had reason to believe my aunt was trickier than that.

It was watching her give my mom the Fae pendant that had made me think of it. She and Antonia shared everything, and had always been immensely protective of each other. And we had that locked hope chest in our living room, a storage room in the basement of the apartment building full of Antonia's stuff, as well as her van, which was parked in our parking spot since we didn't have a car of our own.

I kept Lucas's gaze to steady me. "I'm going to free her," I said. "My friends and I, young as we are, are going in. Are you going to run away and leave it all to us?"

Ronan held up a hand. "She speaks true," he said. "And the House of Talia has already pledged to her." He turned to me. "You must understand, Eloise, that we swore fealty to Strahan as the high king many years 'ago. We are still bound by that and may do him no lasting harm."

"Oh." Why hadn't anyone told me that before?

Wait.

They didn't think I was going to kill him, did they?

That seemed a little extreme. Not to mention totally gross and illegal.

"We will give you warriors to meet Strahan's warriors, but the rest has to be by your hand or Antonia's."

Shields were beaten with sword hilts, and there was so

much shouting it reverberated in my skull. Skin shimmered, teeth grew too sharp. In the lamplight, I couldn't tell if Meg's dress was wool or fur.

I didn't like where this was going. There was nothing I could do about it though. The facts were facts, and we needed the court's help if we were going to succeed.

I nodded.

"Agreed."

• • •

The journey back through the mushroom ring was less disconcerting now that I knew what to expect. It was just as hot as when we'd left, even so close to dusk. The leaves hung listless, the flowers didn't stir. The air was heavy, dead. It was all too easy to imagine bloodstained hobs wandering in the woods.

There were seventeen messages on my phone, all from Mom except one. That one was from Jo, telling me that my mom was also calling her. She'd told her I was fine and would call her back. She didn't mention our plan, of course.

So if I survived, I was dead anyway.

We walked the dry fields in silence, heading out to the road where Jo's car was parked. Meg had been the first to pledge herself to the journey—well, after Lucas. She stared all around her curiously. Her eyes were black, deer eyes.

"Your eyes," I murmured. She blinked, and when she looked up again, her eyes were normal.

The streets were quiet in town, and it was clear where the Host had roamed. Trees had fallen through roofs, thick branches lay across the road, wires were down. The trees in the park had lost most of their leaves overnight; the grass was buried in drifts of yellow and orange, making it look as if it were on fire.

"I need to go home first," I said. Lucas nodded grimly, eyes suddenly hawklike.

I let us in the side door of the building, and we took the back stairs down to the basement. It was damp and dark, rows of locked doors under weak lighting. Our footsteps echoed and the door clanged loudly when it shut behind us. The only light inside was from a bare bulb hanging on a chain.

"It's like a horror movie in here." I looked distastefully at the stacks of cardboard boxes and wavering shadows.

"What are we looking for?" Lucas asked. "You haven't said yet."

"The handfasting ribbon. It's red velvet, an inch or so thick."

Meg raised her eyebrows. "Antonia would have it on her person, wouldn't she?"

I shook my head, opening the first box. It was full of new-wave records from the eighties. "That's what we've all been assuming. But I remember seeing it when I was little. I found it in a music box in my mom's closet. She freaked out and took it away, and I never saw it again. She said it was a family heirloom. Antonia told Strahan she'd lost it, but he didn't believe her. And now I don't think she even could have done that without his knowing it. In the vision, it tied them together, bound the magic or whatever."

"Aye, we've always thought the crowns were the link, but the ribbon makes sense. He'd want it to control her."

"Well, screw that."

We searched all the boxes, found tarnished silver lockets, books on fairy lore nibbled by mildew, old hats, a teddy bear, a painted jean jacket, and the remains of an unfortunate mouse behind a broken juicer machine.

No ribbon.

"Let's try the van," I suggested. It was in the back corner, where the overhead lights flickered annoyingly. It was an extended VW van, the original lime green since painted over in blue. In the back, the single shelf was empty except for a few candles and a box of matches. The bed was made, but also empty. We found a box under the driver's seat, and I got excited until we opened it and found only photographs and an old diary, the pages yellowed.

"Nothing." I pulled the door shut and leaned against it, defeated. "I was so sure it would be here."

Lucas ran a hand through his hair, equally frustrated. "Samhain is in mere hours now."

"I know." There was a lump in my throat.

Meg pinched Lucas, hard. "You're not helping," she chided him. To me she asked, "Did your aunt not have a home of her own?"

I shook my head. "Not as long as I've been alive."

Meg tapped her lips, thinking. "It would be in a place where she could get to it with some ease, if necessary."

I thought so hard I nearly went cross-eyed.

"She doesn't even have a bank account, never mind a safety-deposit box. I always thought it was just because she didn't trust the government or something. When I was ten, I decided she was on the run from the police." I thought harder. "In the movies, it's always in a locker at the bus depot." Lucas waited patiently, his hair the color of antique wood. Something clicked, slowly. "That's it," I whispered. I bounced on my heels. "The old hope chest. Come on."

We hurried up to the apartment. "Mom'll be at work."

We crept inside. Meg was still as a deer in the woods. I was glad for the area rugs, which muffled the sound of our footsteps. The living room was stuffy, windows locked tight. The sun was fully out now, burning the barren field of sky.

The hope chest, of course, was locked.

And I'd been looking for the keys for years, with no success. We didn't have time for a repeat search. "We'll need to pick the lock," I whispered.

Meg smiled. "Let me," she murmured, soft as breath. Even Elvis didn't move from where he was curled up on the couch. She pulled a long straight pin out of her leather satchel. It didn't take her very long at all, a few jiggles, a soft snick, and it was done. I took the candles and the bowl of jelly beans off the top and lifted the lid. Lucas muffled the creak of the hinges with his hands.

The hope chest held jars of rowan berries, dried ivy vines, iron nails, and, in the center, a small pouch. It was soft velvet, like the ones you got at jewelry stores, and it was bound with red thread.

Inside, the velvet handfasting ribbon.

chapter 18
Jo

"They should be here by now."

I was pacing in the field by the pond, where I could keep an eye on the hidden entrance while we waited for Eloise and Lucas. Isadora was perched on a tree branch making hand signals to the Fae hidden in the pines on the opposite side of the water. The sun was sinking behind the park, leaving a thick humidity that made it feel as if we were wearing woolen coats.

"Something's happened," I insisted, pacing faster. "Something's wrong. Oh my God, they ate her liver."

"Ew." Isadora grimaced. "We eat berries, you nutter, not human organs."

"Jo, if you don't chill out, I'm going to poke you with an elf dart." Devin waggled a handful at me to prove his point.

I slowed my pacing but I didn't stop altogether. I rubbed my arms, chilled despite the heat. "Aren't you worried?"

"Of course I am. But she'll be here." He went back to opening and closing his pocket knife. His nervous tic was just as irritating as mine.

"Will you both calm down?" Isadora snapped. "Honestly, amateurs."

The sun sank lower and lower. Twilight rose like smoke, suddenly, maliciously. I could hear Eldric's warnings echoing in my ears.

"There," Devin said just as Eloise came racing between the willows, with Lucas and a girl I didn't know. Eloise's face was red, excited.

I hugged her hard. "You're late."

She hugged me back. "Sorry." She introduced us. "This is Meg."

We smiled at each other. "Well?" I asked. "Did you get help?" She nodded, breathless. "Brill," I said. "I knew you would."

"You?"

"Isadora's lot will protect the pond. Because apparently come Halloween night, this park is just crawling with beasties."

"Great," she said drily. "The courts will meet us in there. They can't take Strahan on personally though. That's up to us."

Meg shivered suddenly. She was graceful as a doe.

"Samhain's unfurling," she said quietly. "We'd best get going, before we're caught out."

"Strahan will have patrols," Lucas agreed. His eyes glittered suddenly. "Down!"

We dropped into the tall grass like we were marionettes whose strings had suddenly been cut. There was a rock digging into my hip. Devin was behind Eloise, his hand on her calf. Lucas had swung himself up into an oak tree.

A woman wearing hard, shiny leather, like a beetle's shell, emerged from a circle of mushrooms. She was armed to the teeth with wickedly curved swords. Beetles crawled over the grass, dust clinging to their pincers. Beetles didn't usually bother me; they were kind of pretty, actually, the way the last of the light caught them in swirls of iridescent blues and greens.

Except when there were hundreds of them.

I had to bite my tongue when one of them walked over my thumb. Did Fae beetles attack? Were they poisonous? If that one got any closer to my face, I was going to bite my tongue clean off.

She walked slowly, confidently, barely looking around. She had no reason to believe we'd be here by the pond. But she was close enough that I couldn't cry out, not even when a beetle got tangled in my hair. Another one followed, falling into the collar of my shirt. I swallowed a scream.

When she'd finally gone and Isadora and Lucas gave the signal to come out of hiding, I leaped to my feet and shuddered about like a lunatic. I shook my hair out, and my shirt, moaning. "I did *not* like that."

"If you're done dancing," Isadora said drily. "Let's go, before any of the others come. They have to pass by the pond to get to the ring."

The swan was making its rounds on the pond. The last of the lilies sweetened the still air. "Could be a sentry," Meg said. "Strahan's from Swan folk, after all, before Talia exiled him."

"I got it," Lucas said, dropping out of the tree and turning into a hawk. His huge wings flapped by my face. It was so unexpected that I tumbled backward and landed on my butt.

"You do that a lot." Isadora shook her head at me.

"Oh, shut up," I muttered, gathering up the wounded bits of my dignity. Lucas circled the pond, then dive-bombed. The swan honked, insulted. Lucas pecked again, going for its eyes. The swan eventually flew off, honking madly. Lucas waited for us on the banks, shimmering back into a medieval prince.

"Just a bird." He shrugged.

I gaped at him. "Warn a body, would you, birdbrain?"

Eloise grinned at me. "Just wait."

I groaned. "It makes me nervous when you're that cheerful."

"Please, you're the troublemaker. I'm the quiet, polite one."

I snorted so hard I sounded like a dyspeptic pig. "Right."

"You're both brats," Devin said soothingly. "Now, move it."

Isadora made a last signal to her brethren, who gleamed briefly like fireflies in response. She floated over the middle of the pond and dropped like a stone. Ripples made concentric circles. She popped back up briefly. "Will you come on? You've got to swim to get to the door, don't you?"

"This is such a bad idea," I muttered as Meg dove in, then Devin.

Lucas waited for me, keeping guard. "Go on," he urged.

I walked into the warm water, feeling a little too much like Ophelia for my liking. My skirt twisted heavily around my legs. I took a deep breath and went under, struggling to open my eyes. Everything went gray-green and hazy. We swam down toward the bottom, batting weeds out of the way. I followed Devin's wildly kicking feet.

Until he stopped kicking.

I couldn't tell what was going on, only that he'd stopped swimming and had decided to float instead. Water filled his clothes so that he swayed gently. I swam closer and tugged on his sleeve. My lungs were already starting to protest the lack of air. He ignored me.

I tugged harder.

He was too busy staring at the watery shadow of a girl under the water. Her hair was long and pale. She was innocently naked; her long hair glistened like opals. She beckoned at Devin. He followed.

Isadora flew past my nose, startling me. She pointed up and then burst through the surface of the pond. I followed, gasping for breath.

"That's a kelpie," Isadora snapped. "She'll kill him." She slapped her small hand on my forehead. "See for yourself."

I dove back down, searching for Devin. The hauntingly beautiful girl wasn't a girl at all. She wasn't even a mermaid. She was a horse.

A big, black, angry horse was drowning Devin because he couldn't be bothered to fight back. I kicked forward frantically, just as Lucas shot past me. He swung his sword at the kelpie. She nearly clamped her teeth over his arm, eyes rolling.

Eloise went up for a breath, then came back down. We both descended on Devin, snarling at the kelpie. She tried to kick Eloise in the head. Lucas swam between them, and used the horse's mane to leap onto her back. He yanked back until she snorted, blowing bubbles. Her seductive gaze broke away from Devin.

He blinked, shook his head. Eloise and I took an arm each and dragged him up to the surface. He coughed out water, trying to breathe.

"What the hell was that thing?" he finally gasped.

"Kelpie," I answered.

"So, you get a Fae prince, El gets a hawk, and I get a psychotic water horse who tries to kill me? How is that fair?" He coughed again. "You guys haven't even read Lord of the Rings," he said again, disgusted. It was his traditional complaint. His teeth chattered. Eloise and I looked at each and then closed in, each kissing a cheek. "Yeah, yeah," he mumbled. "Let's go."

We dove back in, swimming down to where Lucas had chased off the kelpie. I saw the swish of her tail and had no idea where she could be swimming off to in such a small pond. As long as it was away from us, that was good enough for me.

Lucas led us through a dark crevice between two rocks and we emerged in a kind of cave with pink quartz glittering in the walls. We hauled ourselves up onto the rocky cave floor, drenched and gasping. My muscles quivered uselessly. I felt like melted butter.

I wrung out my hair like a rope and then twisted it into a halfhearted braid. The rocks led to a tunnel hung with cobwebs like lace.

"Everyone here?" Eloise whispered. We all murmured, "Here," like it was homeroom.

"Iz, how far is it?" I asked, pushing the webs aside.

"A few minutes yet. We're not even under the rath proper."

Devin was right beside me, holding out his pocket knife like it was a broadsword and he was a warrior out of one of his fantasy novels. I didn't even tease him about it. A rat chittered at us, dodging our feet. Isadora flitted backward toward us, watched the rat shoot down the hall with hard eyes.

"That one was a sentry. We have to hurry or we'll lose the element of surprise."

We broke into a run with no more prodding necessary. There were faint sounds of merrymaking: laughter, some kind of musical instrument being played, footsteps overhead. We went up rough steps carved into the earth, the walls and ceiling turning into a complicated weave of tree roots and little yellow flowers. Isadora looked right fierce.

"Iz, you all right?"

She nodded, showing her teeth and a hungry smile. "I'm looking forward to this."

I was a little worried for her. She might have been some warrior queen over a hundred years ago, but right now she was tiny. And her sword, though sharpened, was even tinier.

The tunnel curved left and brought us to a tarnished silver grate. Lucas shifted to a hawk again and caught the rat in his beak before it could dart through. Lucas tossed the rat and it squeaked, hit the wall, and then lay still. No one said anything. We peered through the grate.

I'd never seen anything so beautiful before, not even Eldric's room. The ceiling was all silver roots dripping red roses and painted glass lanterns. The floors were thickly laid with Persian rugs; the furniture was ornate and hand carved, piled high with silk cushions. Jeweled oil lamps burned next to thick beeswax candles, and there was a fire crackling and snapping inside a massive hearth. The mantel was crowded with more candles, slim tapers of every height and thick pillars carved with roses. Incense hovered and snaked through the hall. A shield bearing a white swan hung on the far wall. Huge tables were covered with every kind of food imaginable: pomegranates, brioche, éclairs, blood oranges, fried zucchini flowers, pink meringues. No wonder Eloise had had such a hard time resisting. My mouth was already watering.

But it all paled next to the Fae in their finest corsets and frock coats, cravats and jewels. A slim blond man with splintered antlers played the harp, his feet chained to the wall. The song was so sad, there were tears on my cheeks.

"Nicodemus," Eloise whispered.

A chained mermaid lounged in a water fountain, her expression both hot and disgruntled. Strahan's guests were dancing and laughing, wings unfurled. Guards with crow feathers on their breastplates surveyed them from every door. I looked for Eldric but the music was so distracting, I found myself swaying, eyes half-closed. My feet itched to join the festivities. I could stand here in the damp, forever, just listening and twirling.

Something sharp poked me in the neck.

"Ow!"

Isadora glared at me, her sword aimed at the same sore spot. "Fae music," she explained. "It bewitches humans." Eloise's eyes were closed and even Devin looked like he was about to break into a jig. Isadora poked them both. "Don't focus on the song," she demanded.

It was surprisingly difficult. In fact, it took such an effort that sweat dripped down the side of my face. Lucas-as-hawk landed on Eloise's shoulder, dug in his claws.

"Follow me," Isadora insisted. "Now!" She barked when we seemed more inclined to stand there humming happily to ourselves. I knew that music would haunt me until I was a toothless old woman.

"There's an archway farther along that will take us to the old kitchens outside the ballroom. It was in ruins when I ruled here. I doubt it's been repaired."

We came out the archway and it was still in disrepair, as predicted. The stones were crumbling, thick with dust. But there was someone pacing, scowling, in a fine black velvet coat.

Someone familiar.

Eldric.

chapter 19

Eloise

Eldric didn't say a word. He just turned on his heel and walked away. Jo watched him go, but I couldn't read her expression.

Lucas shifted out of hawk form, even as Meg's feet turned to hooves though her face stayed human. "We're surrounded."

My heart lurched as the three passageways spilled out crow-guards and beetle-girls. Their weapons were drawn, their dark eyes menacing. Isadora hovered in the dark spaces of the ceiling. "Go," I mouthed at her. "Don't fight," I told the others.

A beetle-girl sneered, showing off her curved daggers. "A wise decision."

It wasn't just that we were outnumbered and would very

likely get our asses kicked. I needed to get to Strahan and my aunt. I knew him well enough to know that he'd want to lord his victory over us, would want to add us to the collection. I would just have to use that to my advantage. It wasn't a perfect plan by any means, but it was the only one I had.

We were marched down another corridor, this one painted with swans and lit with gilded lamps. The captain of the guard glanced at Eldric approvingly when we passed him in the hall. He was leaning against the wall, his face fierce. "Well done, my lord. We'll take them from here."

We were shoved at spear point through throngs of laughing and smirking Fae. Strahan lounged insolently on his throne, crown gleaming. Eldric was now standing stiffly behind him, expression unreadable. Malik was at his side.

My aunt was chained to the wall, dressed in a beaded Victorian gown, her hair tied up with ropes of pearls. There were bruises on her arms. When she saw me, she winced. "Oh, Eloise," she said.

Nicodemus, trapped on his dais, stopped playing abruptly. Strahan smiled. "Welcome, welcome."

Antonia's chains rattled when she pulled herself to her feet. "Eloise, you should've stayed home."

I shook my head stubbornly even though fear made my knees feel watery. "You rescued me, now I'm rescuing you."

"How very noble," Strahan drawled. "And stupid." He watched us carefully, amused. "How charming, the hope of youth. I do believe you think you'll defeat me still."

"It's early yet," Jo muttered, but it was under her breath. Devin reached for her hand.

"How do you like our Samhain ball?" Strahan continued. "The entertainment is the best yet, I think."

Aside from Nicodemus and Cala, there were others: red-vested hobs forced to dance, fairies and sprites hanging from the roof rafters in antique birdcages. They were all perfectly dressed and adorned, and haunted.

Antonia was pale and serious. "Stop this, Strahan," she demanded. "They've nothing to do with this."

"Don't be ridiculous, my dear."

The ribbon was in my pocket and I felt exposed, as if everyone could read the truth of it there. I had to find a way to get closer to Antonia. A spear tip prodded me in the lower back. Jo followed my gaze, then sneered suddenly.

"I've seen better entertainment on a street corner," she said.

I blinked at her. Was she insane? Strahan turned his attention toward her. Eldric closed his eyes briefly.

Jo shifted, pinched my hip surreptitiously. "This is hardly a party," she added. "You rat-arsed git."

Strahan looked totally taken aback. His courtiers muttered among themselves.

Eldric looked like he was going to be sick. But he didn't move from his spot, even though every muscle in his body looked tense.

"I'm sick of your mouth," I jumped in loudly. "It always gets us into trouble."

Jo scowled. "Well, there's gratitude for you. I won't come on your doomed quest next time, and I'll just let you mess about blindly on your own."

"Good, who asked you to come?"

"You did."

Our guards were bewildered, looking at Strahan for orders. Jo took the moment of distraction and yanked hard on the spear at my back.

I didn't hesitate, launched myself into the air, shouldering aside a beetle-girl. I didn't aim for Strahan like his guards assumed I would. They closed in around him and I raced right past. Malik pulled Eldric back and they stumbled dramatically, falling backward in a flurry of limbs, as if I'd shoved them. I hadn't even touched them.

I leaped over a furry hob as if I were hurdle-jumping. I landed badly but close enough to my aunt that I could pull the red velvet ribbon out of my pocket and throw it to her. She caught it, at first confused, then triumphant.

"Very impressive." Strahan shoved guards out of his way. Crow feathers and rose petals flurried around him. "But you're not any closer to escape. And I still have your friends."

Sword tips pierced skin, blood blooming on Meg's and Devin's throats. Jo stood like a tragic Shakespearean queen, pale and proud. Lucas was flying frantically near the ceiling with a piercing cry. Blood dripped from one wing, held at an awkward angle.

"Not all my friends," I said grimly as Ronan and his people poured through the archways like ants overrunning a picnic. Swords flashed, dogs bit. Meg used her hooves to break kneecaps. Howls of pain rang over the sound of clashing swords. Devin tripped once, scrambled back to his feet.

Isadora came shrieking out of the ceiling roots, her eyes wild, her teeth bared in a laugh. Her folk swarmed in after her on their hornet mounts, loosing a silver rain of elf darts. One barely missed Jo, tangling in her hair like a lost earring.

"Watch it," she croaked, swinging her captured spear wildly. She took out two beetle-girls and nearly broke Devin's neck in the process. "Sorry, sorry."

Eldric didn't join the fray right away. He stayed on the dais and though he didn't look at Jo and she didn't look at him, every dagger he threw knocked a weapon out of its path toward her. Arrows and knives clattered around her, as if she had an invisible force field protecting her.

The Seelie courts fought furiously, as the tall grandfather clock watched, like some stern patriarch. Dusk had come and gone; there was one more time of power before Samhain's end. Midnight.

And it was 11:47 now. The pendulum swung rhythmically, hypnotically.

Strahan blocked my view suddenly.

"Run, Eloise." Antonia yanked and pulled at her chains, the ribbon crumpled in her fist. "Run, damn it."

My throat felt like it was full of broken glass, my knees like melting ice. The Grey Ladies floated behind him, shrieking.

The lamps shattered. Frost limned swords and fingers and silk bustles. My teeth chattered. My lips went blue.

"Give me the ribbon," Strahan said to Antonia calmly. His hair was so golden, it glimmered. "And I won't break her bones and suck out her marrow."

That was a little too descriptive for my taste. And since it was what the old lady in the woods had warned me about that night at the party, I didn't even think he was exaggerating.

"Don't do it, Aunt Antonia," I said when she hesitated. "Don't!"

Strahan was annoyed. "You are becoming tiresome, little one." The battle raged on behind him. Ronan cleaved a rat-woman's head from her body. Swan feathers gathered in the corners with the drifts of snow. The wailing of the Grey Ladies was making my teeth hurt.

"Yeah, well, you became tiresome a long time ago." I glanced behind me. "Antonia, do whatever it is you need to do with that thing."

"I need his crown as well," she said, her hair coming out of its intricate twists. "The key," she muttered when I stumbled closer to her. I hadn't noticed it before, hanging on a hook, just out of reach to taunt her cruelly. I grabbed it, tossed it to her, though I was so cold I felt as if I were moving in slow motion.

Strahan flicked his hand and more guards closed in. I threw a vase of lilies at one since it was the closest thing within reach. Water arced over him. The other one moved in, snarling. Antonia's sword, stolen from a fallen guard, caught him across his right arm as she pulled free of the chains. She swung again. Blood and red rose petals scattered over her boots.

"Back off," she bit out.

Strahan's fury had the candles burning higher, the fire leaping up the chimney. Oppressive heat pressed down on us. Sweat soaked my shirt despite the Grey Ladies' icy breath. The clock kept time, impassively.

"Jo! Dev! Unchain the others." I scooped up the iron key and threw it. Devin grabbed it out of the air.

"I'll have that damnable ribbon." Strahan grabbed a sword from a beetle-girl who was clawing at the wound in her chest. A dog yelped. Winifreda was hiding under a feast table, eyes wide with fear. A fairy with lavender wings plummeted past my head. I saw Nicodemus leap off the dais, snarling. The heat kept burning, reddened exposed skin, forming painful blisters. Strahan's sword whistled toward Antonia. She blocked it, grunting. There was another thrust, a parry. Pearls rolled across the floor.

I didn't know how to help.

And then that didn't matter so much.

The crow-guard who had pushed me off the roof of my apartment building grabbed me, scratching my face. It burned, blood dripping. He licked it. I gagged.

"Let. Go." I elbowed him as hard as I could. It wasn't

enough to stop him, but Lucas's talon to the eye was. He screamed, clutching at the bloody gash, jabbing up with a dagger. The blade caught Lucas in the breast, through feathers already matted with blood. He screamed, shimmered, and when he landed on the rug, he was a pale, unconscious boy, blood staining his shirt.

"Lucas!" I tripped over a Redcap hob who grinned before jabbing at me with the fire poker. I kicked him aside. "Lucas!"

My aunt was tiring. The clock kept ticking. A Swan girl, clearly still loyal to Strahan, glided toward me and took my feet out with an ivory staff. I landed hard. I scrambled backward on my elbows but the staff smashed into my ankle. Yelping, I tried to move faster. I kicked out with my good foot.

The roses in the ceiling were drooping, wilting. I wondered if it was the last thing I would ever see. An eagle screeched, knocking the Swan girl off her feet. I used her staff to drag myself to Lucas, resting his head in my lap, the way he'd done with me on the couch. Blood dripped, warm and steady on my knee. He coughed, wincing. His skin was clammy, hair spiky with sweat.

"I'm sorry," he whispered.

"Don't move," I said. "Don't move. You'll be okay." I shifted to kneel beside him, wadding up the torn remains of his shirt, pressing it on the gash under his ribs. "Oh God, please be okay." There was so much blood. I leaned down to kiss him, tears dripping onto his face. They were my tears, because he was smiling. "I knew you'd kiss me eventually."

I half laughed and kissed him again. "Hold on, just hold on."

His gaze shifted over my shoulder, his eyes shifting into those of a hawk. He lifted up, one arm holding me against his chest, the other jabbing with the ivory staff. The end caught the beetle-woman who had been closing in behind me. She staggered, screaming. Black blood spattered. Lucas slumped back to the ground.

He didn't move again. His blood seeped into the rug. I choked back a sob. I couldn't tell if he was still breathing.

The beetle-woman came at us. The gash nearly severing her arm wasn't going to stop her. Her long needle-thin sword slid through the air toward us. I shielded Lucas, trying to reach the staff. It was too far away. The sword point glittered.

And then there was a crack of light as my fierce, tattooed mother appeared, wearing Antonia's pendant and screaming, "Get the hell away from my daughter."

Her baseball bat did a pretty good job of follow-through. "Mom!"

"When I saw the ribbon was missing, I knew you must be here. Of all places." Her face went steely when she saw Strahan hacking away at her twin sister. "Oh, I'm going to enjoy this," she said, taking handfuls of rusty iron nails out of her bag. She shoved a few at me and then began to whip the rest at Strahan. The first one grazed his cheek, the second his hand. He cursed, skin sizzling. There was a noticeable dip in the temperature; the battle between summer and winter was balancing out.

I didn't care.

Lucas wasn't moving, and his blood was everywhere.

I touched his cheek. His eyelids didn't flicker; he didn't even groan. Matted feathers half sprouted from his shoulders. He'd been caught midshift. His wound was too deep.

Lucas was dead.

The battle faded around me, sounds of clashing swords muffled, screams muted.

My beautiful hawk-boy was dead.

I choked on a sob, his blood staining the knees of my jeans.

Mom was still flinging nails like grenades. Isadora's tribe dodged them, hornets buzzing angrily. Eldric ducked but one of them caught his wrist anyway. I grabbed a handful as well and flung them at anything that came too close to Lucas.

Antonia nearly bobbled her sword dance when she saw her sister. "Jaz?"

Strahan fought harder, until a nail caught him square in the eye. He shouted between gritted teeth. The Grey Ladies wept. I threw a nail at them too. It didn't bother them, but the crow-girl behind them wasn't so pleased. The disgusting smell of frying flesh mingled with lilies and roses and heat.

Strahan was distracted enough by his burning eye that Mom had time to dart in and punch him in the other eye. He toppled, his crown flying off and landing at Eldric's feet. Malik smiled.

It was like the battle went into slow motion, even the sounds were distorted, except the clean slice of the clock striking its first of twelve bells.

Midnight.

Mom held Antonia. Devin cradled his arm. I couldn't see Jo at all. Isadora was scratched but still smiling her feral smile. The roses began to fall from the ceiling.

Antonia dropped her sword, the ribbon unfurling from her wrist. It fluttered out of reach.

Second bell.

I wouldn't let Lucas die in vain. He'd want me to keep fighting.

I dove for the ribbon, narrowly losing it to a swan boy with sharp teeth. I drove a nail into the back of his hand. White feathers popped out of his arm as he screamed.

Now I had the ribbon. So what the hell was I supposed to do with it?

Third bell.

Eldric bent very slowly, scooped up the crown. Only his eyes burned wildly; the rest of his face was set in its usual mocking lines.

Fourth bell.

Strahan looked at his son triumphantly. It was suddenly

so hot, it was hard to breathe. Flowers bloomed everywhere—
roses, hyacinths, bluebells; in empty chairs, between boots,
tumbling out of bustles and pockets and mouths. The perfume was so thick and cloying it clogged my throat. The
summer king was pleased, and his power surged.

Fifth bell.

Eldric stepped forward, the hawthorn crown still in his
hands. His wrist was raw, painful from the iron. He didn't
appear to notice.

Strahan made an imperious gesture. "Give it to me."

Eldric's fingers tightened.

Strahan looked nervous for the first time. "I com-
mand you."

Eldric lifted the crown. The battle stopped. The silence
was like molasses, sticky, binding us all together. Jo was suddenly beside me, slipping her hand into mine, silent tears
running down her face. I didn't know if she was crying for
Lucas or for Eldric.

Sixth bell.

Everyone looked at me, at the red velvet ribbon looped
around my fingers. Except for Eldric, who had glanced down
at Jo so quickly I might have imagined it.

We could try and take the crown, somehow get it to
Antonia, so she could break Strahan's rule. Or I could trust
Jo's instinct and give the ribbon to Eldric.

I looked at Antonia. "He's my son," she whispered.

Seventh bell.

Eldric goggled at her. "You admit it?"

"I've never denied it," she murmured softly, sadly.

"She's lying," Strahan seethed. "She abandoned you. She doesn't love you any more than she loves me. I took care of you."

Antonia drew herself up. "I didn't leave you behind, Eldric," she said. "He stole you from me. I tried to get you back but once you were old enough to show me partiality, I knew I had to stop trying. He'd have killed you for it."

"You left me alone."

Eighth bell.

"Not for a single moment," she told him. "Malik was always with you."

I wasn't sure who looked more stunned, Strahan or Eldric.

"Why else would I have returned every year? And run so far?" She shook her head. "Not for him, not for these courts, or that crown. For you."

"Enough of these games," Strahan finally said. "I am the rightful king."

Ninth bell.

"You *were* the rightful king," Eldric's torn sleeve revealed burn scars on his arm.

"I trust you," Jo whispered so that only I could hear. I wasn't even sure if she knew she was speaking out loud.

Eldric put the crown on his own head, the wildly flickering candles catching the embroidery of his frock coat. Malik looked proud, like a real father ought to.

I shoved the ribbon at Eldric before I could change my mind.

Tenth bell.

Strahan pounced on me like an enraged cat. He scratched at my face, pushed a ruby dagger under my chin so that my head fell back. "Destroy it," I yelled to Eldric, trying not to move my throat.

Eleventh bell.

Eldric threw the ribbon into the Samhain fire, the silver crown on his brow and the blood of both his parents giving him the power to break the binding spell.

The tip of Strahan's knife cut into me, drawing blood. It felt like a bee sting. My mother made no sound but every part of her screamed. The knife cut deeper and deeper and then jerked loose. Strahan gurgled, blood staining his teeth.

Nicodemus's antlers were shoved straight through Strahan's back and into his chest. My gentle poet friend looked grim, satisfied.

Twelfth bell.

Behind him, Lucas stirred. One arm shifted to a giant hawk's wing, shifted back. He coughed, groaning.

He was alive.

I burst into tears.

He smiled. "That's a rather soggy reception," he croaked.

"I thought you were dead."

"Not dead." He winced, pain lancing through him when

he tried to move his shoulder. "Just out cold. Though I hear a kiss from a pretty girl can heal anything."

"Isn't that a kiss from a prince?"

"Let's try it the other way. I don't fancy kissing Eldric."

I chuckled, kissing his face, his jaw, his hair. My mouth finally closed over his, and it was a slow dance of lips, so slow and thorough I couldn't help but fall into it. For a long, delicious moment, the world narrowed down to his tongue touching mine, to the feel of his hair under my fingers, the press of his chest against me.

When I pulled back he smiled. "Better already."

epilogue
Jo

I hadn't seen Eldric since the night he became king of the Seelie courts.

He'd said good-bye; taking the crown didn't change that. If anything, it made things more complicated. I was trying not to think about it.

Eloise's aunt was finally free. In fact, she had just signed the lease on her first apartment. Eldric was apparently slow to trust Antonia, having been raised to believe she had purposely abandoned him. The Hart tattoo on his arm had been one of his rebellions when he wanted to anger Strahan. Antonia and Lucas both told Eloise about Eldric, and she told me. Secondhand details hurt, but they were better than nothing at all.

"Eloise just shared her chocolate with me voluntarily,"

Devin said from behind me. We were at the farm, eating everything we could get our hands on. I was at the kitchen window, watching the rain soak into the fields.

"You deserve it," I agreed, glancing over my shoulder at him. His arm was in a cast. "You were brilliant."

He frowned. "You two have been nice to me all week," he said suspiciously. It was true. After he had his arm set, we'd been extra nice to him. "It's freaking me out," he added. "Stop it."

Eloise grabbed the chocolate, stuffed it into her mouth. "Better?" she asked, chewing.

He looked satisfied. "Yes."

I turned back to the window. The weather was cold and damp. A constant, dreary drizzle of rain coated the trees and the fields. It was miserable and wet and we loved it. In the misty gray shadows of the apple orchard, I saw a silhouette.

My heart leaped.

I raced outside, not bothering with a raincoat or rubber boots. Mud squelched under my shoes. I burst through the gate, searching the rows of wet trees. The smell of rotting fruit was thicker than usual, almost like cider. I could get dizzy off the fumes. I checked the last row. My shoulders slumped.

I'd imagined it.

There was no one in the orchard. Eldric was somewhere in the Fae lands, doing whatever it was Fae kings did. I turned around, sighing.

"Looking for someone?"

I'd know that voice anywhere. Eldric leaned back against a tree, drops of water clinging to his hair and his eyelashes. He wasn't wearing the crown or a silk coat, just his usual T-shirt and torn jeans. My dress didn't change, but it suddenly felt like a velvet gown.

I swallowed. "You're here."

"And where else would I be?" He pushed away, coming toward me. I felt nervous suddenly for some reason. He ran his fingers through my hair, dislodging raindrops. "It's raining," he said.

My smile trembled. "I *told* you you were the good guy."

"Nothing's changed," he said softly.

I paused. "Then why did you come?"

"Because everything's changed," he said, with the wicked grin that always made me lean toward him, like a sunflower to the sun. "No one can know about us," he murmured. "Not until I'm a stronger king and know what I'm doing. The Seelie courts are gathering under my banner, but I can't be sure yet who will be loyal. And not until you know what you're getting yourself into."

"*Is* there an us?" I whispered.

"There'll *always* be an us," he said, sliding his hand down to my lower back and pulling me against him.

I felt like laughing, like there were too many emotions inside me. "Are we done with the talking yet?" I asked, wrapping my arms around his neck.

He bent his head, stayed there with his lips just barely touching mine. "I thought girls liked to talk."

I nipped at his mouth.

"I have something better in mind."

acknowledgments

They say a village raises a child and it's much the same with books. I may be the writer working alone in her studio, but there are many hands that made this book better. Many thanks to my editor, Emily Easton, who helps me improve my stories, and to all the known and unknown assistants, publicists (props to Deb Shapiro and Emma Bradshaw!), copyeditors, art directors, bookshops, and librarians. Thanks also go to Marlene Stringer, agent extraordinaire.

And to my friends and family. I wrote the first draft of *Stolen Away* by hand in a notebook over the month of December while holiday madness thrummed around me. Thanks especially to my husband who brought me dinner two hours before midnight on New Year's Eve so I could finish the last chapter before the year ended!

ALYXANDRA HARVEY is the author of the Drake Chronicles—*Hearts at Stake, Blood Feud, Out for Blood, Bleeding Hearts, Blood Moon,* and *Blood Prophecy*—as well as another stand-alone novel, *Haunting Violet.* Alyx likes medieval dresses and tattoos and has been accused of being born in the wrong century—except that she really likes running water, women's rights, and ice cream. She lives in an old Victorian farmhouse in Ontario, Canada, with a few resident ghosts, her husband, and their dogs.

www.alyxandraharvey.com
www.thedrakechronicles.com
www.facebook.com/thedrakechronicles

THE BATTLE FOR VIOLET HILL HAS BEGUN . . .
AND THE DRAKES COULD LOSE
ONE OF THEIR OWN.
FOREVER.

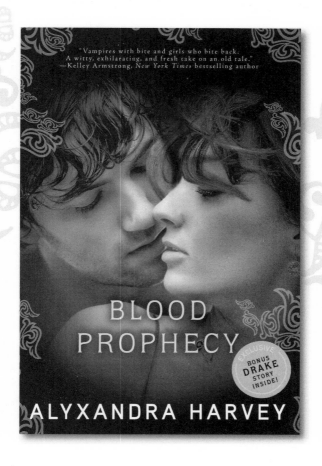

"Vampires with bite and girls who bite back.
A witty, exhilarating, and fresh take on an old tale."
—Kelley Armstrong, *New York Times* bestselling author

BLOOD
PROPHECY

EXCLUSIVE!
BONUS
DRAKE
STORY
INSIDE!

ALYXANDRA HARVEY

DON'T MISS AN EXCITING EXCERPT FROM
THE FINAL ADDITION TO THE
Drake Chronicles—*Blood Prophecy* . . .

Sunday afternoon

I spent most of Sunday dialing Nicholas's cell phone even though I knew he wouldn't answer. There was no reception at the camp, but I was secretly hoping he'd gone back to the farmhouse. It was early November and the sun had only set about an hour ago. It was too early for him to answer regardless of where he was. I called Bruno, just to feel as if I was accomplishing something. "Any news?" I asked.

"Afraid not, lass," he replied, sounding tired. "We'll be sending a message in a few hours. And waiting to get information from those still loyal to us at the camp."

"And Nicholas?" I almost ached just to say his name. Everyone was always so worried about Solange being hurt because she was so unique, or about me because I was human. It had never seriously occurred to me just how hurt Nicholas could be. The Drake brothers just seemed to have the kind of luck that saw them through bad places. I never imagined that their luck could run out.

I couldn't think like that. He wasn't missing, he wasn't dead. In fact, he might very well be Solange's only hope. I had to hold on to that. "Madame Veronique hasn't murdered anyone yet, has she?"

"No. You know the Drakes are harder to assassinate than that. So don't make yourself sick."

"Sheesh, one little breakdown and everyone fusses," I teased. When Nicholas first went missing, I'd climbed onto the roof of the dormitory and screamed until Theo, the school nurse, threatened to sedate me. With the kind of year I'd had, I figured I was allowed a little primal scream therapy. "I'll see you soon, Bruno."

My homework was therapeutic: kickboxing, track, and practice at the gun range. My mom would be horrified at just how relaxing it was for me to watch those targets spin. I was heading back to the dorms when I spotted Jenna in the archery field with her crossbow. I made a detour. Archery was my favorite class and Jenna's aim rivaled mine. I watched her arrows slam into the targets and itched to hold my miniature crossbow. Jenna turned when she heard my footsteps.

"Are you okay?" we asked in unison.

She lowered her crossbow. "Just a headache. I'm off classes for a few days, but I just couldn't sit around anymore." Her red hair was in its usual ponytail, a bandage on her temple. "You saved me. If you hadn't sent Spencer to find me, I probably would've ended up as a vampire's next meal."

"I didn't save you," I said, flinching. "It's my fault you were there in the first place."

She shrugged. "Who knew civilian parties could be so dangerous?"

I snorted. "Now you know." Since this was Violet Hill, that wasn't even the scariest party I'd ever been to. "And I'm sorry."

"Hey, you got me back home. We're even." She frowned. "Is it true you saw the Blood Moon camp?"

I nodded. "Yeah. Pretty cool. You know, if my best friend hadn't dragged me out back with the intention to drain me dry."

"Dude."

"Yeah."

Jenna shook her head, then winced, her hand touching her temple briefly. "I thought Solange was this delicate little thing."

"She's sick," I said steadily. I thought of the bats that followed her around. "Does rabies make people crazy?"

"I have no idea. You think Solange has rabies?"

"I guess not." I wrinkled my nose. "But the bats are new. And weird. Everything's weird."

Kieran pulled up into the student parking lot behind us, distracting me from any other theories. There were so many *Hel-Blar* roaming the area that the school was now allowing third-year students to patrol, not just fourth years like Hunter. As a third year I needed to be with a fourth year or an alumnus, and I could only go during certain classes. Since Hunter and I both wanted to keep an eye on Kieran, we alternated forcing him to patrol with us. Plus, it got me off campus, which was a bonus. I wasn't in the mood to deal with prejudice and bullies tonight. We both needed the distraction as we tried to figure out what to do about Solange and Nicholas.

Nicholas.

Nope, couldn't think about that right now.

"See you later." Jenna waved at Kieran and headed back to the dorm.

"You know that you and Hunter aren't even remotely subtle," Kieran told me through the open window.

I just grinned at him. "Wave to the top-floor corner window over there. Lia's got a crush on you."

Kieran's ears went red. "How does she even know I'm here?"

"I told her you were coming," I said, sliding into my seat. I dropped my knapsack full of weapons at my feet.

"You're a menace."

"I was twelve once." I shrugged. "A little crush in a place like this can make a difference. She's got to think about something other than vampires."

"What, like you?" he remarked drily, reversing out of the parking spot.

"Come on, drive like you're cool," I urged him, ignoring his very valid point. "Pop a wheelie or something. It'll give her something to swoon over."

He laughed despite himself. "I can't pop a wheelie in an SUV, you lunatic."

We left the school behind, exchanging the security lights for dark fields and snow-choked orchards. We startled a cat, and a coyote darted across the road, but there were no fangs or pale eyes. I tried to twirl my stake through my fingers as if it were a magic-trick coin.

"Turn left here," I said about fifteen minutes later.

"I know what you're doing," he told me, but he turned anyway. The road cut through thick bushes and red pine groves. The moon was bright enough to cast blue moonshadows over the snow. If I squinted I could just barely make out a house light through the trees, close to the mountains. We passed the familiar landmarks: the lightning-struck ash, the boulder shaped like a bull, the hill where wild daffodils grew in spring.

My phone rang the very second we crossed onto Drake land.

"Lucy Hamilton, you just keep on driving."

I gulped at Helena's stern voice. "Oops. Bye!" I wrinkled my nose at Kieran. "Busted. Keep driving."

We headed into town on the only country highway in Violet Hill. The high beams glittered on frost and ice and the wet black pavement. House lights began to pierce the gloom.

"I'm on campus duty," Kieran said as he turned in the direction of the arts college tucked in by the lake. It made sense, since he looked the part, even if he wasn't covered in tattoos or paint like most of the other local students. Violet Hill had a small arts college, mostly catering to visual arts and literature students. You got to know the look of them after a while.

"Still going to the Helios-Ra college in Scotland?" I asked.

"Let's just get through tonight," he answered.

We walked through three dorm parties and two pubs, but they were clean. I peered into all the bushes, looking for *Hel-Blar*. Wherever they were feeding tonight, it wasn't here.

It wasn't until a couple of hours later, when we were heading back to the academy, that we saw something. A concert had ended in one of the bigger pubs, and the cold streets were crowded with students and taxis. There were girls in short skirts, guys holding one another up, and couples making out as they wandered home.

And a slender girl oblivious to the cold, standing in the snow in a thin dress. No, not just standing.

Feeding.

"Stop!" I yelled. "Stop, stop, stop! That's Solange."

Kieran practically wrapped the SUV around a mailbox in his hurry to pull over. Someone cheered, thinking it was funny. I flung myself out of my seat before the wheels had stopped moving. Kieran grabbed my arm as I darted past him. Momentum swung me around so I was facing him, spitting curses. "The hell, Black."

"It's called stealth," he snapped back, jerking me down behind the cover of the SUV. The fumes from the running engine turned to fog in the cold air, obscuring us. Kieran passed me a stake but I already had one in my hand. "And clearly, neither of you have it."

He was right.

Solange stood near a circle of yellow light from a street lamp, clutching a girl in paint-splattered jeans, with short spiky hair and a nose ring. Her fangs gleamed as her red lips lifted in a delicate snarl. Seeing her wearing red lipstick and a long dress was nearly as weird as everything else. She hated dressing up.

"Shh," Solange ordered when the girl struggled briefly. The girl went silent obediently. No one noticed them, but that was through sheer dumb luck. Any minute now someone would glance their way, someone would scream. Or the girl would die.

Because Solange was still drinking.

"Anyone could see her," I whispered, horrified.

"And she doesn't care," Kieran agreed grimly. "If any other Helios-Ra saw her like this they'd shoot her on sight, no questions asked. And they'd be within treaty rights to do it."

Solange seized the girl by the neck, tilting her head to a near-breakable angle. Her fangs sank deeper through skin and flesh, blood trickling slightly as if she were biting into a ripe peach. The girl made a fist just before her arm went limp. She struggled briefly, then just dangled. There was no pretending it was two drunk room-mates holding up each other.

There was too much blood for that.

Solange looked enthralled, manic. Deadly. So I did the only thing I could think of.

I threw a snowball at her head.

It didn't hurt her, of course, but at least it made her pause. She glanced up, lips curled. I scrounged around the ground until I found a rock at the edge of the flower bed behind me. I threw it as hard as I could and it hit her on the temple. She hissed, blood me welling on her pale skin. The girl in her arms slumped to the ground unconscious, moving so gradually, she could have been water freezing into an icicle.

Solange looked right at me then, and even through the fog of exhaust fumes, her glance was cold and sharp as a needle.

And then she smiled.

"That's definitely not her," I muttered. "And I'm getting that bitch out of my best friend."

"But not tonight," Kieran said, still crouched next to me, his jaw tight as bowstring. "Tonight we have to save them both. And soon."

He was right.

"You run faster than me," I said, straightening up. "So I'll pull focus while you get her the hell out of here."

I walked around the front of the car and stood in the middle of the street. "Wooo-hoooo!" I yelled, as if I was drunk and very, very annoying. Glances flickered my way but it wasn't enough. I looked at the building in the opposite direction of Solange, reading the sign over the door. "Free keg at Kinsley Hall!" I yelled.

Not everyone detoured to take advantage, but at least they were all looking at the crazy girl in the road and not the guy in black cargos chasing down a bloodstained waif of a girl who ran like a deer.

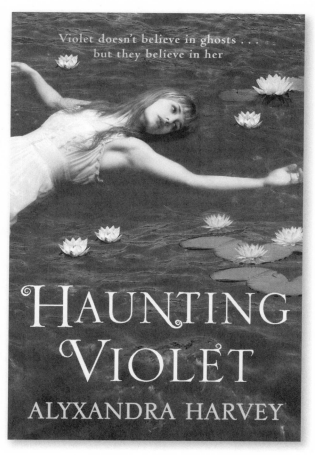

Read the Drake Chronicles

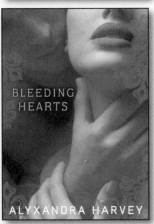

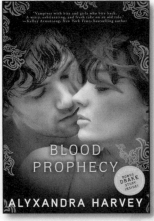

from the beginning . . .

Ruling Passion—includes *Hearts at Stake,*
Blood Feud, and *Out for Blood*

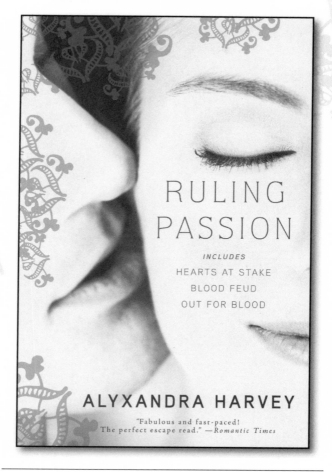

The passion continues with three original e-novellas featuring your favorite characters from the DRAKE CHRONICLES ...

Available in e-book only

WALKER BOOKS
AN IMPRINT OF BLOOMSBURY
www.bloomsbury.com
www.facebook.com/BloomsburyTeens

HUNGRY FOR MORE GRIPPING TEEN FICTION?

JOIN THE CONVERSATION at
www.facebook.com/BloomsburyTeens

The official Facebook Fan Page for Bloomsbury & Walker, publisher of acclaimed books for teens

You'll find out about monthly giveaways, weekly polls, book discussions, exclusive content, author events & more!

DATE DUE